SUMMER MELODY

TODDIE DOWNS

Booktrope Editions
Seattle WA 2012

Cover Design by Greg Simanson

Edited by Sarah Callendar

This is a work of fiction. Names, characters, places, brands, media, and incidents are either the product of the author's imagination or are used fictitiously. Any resemblance to similarly named places or to persons living or deceased is unintentional.

PRINT ISBN 978-1-935961-44-4

EPUB ISBN 978-1-62015-048-1

For further information regarding permissions, please contact info@booktrope.com.

Library of Congress Control Number: 2012914560

ACKNOWLEDGMENTS

It apparently takes a village to write a book. I mean, technically, there's generally only one writer – in this case, me. But there are so many additional people who give feedback, tell you when you're sounding brilliant, or conversely when you're sounding too clichéd or melodramatic. Once you're lucky enough to have a publisher interested in your work, then there are more people who become invested in giving your book the best chance to survive out there in that big world of books and readers. And then, if you're really, really lucky, your book finds some readers, and in the very best of worlds, that book resonates with them in a special way.

Heartfelt thanks go out to my very first readers and supporters in my writers' group in Cleveland Heights, Ohio, most notably Lisa Ferranti and Mary Rynes. Anne Mini provided my first experience with a professional edit of my work and made it the kind of collaborative experience that all first-time writers dream of. My first round of beta-readers consisted of Betty Olson, Greg Downs, and Julie Garcia; their eagle-eyed sense for detail and continuity helped more than they can know. My Seattle writers' group, made up of Anne Mini, Caleb Powell, Cindy Willis, and Layne Maheu, gave me many needed boosts of encouragement when my skin was not as thick as I needed it to be. When I was getting ready to submit *Summer Melody* to Booktrope, my second round of beta-readers gave me more advice and reassurance, so thanks to Sarah Schubert, Emily Schubert and Jessie Kellogg-Smith. A special thanks to novelist Tess Hardwick for vouching for me and my novel to Booktrope in those introductory days.

My team at Booktrope has been amazing, and exceedingly hard-working. Every writer deserves a team like this standing behind her.

Thanks go out to Ken Shear, my publisher; Sarah Callendar, my editor; Sophie Weeks, my book manager; Greg Simanson, my designer; and Susan Ethridge, my proofreader.

Finally, thanks go to the sadly now-defunct Bibo Coffee, where I sat every Sunday afternoon writing and revising, and to my family for treating my dream of being a writer like it wasn't even in question. Their belief in me has been unquestioning and unceasing. And thanks to any reader who picks up this book and gets even this far in the reading.

~1~
JANE

CALL ME EEYORE, JANE THOUGHT as she trudged down the sidewalk on her way home. Nice day, if you liked that sunshine sort of thing. The last day of school always made her feel hopeless. Not that she liked eighth grade all that much, but at least it was something to do in this town where the year's highlight was the Pink-and-Green Parade, with the villagers all dressing in their Izod polos and sauntering down Main Street for the tourists. Summer's perky sunshininess annoyed her; it was just a cover-up for sweat and discomfort. With no job and no access to air conditioning or a pool, Jane looked forward to the next three months with all the enthusiasm of a dog being taken to the vet.

Jane's hair fell into her face as she kicked at the pebbles on the concrete. They skittered like raindrops down the long hill. A group of boys from the middle school was twenty paces ahead. Random syllables floating back in her direction suggested that they were not exactly debating quantum physics. Concentrating all her powers of wallflower-enhanced invisibility, Jane watched as they hooted and high-fived one another. One of them had probably farted.

The boys stopped in front of a small bungalow where a child about five or six years old was playing on the porch. Jane knelt down and pretended to tie her shoe so that she did not have to overtake them. Her t-shirt, two sizes too big, grazed the sidewalk. She didn't know why the boys had stopped, but she knew this house. This kid was always on the porch, oblivious to the rest of the world, lining stuff up in perfectly straight lines. Some days, it was cars. Some days, it was blocks. Today, it was cars. The boy sat cross-legged on the floorboards, bangs in his eyes. There was something not right about him, doughy, like a loaf of bread not completely baked through.

"Hey, kid," one of the boys yelled. The child continued to move his cars back and forth, back and forth. He didn't look up.

"Yo, retard! I'm talking to you!"

Still the boy ignored them. No, he wasn't ignoring them- it was as if they did not really exist for him, so there was nothing to ignore.

Jane, still kneeling, picked at a scab on her ankle. Just leave him alone. She contemplated turning back and walking the long way home, but figured she'd draw more attention that way than if she simply stayed put. And attention was the last thing she wanted from these morons. They might be a couple years younger than her, but everyone knew about them. They were the guys who had played keep-away with that blind kid's cane until a teacher finally stopped them.

One of the boys picked up a pebble and chucked it at the child. Its aim was true, glancing off the boy's cheek. Now the boy looked up, puzzled and in pain, but he made no sound.

Jane could see a deep red bead forming on his cheek. "Goddammit." She stood and rushed at the six boys, arms curled up to her chest and her hands balled in fists, yelling what she hoped was a frightening war cry. The boys turned, and with grim faces, began moving toward her like a tidal wave. Just before she collided with them, the two in the middle grinned and moved aside to create a gap. With nothing to slow her momentum – like, say, a body – she tripped on a sidewalk crack and fell hard, landing on her hands and knees.

"You assholes!" Her voice quavered as she stood up. "Beating up on a little kid – ooh, you're cool. I should call the cops." She walked right up to the biggest boy and pushed him with hands scraped and raw from the sidewalk. "You wanna hit a girl, too?"

The boys backed off with their hands raised in mock surrender. "Whatever," the largest one laughed. They started back down the sidewalk, swarming like bees. As they walked off, one of them said, "It's good that retards stick together." They started a solidarity round of arm-punching.

Jane stood guard over the porch until they disappeared, trembling from the adrenalin, her hands and knees stinging. Then she turned to the house and the boy, who had returned his attention to his cars. A thin stripe of blood trickled down his face.

Shuffling up the steps to the bungalow, her knee aching, Jane rang the doorbell. After what seemed a long time, a pleasant-looking blonde looked out of the screen. She appeared too young to be a mom; she must be an older sister, or a babysitter. Her t-shirt was knotted above her belly button. "Can I help you?" she said.

Jane glared at her, figuring she was as much to blame as anyone, leaving a child like that unsupervised. "I just wanted to let you know that some boys were throwing rocks at him." She gestured toward the boy, feeling weird that she didn't even know his name.

The blonde's smile disappeared. She rushed out to check on the boy. Kneeling beside him, she pressed her fingertip lightly to the scrape, which had stopped bleeding. The boy put his car on the floor but did not look up. He had not uttered a word or cried a tear this whole time.

"Oh crap, oh crap, oh crap, Pam is going to murder me." She turned to face Jane and said with a pleading whine in her voice, "This has never happened before, I mean, I figured he'd be okay. I was just on the phone with my boyfriend. I mean, Charley's so quiet, who'd want to pick on him?"

Jane backed away to the edge of the porch, ready to bolt back to the safety of being anonymous. "Hey, it's none of my business. I just wanted someone to know, y'know?"

The blonde looked again at the scrape. "It doesn't look too bad," she said. "A Band-Aid oughta do it." Calmer now, she looked up at Jane. "What exactly happened? Charley's mom and dad will want to know."

Jane replayed the story as matter-of-factly as she could, then said, "Look, I gotta get home." She started backing down the stairs.

She wished she could think of something clever to say to the boy as she made her exit, but as usual, she came up with nothing. The boy did not look away from his cars as she left.

The young woman called to her. "Hey, thanks for what you did. What was your name again?"

* * *

Jane felt reassured when she finally turned onto her street and saw her house, the third ranch house on the left – the one with the red shutters. She'd been afraid that she would run into those boys again, or worse, that they would be waiting for her on one of these streets. So the sight of the yellow checked curtains fluttering from her front bedroom window seemed welcoming, almost like they were waving to her. Jane made sure to step on her lucky tree root on the oak in the front yard, and went inside.

As she slipped into her bedroom, Jane was relieved she'd somehow managed to miss Davey and her mom. They must be in the back yard. She flopped herself on her bed and pulled her teddy bear close.

What had she been doing, standing up to those boys? Aside from committing social suicide, that is. The only saving grace was that it was the last day of school. If school were still in session, the story'd be out before the bell for homeroom.

They called me a retard, she thought, trying to swallow the lump that had formed in her throat. Was that what people really thought about her? Was it too much to ask just to feel normal for once?

The door to Jane's bedroom swung open.

"Don't you ever knock?" She rolled away from the door so her face wouldn't be visible.

"Mom says to come out and start helping with dinner." It was Davey, maddeningly content and normal. "That is, if you're done being depressed and all."

"You don't know anything," Jane said, still facing the wall.

"Oh, please, you're not even fooling anyone. You do this all the time – poor me, my life is soooo awful. What's so bad, anyway?"

Jane wondered if she concentrated really hard, whether she could make him explode.

"You wouldn't understand, you're only ten."

"Ooh, like fourteen's so much older. Are you having a period? Miles says his sister gets all weird when she gets her period."

"I am SO not talking to you about any of this." Jane was actually relieved her period had not decided to show itself yet. The idea of having to wear a pad, or – God, no – a tampon, was just too disgusting for words.

"Blah, blah, blah. Mom says to come out now." Davey neglected to close the door as he left.

Jane wiped her eyes with the back of her hand. Time to get tough. Her mother couldn't suspect anything was wrong or she'd have Jane in one of those "you're a winner" discussions that made Jane want to kick someone, preferably her brother. Those talks had started after the divorce, as if her mom were trying to convince Jane and herself that it was all going to be okay. As if.

Bonnie glanced up from chopping a cucumber as Jane walked into the kitchen. Her knife pounded out a rapid drum beat, the pale cool slices sliding onto the cutting board. Her mom grooved to the beat she was making, dipping her shoulders as she chopped. Jane slowly shook her head. Her mother was always doing goofy crap like this.

Bonnie looked up and smiled at Jane. "You caught me," she said with a shrug. "Me and my rocker fantasies. Can you lay the table while I finish making a salad?"

Jane shrugged. She began to pull plates down from the cupboard.

"Is everything okay? You seem kind of quiet."

"I'm fine," she said in a monotone.

"Yeah, you sound ducky." Bonnie sighed. "Look, I'll drop it, okay? But if you need to talk..."

Jane met her mother's gaze to convince her that nothing was wrong.

"Okay, then. Just try to cheer up a little. The weather's nice, school's out, what's not to be happy about?"

"I said, I'm fine." She concentrated on aligning the silverware perfectly, as if she might actually give a darn about it.

Bonnie gave the salad bowl an approving pat and set it on the table. "Oh, this might interest you. I was talking to Aunt Vivian, and she mentioned that Meg might be stopping by tonight."

This did interest Jane. She hadn't seen her cousin in a couple months, way longer than usual. Meg was the coolest person Jane had ever known. Even if she was twenty-four, she was probably the person Jane most wanted to be like, because she wasn't afraid of anything. She had dyed the ends of her short spiky hair magenta to piss Aunt Vivian off a couple years ago, but then decided she really liked it. She'd offered to give a similar dye job to Jane, but Jane figured the last thing she wanted was to stick out. Meg had moved out of Aunt Vivian's house, and now she lived in a basement apartment with two roommates who were *guys*. She told Jane that they were the only ones who answered the ad who didn't seem prohibitively psychotic. Aunt Viv had nearly had a stroke when she found out Meg was living with guys. It was great.

"Jane, can you find your brother and tell him that dinner's on the table?"

Jane craned her head in the direction of the screen door. Outside, she could see Davey practicing his dribbling. "Hey, dinner's on!" she hollered without moving.

"I probably could have managed that myself." Bonnie removed the casserole from the oven. "Next time, could you mobilize your butt to the door before you shriek?"

Jane shrugged. Whatever. She didn't say it out loud, though. "Whatever" was one of those words that could send her mom off the deep end and lose Jane her TV privileges for a week. She flashed back to the bully that afternoon saying "whatever," and felt herself flush hot and embarrassed.

Davey came running in. He draped himself onto a chair. "What're we having?"

"Chicken casserole."

"Is it that 'Kitchen Helper' again? That stuff is gross."

Bonnie shot Davey one of her "try that again and see what happens" looks. "You want to start cooking meals, be my guest."

Jane was surprised. This was good. Little Mr. Perfect never got called on the carpet.

"You can make whatever you want, provided it's edible and contains something other than sugar."

Davey grinned. "Hey, that'd be cool! Can I make dinner tomorrow? I could make macaroni and cheese."

Bonnie smiled. "Sure."

Apparently, all was forgiven. Too bad.

Over dinner, Bonnie asked how the last day of school had gone. Jane gave her standard response: "Fine." Vague overall, but positive enough not to cause more questions. No way was she going to mention her encounter with those boys.

Davey, as usual, gave a blow-by-blow account of his day. Jane began picking at her fingernails under the table. "It was good. We just played games and watched videos. Matthew Eden burped for like twenty seconds. He got through two-thirds of the alphabet before he ran out of breath."

Bonnie shook her head. "I'm pleased to know that my tax dollars are being so wisely used."

The screen door slammed. Meg poked her head through the doorframe. "Hey, guys!" She bumped into the corner of the wall, ricocheting off like a pinball and stopping just short of the table edge. Rubbing her temple, she shrugged as if to say, "What can you do?"

Wandering over to the cupboard, Meg said, "I was hoping you were having dinner. I'm starved!" She found a plate in the cupboard, grabbed a fork and sat down in a single, smooth glide.

Bonnie laughed. "Why don't you join us?"

Meg stopped, fork suspended in mid-air. "Oh, man!" she whined sarcastically. "I have to use manners now?" Switching to her normal voice, she said, "Sorry. I'm a little scattered today. I barely know my ass from a hole in the ground."

Bonnie raised an eyebrow. "Language, Meg," she said, looking at Davey.

Meg snorted. "Oh, I bet he says worse when you're not around."

Davey giggled, happy as a just-patted puppy.

Jane rolled her eyes. Davey always got all the attention. She said, "Did you know the seniors stole the school flag and replaced it with a banner made out of underpants? Each pair had a letter spelling out 'Class of '92.'"

Meg laughed. "The old underpants-banner trick. Brings back memories." She grinned at Jane. Jane felt a happy flush under the glow of her cousin's approval. She took a bite of casserole, trying to act nonchalant.

Bonnie turned her attention back to Meg. "So Meg, where have you been? We've missed you."

"I missed you guys too. Jane, I especially missed our laundry dates. But I did have a good excuse. You're not going to believe it." Meg pursed her lips, like she was considering options. Her voice dropped, low and conspiratorial. "I don't know if I should say anything about it. I haven't even told my parents yet." Now she started twisting her hair around her finger.

Oh, God, it was probably a guy. Yawn. Jane stared at her casserole with heightened interest. "Fine. I don't really care, anyway." Hopefully they'd break up soon and Meg would get back to normal.

Bonnie stayed quiet, refusing to enter the game. Davey jumped right in, though. "C'mon, Meg. Tell us!"

Jane rolled her eyes; God, scratch his tummy and he'd probably shake his leg.

"Okay," Meg said. "Here it is ... drum roll, please ... " Davey began to thump the table, making the silverware jiggle.

"I'm engaged."

Jane picked at her fingers under the table with intensity. She did not want to look at Meg. Bonnie and Davey jumped up and enveloped Meg in a group hug, although Jane saw her mother had her "loving concern" expression on.

Meg unfolded the basic story. She had met Brady at a folk convention, in between the headline act and the banjo workshop. It had been love at first sight, of course. Brady had been lying on a blanket on the hillside, reading some Dylan Thomas, when Meg tripped over him. Her sandal slipped off her foot, and the shoe began tumbling down the hill, stopping to rest several feet from them. Brady had jumped up and gone to fetch the errant sandal. When he returned, he got down on one knee and replaced the sandal gingerly on Meg's foot.

At this point, Jane interrupted. It had been undying, instant love with ninety-nine percent of Meg's previous boyfriends. "So he's a shoe salesman?"

"No, doofus. He teaches second grade. God, I felt just like Cinderella."

"Cinderella's punked-out stepsister, maybe. C'mon, Meg!"

Davey butted in. "Geez, Jane, what's your problem? He sounds nice."

Jane positioned her hand under the table – out of her mother's line of sight but still in Davey's – and shot up her middle finger.

Meg laughed and continued her story. After her knight in shining t-shirt saved her sandal, they sat down on the blanket and talked – and eventually, made out until most of the audience had gone home. "I'm surprised no one threw water on us."

"That's gross," Davey said with a groan.

Meg grabbed Davey's nose and gave it a tweak. "Not as gross as the Wet Willie I'm going to give you!"

Davey twisted away from her. From a safe distance, he stuck out his tongue.

"So, last night," Meg said, "Brady asked me to marry him and I said yes. Pretty cool, huh?"

Oh, this was the perfect ending to the day. Jane stared at her napkin and tried to breathe evenly. Under no circumstances would she cry.

Bonnie smothered Meg in a hug. "I'm so thrilled," she said. "How do your mom and dad like him?"

"Believe it or not, they both think he's great! I thought Mom was going to jump him after he brought her flowers when he met her the first time. And after Dad found out that Brady was All-State in basketball during high school, well, that was all he needed. I'll head over there next to give them the news, but I just wanted to tell you guys first." Meg paused. "Jane, you're not saying much. Are you OK?"

Jane stared at Meg, unblinking. "Are you pregnant?" she asked.

Davey started giggling. Bonnie choked on her water, but as soon as she stopped the convulsive coughing, she admonished Jane with a "That's enough!"

Meg looked calmly at Jane, seemingly unfazed by the question. "Brady's one of the good guys, Jane, okay? We're getting married because we love each other, and we don't see a reason to wait. Neither of us is much of a planner. In fact, we probably would have eloped, except that his mother would have dropped clean over dead. Anyway, I think you'll like him if you let yourself, but if you don't, y'know, well, that's your deal."

Jane mumbled, "Sorry," under her breath and excused herself from the table. As she skulked back to her room, head down, she heard her mom apologize for her behavior.

Davey said, "I think she's got her period."

Meg laughed. "No sweat, it's cool. Listen, I gotta scram. I've got to go see Mom and Dad, then I'm meeting Brady, and we're gonna slam out all the gory details of the big day. Later!" Jane heard a noisy kiss being planted, presumably on Davey, and the screen door slam.

She threw herself down on her bed and hid her head under the pillow. Why didn't she feel happy for Meg? She didn't even get to see her all that much anymore since Meg started working at the store full-time, maybe once a month. And it wasn't like she told her secrets or anything, although it would've been nice if Meg had told her before everyone else. Jane had never minded Meg's boyfriends that much before, even serious ones. She couldn't figure it out – it was all too weird. She had a bad feeling about this summer.

It only got worse when the phone rang, and her mom called out, "Jane, phone! It's some lady named Pam Burke, says you saved her little boy today from some bullies!"

Oh hell.

~ 2 ~

BONNIE

Bonnie inhaled deeply as she drove through the valley, listening to Carole King on the oldies' radio station. Ironic that the only peace she had in any day was her forty-minute commute, three times a week, to visit her mother at Whispering Woods. Whispering Woods – what a name. There was Parkland Villas, Deer Hollow Run, Canterbury Hills: names designed to evoke a sense of opulence and ease, sanctuaries where one could while away the hours playing Whist with characters lifted out of *The Great Gatsby*. Or contemplate a life well led while staring at the deer grazing in a wooded glade. But what none of these homes could disguise, with their floral wallpaper borders and cozy walnut-stained wainscoting, was the antiseptic weariness. It clouded the air like fog.

Whispering Woods had been no better, no worse, than the others, but it had the advantage of being closest to home, and it overlooked an actual pine forest. Bonnie doubted whether Elizabeth ever looked at the scenery. The location, however, made it easier for Bonnie to bear the visits. That was something, at least.

Dusk was beginning to fall, so Bonnie flicked on her headlights. The air circling around her neck from the cracked window was unusually cool and crisp for an early June evening in Ohio. Bonnie was glad she'd remembered to tie her hair back: the last time she'd driven with the window down and her hair loose, she'd arrived looking like she'd been given a beehive – or a wasp's nest – by a crazed hairdresser. It had taken a full fifteen minutes in the lobby's bathroom to unsnarl her hair enough to make herself presentable to Mother.

As Bonnie started the long series of lazy S-curves that led out of the valley toward Parkington, she spied a mother deer and a fawn skirting the edge of the woods. She automatically slowed. Sure enough, one deer, spooked by the car's headlights, bolted out into the road, only twenty or so feet away. The second deer followed close behind. Once the mother and baby had cleared into the forest on the other side, Bonnie resumed her course; before long, she had pulled into the u-shaped driveway of the nursing home. The heady smell of honeysuckle bushes lining the drive greeted her as she made her way toward the entrance.

Bonnie walked into the airy vestibule and waved to the nurses sitting behind a large central desk. They smiled and nodded as she passed. Stopping at an ornate gilt-framed mirror, Bonnie quickly checked her appearance. Hair was still neatly pulled back, lipstick fresh, and neither too pale nor too "tarted up," as her mother would put it. It should do. When she reached Elizabeth's room, she stopped at the slightly ajar door. She took a deep cleansing breath, steeled her shoulders, and knocked. There was no reply, as per usual. Bonnie entered.

"Hello, Mother," Bonnie said to a shadow in the corner of the room. "Why are you sitting in the dark?"

Elizabeth shushed Bonnie and raised one hand, pointer finger raised. "Listen," she whispered. The room was silent but for the occasional sound of footsteps echoing down the corridor.

Bonnie walked over to the corner where Elizabeth was sitting and switched on the table lamp. The light illuminated the space just around her, magnifying the shadows on the wall behind.

Elizabeth laughed, a sharp expulsion of air that could have been mistaken for a cough. "Yeah, run for the hills, you bastards," she said with satisfaction, staring at her dresser.

"Who's running for the hills, Mother?"

She looked at Bonnie as if explaining the obvious to a slightly dim child. "Why, the rats, of course. Place is teeming with them. Sneaky little rodents."

Oh. She was seeing the rats again. She seemed to go on jags with this particular hallucination, scaring the bejeezus out of Bonnie the first time she had mentioned it. It took two aides searching the room before Bonnie could be persuaded they were only in her mother's mind. Now, she just let the reference pass. Mother would forget she'd mentioned it in a minute.

Elizabeth peered at Bonnie more closely. "Who are you?"

"It's Bonnie, Mother. Your daughter. How are you feeling today?" Bonnie settled onto the foot of the bed, automatically smoothing out the chenille bedspread she'd brought over during the move from her mother's house.

"Rotten. They don't feed us here. Place ought to be reported. It's appalling." Elizabeth narrowed her eyes. "Daughter, huh? You don't look like any daughter of mine. What's your name?"

"Bonnie."

"I would never give a child of mine such a common name," Elizabeth harrumphed. "Well, you might as well stay. No one ever visits me." She raised her arm and waved her hand, a queen granting an audience.

Bonnie closed her eyes and rubbed her temples. Honestly, Jane's fourteen-year-old histrionics didn't exasperate her as much.

Every time Bonnie came here, she was torn between a desire to bang her head against the wall repeatedly or put her mother over her knee for a good spanking. She had long ago abandoned the idea that Elizabeth would recognize her. But the irrational hope remained that she might at least recall that she'd just seen Bonnie only a few days ago.

Because it was true: no one else visited. Vivian was useless. Bonnie didn't know what the fallout had been between Vivian and Elizabeth years ago, but whatever it was trumped her older sister's more general adoption of the martyr role. She always had some other commitment vying for her time that precluded a visit. Frankly, it was easier making sure Mother was taken care of without Vivian's input.

"Hey!" Elizabeth snapped. "You there, scratching your head. Are you sick? Did you come here to pass along your germs? Don't think I don't know what you're all up to. If it's not the rats, it's the germs, trying to kill me. I won't have it!"

Bonnie placed her hands in her lap. "It's always such a relief to know that at least your paranoia can survive Alzheimer's."

"Don't you sass me, missy. I'm your elder."

Bonnie sighed. "Yes, ma'am." Trying to make her voice sound cheery, she asked, "Mother, would you like to take a walk with me?"

"Don't be stupid, girl. Do I look like I'm in any condition to walk? I'm practically at death's door. I'll probably be dead by the time you come to visit again." Elizabeth gave a little hiccup of a sob and clutched her woolen lap robe tighter, like a security blanket.

Bonnie bit her lips to hide a smile. Her mother could walk faster than most of the aides, as she had demonstrated in several impromptu escape attempts. Rising from the bed, she walked over to her mother and kissed her on top of her head, lips touching fine-spun silver. "You always say that, Mother, and you're always here. Why, you'll probably outlive me, or at least your mouth will."

Her mother glared at her. "Don't be impertinent."

"You're right, Mother. I apologize." Bonnie recognized with discomfort the same robotic roteness that Jane occasionally used in her apologies.

"So what did you bring me? You did bring me something, right?"

How typical that Elizabeth would never remember Bonnie's name but could somehow recall that Bonnie always brought a food offering. She dug through the detritus of wadded Kleenex and store receipts in her purse and found the bag of orange shortbread cookies she'd made yesterday. Elizabeth clutched the proffered sack with one delicate hand, fumbling with the other to get one of the shortbread squares out. Her fingers were long and spidery, their skin translucent as parchment. She brought the cookie to her mouth with a slight tremor and gnawed on it absent-mindedly, looking off into the distance.

She seemed now to have forgotten that Bonnie was even in the room. Every thirty seconds or so Elizabeth would lick a spittled crumb off her lips, habitual as a blink. After a few minutes she brought the half-eaten cookie back down to her lap, although she continued intermittently to lick her lips.

Bonnie felt a small thrum of concern ignite deep in her chest. This was new. Never before had Mother lost her focus during the act of eating, heretofore as precious to her as any act of intimacy. She might tune out during a conversation, close her eyes in mid-sentence, but eating? Bonnie examined her mother more closely, looking for changes. It was possible that Elizabeth appeared slightly thinner, but it was hard for Bonnie to say, since she saw her so often. She would have to ask the nurses before she left for the evening. They could check her weight log.

Elizabeth was nodding off now, her head cocked over to the wing of her chair. Her eyelids drifted shut for several seconds, then slit open not even a quarter-way as she unseeingly gazed at some moondust before her. They closed again, heavy with the slowed blinks that reminded Bonnie of her children when they were babies.

"The eagle has landed," Bonnie whispered. She rose and stole the slobbery cookie off her mother's lap. She did not want to wake Elizabeth, but couldn't stop herself from attempting lightly to dust the crumbs away from her lap. Tucking the bag of shortbread into her jacket pocket, Bonnie smoothed the lap robe over her mother's legs.

"Bye bye, Mother. Happy dreams. I'll see you in a couple days." Bonnie bent forward and brushed a light kiss onto her mother's cheek. Elizabeth did not stir.

One of the evening shift nurses, Daisy, was working on charts out at the nurses' station. She rose to greet Bonnie, and placed her hand on the small of her back. She appeared to be about eight months and twenty-eight days pregnant.

"I suppose you're tired of having people ask," Bonnie said, "but when are you due?"

"Two weeks from now, believe it or not. He's gonna be a big boy!" Daisy chuckled and shook her head.

"Your first?"

"Third."

"Wow. Well, I wish you a quick labor and a good epidural," Bonnie said.

"Thanks." Daisy looked like she wanted to get back to sitting, casting sideways glances at her charts. "Was there something you wanted?"

"I just wanted to see if anyone's noted anything different about Mother's eating recently."

Daisy furrowed her brow. "Well, she's definitely not as interested in the food in the dining hall these days, but if you'll hang on a sec, I'll check." She pulled Elizabeth's chart from a revolving lazy Susan and flipped it open. "She *has* lost a couple pounds since last month. I'll leave a note for the doctor. Maybe we'll get her put on a calorie supplement." She gazed up at Bonnie sympathetically. "I don't think it's anything to worry about yet, okay? We'll keep an eye on it, though."

As Bonnie turned to leave, Daisy called to her. "Ms. Stanton?"

Bonnie pivoted back.

"Your mom's been talking a lot the last few days, calling everyone 'Dot.' She usually thinks we're someone else, but this is the longest she's stuck with one person. Do you know who 'Dot' is?"

"That's my aunt. Mother's sister."

"Well, that explains it, then." Daisy nodded, apparently satisfied with the answer. She began to turn back to her charting.

But now Bonnie's interest was piqued. "So what has Mother been talking to Dot about? Has there been a particular topic she's stayed on?"

Daisy quickly scanned Elizabeth's chart notes before answering. "Nobody's written anything. If she was agitated while she was talking to Dot, we'd have noted it. So I doubt there's anything to worry about."

"I wasn't worried, just curious." Bonnie repositioned her purse, which had slipped off her shoulder. "You'll let me know, though, about the calorie supplement?"

"Absolutely. Have a good evening."

Back in the car, she sat, hands resting on the steering wheel. The keys were in the ignition, but she made no move yet to start the car. Dot. It had been years since she'd died, years since Bonnie had thought about her, but the memory of her was vivid and comforting. Dot had been as round and cushiony as Elizabeth was angular and sharp. She'd smelled of yeast and sugar, and she had loved Bonnie. Even though Bonnie knew relatives weren't supposed to have favorites, she knew with a happy certainty that she was Dot's. Until she was seven years old, she'd spent several weeks every summer on Aunt Dot's and Uncle Joe's farm. She'd help with chores, play with the lambs and piglets, shadow her aunt's side in the kitchen as she baked. Vivian had never come, preferring to stay in town with her school friends, so these summers were like Bonnie's special secret.

She always felt vaguely traitorous when she wished for Dot as a mother, and would try hard not to think such thoughts. But each time Dot brushed Bonnie's hair, twisting the golden strands into braids, and each time she let her crawl up into her lap, even though much too old for such a thing, Bonnie felt the ring around her heart tighten. She'd wished that she could be Dot's forever.

In July of Bonnie's seventh year, it had all ended. Bonnie had been in the garden picking green beans. Even though she was wearing a broad hat, she could still feel the sun beating through the loosely woven straw onto her neck. Hairs escaped from her braids and lay limp, plastered by sweat. Dot had come bustling out, her face mottled and glistening with recent tear tracks. She'd pulled Bonnie into a tight bear hug, a tangible dampness on her apron.

"Honey, I've got some bad news for you. Your mama was just on the phone. I'm afraid that your daddy has passed on. We're going to need to get you packed and home."

Bonnie had stared at Dot, barely comprehending. She wasn't quite sure why she didn't feel like crying; she didn't really feel anything. "Home" seemed another world away. Her father had been an invalid for so long, bedbound by a bad heart, that his death did not come as a surprise. She gestured helplessly with open hands to the garden. "What should I do about the green beans? I've still got lots to pick."

Dot bit her lip and teared up again. She cleared her throat and dabbed at her eyes with her apron. "Oh, Bonnie, don't you worry about that. Joe'll be able to handle it."

The ride home was quiet. Dot wouldn't let Bonnie turn on the radio as a sign of respect for the departed. Bonnie didn't feel much like music, anyway. She'd never been able to have much interaction with her father because of his health. He was pretty old, as old as some of her friends' grandfathers. Once or twice a week, Elizabeth would schedule Bonnie to entertain her father with tales of school or a game of checkers. Bonnie enjoyed these visits. Father always let her beat him, missing obvious moves and then trying to cheat outrageously. When she caught him, he'd lay his hand on her shoulder, then pretend to be sad as he moved his reds back along the diagonal. Thinking about the checkers made Bonnie want to cry. But she was mad as well. Why couldn't he wait to die until after the summer was over? Why'd he have to ruin the rest of her summer?

She pinched herself hard on the inside of her forearm in repentance, and tried to think nothing for the rest of the ride home.

As she reached the stoop, before she even opened the door, Bonnie could hear her mother issuing orders like a drill sergeant. "Thank God you're home. There's a million things to do. Dot, are you staying? Bonnie, you're filthy. Go to your room immediately and get washed." Elizabeth did not sound especially sad either, more like she was running a business. Dot's head was bowed, and every so often she took out her handkerchief and blew with gusto. As she went to her room, Bonnie felt guilty - she realized that the only one who seemed even remotely sad about her father's death was Dot, who was only related to him by marriage.

After the funeral, which was disconcertingly sunny, family and friends departed. Bonnie sought refuge in her room, but left the door cracked. She heard Dot's and her mother's voices in the kitchen. Her own name came up in conversation.

"So Elizabeth, you know that if you need anything at all in the coming days, you just call, all right?"

"We'll be fine, Dot. Things will probably be easier now that I won't have to be a nursemaid anymore."

"Yes, of course. But... you'll be getting less pension. Do you have a job lined up? Who will watch the girls?" Aunt Dot raised this last question slowly, almost like she was afraid.

"It's a small town. Someone's bound to need a clerk or a bookkeeper somewhere." Elizabeth paused. "And the girls are perfectly capable of taking care of themselves if I'm not here. Vivian's fifteen, for goodness' sake."

Bonnie narrowed her eyes. Her mother did not have to use that smart tone of voice with Aunt Dot.

There was a long silence, broken finally by Elizabeth. "Oh, for God's sake, Dot, spit it out."

Her reply was so quiet, Bonnie had to sneak up right next to the door to hear what she was saying. "... you know Joe and I couldn't love Bonnie more if she was our own. So I was just thinking that, with this being such a difficult time and all, well, if you wanted to let her come live with us for a while ..."

Bonnie realized she was holding her breath.

"You don't think I can take care of her." Elizabeth's voice was low and dangerous. "You think you can do a better job."

"It's just that Bonnie is so happy on the farm, you just wouldn't even recognize her."

In her room, Bonnie winced, knowing that her mother would take *that* the wrong way.

Dot continued in a great rush, as if hoping Elizabeth would lose her place in the conversation. "And anyway, Lizzie, you treat that child differently than Vivian, you know you do. It's as if when Pete died, you did, too. And Bonnie's suffered for it."

Pete? Who was Pete?

Bonnie heard a plate or teacup or something crash and break. Her mother was shouting now. "You promised you'd NEVER talk about that! You promised." Elizabeth's voice broke raggedly. "

Furniture scraped on the linoleum. "Lizzie, I'm sorry; I didn't mean it. Please think about what I asked. Bonnie's lonely and we love her so much."

"Just leave. I'll tell her you said goodbye. Go."

Bonnie eased the door closed and sank down on the floor, cradling her head in her hands. Everything good had to end sometime, right? She felt extra guilt realizing that she felt worse about losing Dot thanshe did about her own father. Her mother continued to storm through the house, upending furniture and muttering to herself loudly. A screen door opened and wheezed shut. Dot was gone.

~3~
MEG

Meg puttered around the exhibit area of Yesteryears, adjusting tops and hanging up new merchandise. She loved this time of morning, an hour before they opened, when she could work with the radio on and the lights off, natural light streaming in the storefront's wall of windows. The shop had just obtained a collection of antique aprons made out of cotton feed sacks in excellent condition, the prints still vibrant and bright. Meg wandered around the display, assisting the mannequins in tying the aprons around their waists. The store was beginning to resemble a scene from *The Stepford Wives*.

A small bell tinkled someone's arrival. Carla walked in the front door, grinning as she viewed Meg's handiwork.

"Already dreaming of being a housewife?" Her Jamaican accent was faint but still carried a musical lilt.

"Oh, about as much as you're dreaming about dying your hair blond."

Carla waggled a dreadlock at her, smiling. As she fingered the weave of the aprons, she said, "Mmm, these are really nice. Very retro. I wonder if we'll sell a single one to anyone who actually cooks." She walked over to the wall and started flicking on overhead lights. "Speaking of domestic hell, how are you and your prospective in-laws getting along?"

Meg began updating inventory on the computer. "I love Brady's dad. He's a total pussycat. And Mona's actually not so bad, in a frigid, WASP-y sort of way. We met for lunch last week – her club, of course – so that I could see the place before she booked it for the reception. She managed to book the church for the date we wanted, which is a freaking miracle, considering it's only a couple months away."

"Is she still pissed about that?"

"What, that the wedding's so soon? Probably. But she'd never say anything to me about it. I can mostly tell because Brady's bending over backward now trying to accommodate his parents and their Santa's list of invitees."

Meg loaded a new receipt roll into the cash register. "So what about your weekend? How was the concert?"

As Carla started to answer, the phone rang. Meg answered. "Yesteryear's Vintage Clothes."

"Meg, is that you?"

The voice on the other end was familiar, but Meg couldn't place the edgy tone. "Speaking. How can I help you?"

"Meg, this is Mona."

This *was* a surprise. "Well, hi, Mona. You don't sound like yourself. What's up?"

"I'm at the hospital, St. Elizabeth's." Mona's voice sounded tight, brittle as a twig. "Brady's been hurt."

"Are you sure?" Meg realized how stupid that must sound. Before Mona could answer, she said, "Sorry, I didn't mean that. But I just left him a couple hours ago and he was fine. What happened? How bad is he?"

"He was apparently mugged while he was walking Barkley."

Meg's hand ached, and she realized she had a white-knuckled grip on the phone. She consciously took a deep breath and tried to relax her body.

"His ankle is broken. He's got cuts and bruises everywhere. The doctors have said he has some broken ribs as well, and he has to go to surgery now so that they can set his ankle. He's never had surgery before."

With these last words, Mona's voice twisted and caught like fabric on a nail. The receiver went silent for a moment and then she resumed, her voice recomposed. "I apologize for not calling you sooner. It took me some time to find your work number. Do you want to meet us here? Or, if you're busy, I can call you later with an update."

"Of course I'm coming over! I'm leaving right now." Meg's mind was racing. A thought tripped over part of what Mona had said. "Oh, Jesus, Barkley. Is Barkley okay?"

"The police told us that they picked him up when they found Brady. They're keeping him in the animal shelter until someone comes to pick him up."

Meg's heart twisted for the poor Basset. She knew he would be howling like an abandoned child. Hoping she didn't come off as a total flake, she asked, "When is Brady going into surgery? Is he conscious? If he's heading in before I'd make it to the hospital, I should probably go pick Barkley up."

"Yes, that's a good idea." Mona sounded tired, like she didn't care what Meg did. "We'll see you in a little while, dear."

"Kiss Brady for me?"

"Of course."

Meg hung up the phone and stared at it, unmoving.

"Hey, Meg, are you okay?"

Meg turned to face Carla. "I have to go." Her forearm was numb from holding the phone so tightly. "Brady was mugged this morning. He's in the hospital."

She said the words as a matter of fact, a news bite, an act that had happened to a random stranger. Not to Brady. See? The words just floated away, absorbed into the air. If this really involved Brady, surely the gravity of the words would have sent them crashing in shards around her feet.

"Shit, man. That's low." Carla's face was drawn in concern. "Go, already. Don't worry about this place." As Meg gathered her tote bag from the back room, she added, "Call me if you need anything, 'kay, Meggers?"

Meg drove on auto-pilot all the way to the animal shelter. She was fairly certain she stopped for red lights and stop signs, and she hoped she signaled her turns. Every once in a while she wiped a wetness from her cheeks, although she was not aware of crying. She pictured Brady earlier that day, stretching before his morning run in his sweat shorts and holey T-shirt, a ball cap tamping down bed hair. She loved how before a run he'd start talking to her, his head buried into his knee as he stretched his quad muscle, then get so involved in what he was saying that he would come out of the stretch and have to start over. He just had to be okay.

Barkley was a mass of quivering flesh rolls. He greeted Meg with the mixed message of joyful tail wag and mournful eyes of the condemned. After the attendant handed him over, she clutched him like a squirming baby, burying her face in his neck.

They piled into her beaten-up VW Bug. "Fasten your belt," Meg said to the dog, then reached across him and fastened the shoulder strap over his stubby body. Barkley sat motionless, too timid to move.

Brady was in surgery by now. What if there were more serious injuries? Sometimes people had internal injuries that didn't show up right away. Okay, so she only knew this from watching *St. Elsewhere* reruns, but it really did happen. What if he were dead? He couldn't be dead.

Meg started talking aloud to drown out the scary thoughts in her head. "So Barkster, the plan is I'm going to drop you at my place and then go see your dad, okay?" Her voice seemed far away to her. She dangled her fingers in front of his nose when they reached an intersection and let him lick her fingertips. Trying to keep her voice light for the dog, and really, for herself, too, she said, "What happened this morning, Pops? Did some mean mugger boys get in a fight with you and my guy? I bet you were pretty ferocious, huh? Showed them who's king of stumpy land?" She wasn't fooling anyone. She could literally feel her heart thump against her chest like a prisoner trying to escape.

She started to feel weepy. On the one hand, she was worried like crazy about Brady, but on the other hand, she was pissed. They had argued about how and when to navigate the neighborhood safely. Their apartment was on a clean, tree-lined street. But once you ventured more than a block or two away from his building, the neighborhood faded, became a bleaker version of itself. Wire fences and gates warped and bent in the postage stamp-sized yards, and windows had boards or bars across them to ward off intruders. The kids in Brady's class came from this neighborhood, and they knew how to stay safe, as far as they could. But just as Brady was always trying to fashion lessons to equalize the kids in his class, he also held to this notion that if he refused to operate on society's racial biases, he would be making a difference. And this translated into actions like running or taking the dog for walks wherever he wanted, regardless of time of day or whether the area was isolated or populated. So he'd walked around with blinders on, and this is what happened. The I-told-you-so tasted bitter in Meg's mouth.

"I love your dad, but he can be a real moron," Meg told Barkley as she parked the car in front of her duplex apartment. The dog softly whined. When they got indoors, she hoisted Barkley up in her arms and deposited him in front of the couch, then got him some water.

"I don't have any dog food yet, so you'll have to make do with Cheerios." Getting down on all fours directly in front of the dog, Meg planted a kiss on his unibrow. "I'll take good care of Dad and get him back home to you, okay, Pops?" She wrote a quick explanatory note for her roommates – given how seldom either of them was home and/or sober, it was conceivable that they wouldn't even notice the dog – and left again.

At the hospital, Meg checked in at Patient Information and got directions to the Surgery waiting area. As soon as she spied Arthur, sitting uncomfortably on an overstuffed vinyl chair, she began running, calling, even though he was a good seventy feet away.

"Oh my God. How is he?"

As she reached him, Arthur stood and clasped her hands in his.

"Brady's out of surgery. He's in Recovery right now." Arthur's voice was calm, but he still looked relieved.

"Can I go see him?" Meg felt her heart racing, as if she'd been held underwater and was only now being let up for breath.

"I'm sorry, Meg. Mona's back with him now, and they are pretty strict about only letting one family member in at a time until he gets back to his room."

"I need to see him. I need to make certain he's okay." Meg wanted to stamp her foot in frustration. "He *is* all right, isn't he, Arthur?"

Arthur took her hand and patted it. "He's going to be fine. The surgery went well. They put some pins in his ankle, so he might set off a few metal detectors from here on out, but he'll make a complete recovery."

Meg sank down onto a chair. She felt tears spring to her eyes. Dammit, she didn't want to wait. And yet, her mind had concocted all these scenarios of what must have happened, and she was terrified to witness the evidence of how close he'd truly come to getting killed.

Arthur sat next to her. "He's a strong boy. He'll be fine, Meg. Are *you* holding up?"

"A little bit. It certainly seems like more than a few hours since I saw him last." Meg massaged her temples. "Have you talked to the police?"

"Just momentarily. I'm sure they'll be back once Brady's recovered a little, although I doubt the case will be much of a priority. The prevailing theory is that he got beaten more severely when those thugs found out he didn't have his wallet or any cash on him."

Meg squeezed her eyes closed, but she couldn't shut out the vision of Brady lying bruised and beaten on the ground. "I just keep thinking this can't have actually happened, that there's been this giant mistake. I don't know." She gave a rueful smile. "Maybe my blood sugar level is tanking."

"Look, Brady won't be in Recovery for long. I was going to walk down to the cafeteria and get some sodas. Why don't you come with me, keep me company? Maybe he'll have been moved to a room by the time we get back."

As they headed toward the cafeteria, she listened to the rhythmic clip-clop of the soles of their shoes on the scuffed linoleum, and stifled the utterly inappropriate urge to break into one of the jump-rope rhymes from her childhood: *Miss Mary Mack, Mack, Mack, all dressed in black, black, black, with silver buttons, buttons, buttons, all down her back, back, back.* She doubted if Arthur had ever heard of it. What were these thoughts? Was she being hysterical? She couldn't afford to have a breakdown.

"I hate hospitals," Arthur confided to Meg in a hushed voice.

"But you're a doctor. Isn't that like a mountain climber being afraid of heights?"

Arthur chuckled. "Maybe so. But I can't help it. I don't like the smell, I don't like the way the light falls on the walls. I get very claustrophobic in hospitals. I'm much happier in an office."

Meg knew what he meant. A prankster could blindfold her, drive her around for hours, and deposit her in a hallway just like this one, and she'd be able to identify it as a hospital before they got the blindfold off. Every one she'd ever been in had that same bleachy smell that they tried to camouflage with faux-lemon scent. And the fluorescent lights in the hallways cast a sickly green glow onto the white walls.

They reached the cafeteria and made choices using the "least of all evils" approach. Meg suspected Arthur might be dragging out the process to keep from having to make awkward conversation until Brady was moved out of Recovery to his room. After they paid for their items, Arthur glanced at his watch and nodded. "Shall we, my dear?"

Arthur confirmed in the waiting room that Brady had been moved. As they began walking to the orthopedic wing, Meg's stomach was in knots. God, please let him look okay, be okay.

A nurse came out of Brady's room as Arthur and Meg approached. "Are you more of Brady's family?"

Meg glanced at Arthur. He caught her gaze and smiled. "We are. May we come in or do we need to wait a bit?"

"No, your timing's perfect. He just got here a few minutes ago. He's as comfortable as we can make him at the moment. Mrs. Campbell is in there with him. I wouldn't stay too long though; he's still kind of out of it, which nothing but sleep will cure."

With legs feeling weighted with wet sand, Meg entered the room. Mona was sitting in a chair beside the hospital bed. The bed itself appeared to be occupied by an actor – one of those extras from a hospital TV movie-of-the-week. Welts and bruises covered Brady's face. His eyebrows and cheek features were swollen, exaggerated, a doll's face stuffed by an incompetent doll maker. A wide bandage, already soiled the deep red-brown of dried blood, covered his nose. Brady's hospital gown draped over him loosely, exposing a slim line of butt cheek. His left ankle was casted and raised in a kind of Rube-Goldberg-looking traction device.

Meg had expected to feel shocked or repulsed, and had been rehearsing a benign lie about how well Brady was doing. But all she saw was *her* Brady, and her relief at this made her almost giddy. Afraid to touch him for fear of hurting something, she kissed him on top of his head. She hoped she'd found an unscathed spot. "Hey, baby. You look like shit."

Even though Meg meant it to be light, Mona recoiled ever so slightly in her chair, re-crossing her arms. She readjusted her already perfect posture so that now her pencil-skirted knees brushed against Brady's bedspread. Meg realized that everything about her at this moment projected her staking her claim as Brady's protector. She bristled at the implication.

"Meggie." Brady's eyes swirled, unfocused. "You look like an angel."

"Those must be some kickin' drugs."

"Mmmm," Brady replied.

Meg took that as a yes. She took his hand and stroked his fingers. "I got Barkley and took him home with me. He's probably eating Cheerios and watching the soaps even as we speak."

"Uh-huh." Brady's eyelids drifted closed, then popped open, then started to lower once more.

Meg laid his hand gently on the bed. "You sleep now, hon. It's okay." She moved over to the foot of the bed and gingerly perched on it. "He doesn't seem too awful," she said to Mona, wanting to share her relief.

Mona's face was marble, expressionless, a Roman statue. Only a small contemptuous pinch to her lips indicated anything other than neutrality. "They've cleaned him up a lot since he first got here. And once the painkillers start wearing off, he won't be doing as well. He will need a significant amount of assistance to come through this ordeal."

Suddenly, Meg saw what Mona wanted her to see. She saw the bruises and bandages and damage and need, and more than anything, what she wanted now was to leave – abandon this broken man to his concrete mother, whose iciness unnerved her as much as Brady's injuries. She was sure Mona despised her. Meg's scalp itched, and as she repressed the urge to scratch, the itch traveled over her entire body. She wanted to scrape her fingers down her flesh until she drew blood, until needles of pain dulled her senses to what she saw in front of her. Meg clenched her fingers into her palms deep enough for her nails to indent the skin.

She stood. Her words faltered. "I wish I could stay longer, but I really need to get back to the store and check on things, and I should probably stop and get some dog food for Barkley. I'll come back later this afternoon or this evening."

The excuses sounded artificial to her even as she said them, but she maintained eye contact with Mona as she lied. Like staring down a lioness.

"It was good of you to come." Mona's tone was polite, evenly modulated.

"I'll walk you out." Arthur had been standing in the corner of the room this entire time. Hospital rooms were so insane. There were never enough chairs, and someone was always odd man out, standing in the corner like a child in time-out. Mona raised a hand as if dismissing them both.

As they exited the chill of the hospital wing, drawn into the warm sunshine, both Meg and Arthur inhaled the fresh air with deep, open-mouthed gulps. They smiled uncomfortably as each noticed the other doing it.

"I feel guilty leaving." Meg rested her hand on the VW's door. "Mona looks like she's in there for the long haul."

"She's his mother. It's part of the job. And there's history there, of course."

Was there something Brady hadn't told her? Something big she didn't know about him? Meg felt suddenly as if she were observing their engagement from the outside in, skeptical that two people who had been together so briefly could have any foundation on which to build a marriage. "Oh?"

"Brady had meningitis as a child. It came on very quickly, very violently. We almost lost him." Arthur cleared his throat.

"Mona didn't leave his bedside for over a week, except to use the bathroom. I think she felt she was the only thing standing between him and Death."

Meg was torn between feeling a magnified respect for Mona, and jealous of the strength of her passion for her son. She felt like such a coward.

Arthur's forehead was creased with the memory of that long-ago trauma. She reached out and squeezed him in a bear hug around the middle. There was so much of him in Brady: it was like fast-forwarding twenty-five years.

He awkwardly accepted the hug, maintaining his rigid posture and patting Meg on the back in the manner of someone who is trying to help a coughing victim. She stepped out of the hug, hoping she hadn't embarrassed him.

~4~
JANE

Jane sat on the couch, idly fingering a nickel-sized hole in the upholstery's broad weave. Charley sat on the floor in front of her, systematically lining up his Match-Box cars into perfect rows, like he was overseeing parking in the world's widest drive-in movie. Jane had been babysitting him for more than a week now, and each day was exactly the same as the last. What had she gotten herself into?

On her first day of work, Mrs. Burke and Charley had met her at the door. After telling her not to worry about that "Mrs. Burke nonsense," Pam had introduced Jane to Charley. He'd stared at the plaid checks on her blouse, then turned and walked back into the kitchen.

In the dining room, Pam went over the routine. Jane listened with half an ear, trying to watch Charley at the same time through the cutaway in the wall that separated the dining room from the kitchen. He was sitting at the kitchen table, eating cereal, swinging his legs under his chair like the pendulum on a grandfather clock. His jeans hung down over his feet. In this context, he looked like any other five-year-old.

Pam told her that Charley had a condition called PDD-NOS that fell on the autism spectrum. Jane had been wondering about whether babysitting this kid was a good idea in the first place, and now she really felt nervous. She didn't even know there were different types of autism. When she asked, Pam said the whole thing was really confusing, and that basically, kids with PDD-NOS showed a lot of the same symptoms as children with autism. The worry must have shown in her face, because Pam held up a hand as if to stop a protest, and said that if Jane just followed the day's schedule to the letter, she'd be fine. Charlie knew his routine better than anyone else, so for the most part, Jane should just let him do his thing. Lunch was a peanut butter and jelly sandwich on white toast, sliced on the diagonal. Charley would either get very upset, or just not eat, if there were any deviation. The other part of the day that could not be tampered with was Charley's show, on from three to three-thirty: *Food Frenzy*. He knew what channel he needed and would turn the television on at the right time.

"It's his favorite show. And it's the only time the television should be on." Pam eyed Jane to see if this was going to be a problem. As if. There was nothing on during the day anyway except talk shows and soap operas. Ick.

"Will he talk to me, do you think?" If not, a little quiet wouldn't be so bad. A nice change from Davey – who never, ever, shut up.

Pam scrunched up her nose. "Maybe, maybe not. He doesn't talk to most people, just me and his dad. It sort of depends on how comfortable he gets around you."

When Pam left for work that morning, Charley walked with her to the door. He didn't look sad or upset, and he didn't kiss her goodbye. Pam didn't try to kiss him, either. Their only contact was Charley briefly pressing his palm against hers. It reminded Jane of that scene from *E.T.* where the alien and Elliott touch fingers. Maybe Charley was part alien. After Pam left, he shuffled back to the dining room table to finish his cereal. His face never changed its half-asleep expression.

After breakfast was done, he lined blocks up as precisely as if he'd had a ruler in front of him. This took forty-five minutes. Then he went to use the bathroom. Jane knew he was done after she heard the water: on and off and on and off and on and off. After he came back into the living room, he took his basket of coins off the shelf, and sorted them into pennies, nickels, dimes and quarters. After he sorted them, he put them all back into the basket.

In all this time, he did not glance at Jane once. He might as well have been alone in the house. Her being there was so pointless. Jane normally did not have destructive impulses, but a fantasy entered her mind about whirling the basket of coins over her head like a helicopter blade, scattering them to all corners of the room.

The only voice Jane heard during that day was that doofus Pierre Miller, who hosted *Food Frenzy*. She'd never watched it before. This guy Pierre was the traffic reporter for one of the local stations, so he must have thought this show was his ticket to the big time. Poor guy.

At two fifty-nine, Charley stood up and turned on the television. Jane had not seen him consult a clock, so how he knew the exact time was a little freaky. As opening strains of an accordion polka streamed out of the tiny TV speaker, a deep voice boomed, "Are you ready to shop?" Charley hopped like he had to go to the bathroom. He actually clapped his hands. Jane couldn't believe this was the same child. It was like someone had plugged him in. He settled himself on the floor, sitting cross-legged about a foot away from the television screen, staring with a big grin on his face as he rocked back and forth.

On today's show, Pierre Miller was at the ShopMart in Monroe Heights. He'd adopted this weird French accent, which Jane had never heard him use in his traffic reports. Why he thought this was a good idea in *Ohio* was beyond her. And he wore overalls, like he was some sort of farmer – really, it was kind of offensive to actual farmers, when she thought about it.

In the first game, Miller shouted, "It's time for a pickle party," which caused Charley to writhe on the floor, giggling. The game consisted of five shoppers who had to fish for kosher dill pickles out of a giant vat using five-foot forks. It was humiliating, even if the prize was one hundred dollars. After the commercial break, the contestants played a version of tag, and then a scavenger hunt, all involving food in the store. Miller tried to be funny as he introduced each segment, shouting out lines like "We're gonna win bo-coo bucks now!" or "Soo-wheee! Someone's gonna pig out tonight!" The show was so lame, like a tacky version of *The Price is Right*. Jane was relieved when it ended, but a little sorry to see the animated version of Charley retreat as well.

And here they were again, eight days later, the start of a brand-new identical day. In the entire week, Charley had not said a word. Jane was starting to lose her mind from the quiet. As Charley lined up his cars, Jane picked up the *Better Homes and Gardens* magazine lying on the coffee table. She'd already leafed through it four times this week. She prayed that by some miracle, she'd find a story that she hadn't already read, and that it might even be remotely interesting. She set it down after only a few pages, unable to work any magic to transform the newest recipes for asparagus into stories about something cool – maybe about people recovering from brain surgery. It would be so cool to be a brain surgeon. She didn't even like asparagus – it made her pee green.

"Hey, Charley." Jane tried to make herself sound enthusiastic.

He did not look up.

"C'mon, Charley, look at me."

Still nothing.

Jane sighed. If she weren't such a chicken, she'd quit today and find another job. It was depressing being so invisible. She scooted to the floor and tried rocking back and forth like Charley. It felt good, like being cradled in the ocean. Shoot, maybe she was a little autistic herself.

As she gazed at a spot on the wall, she realized something weird. There were no photos of Charley anywhere. No family pictures, period. She couldn't remember ever being in a kid's house where there weren't school photographs or vacation pictures or something framed. At her home, Mom had a big collage that held all her school pictures, from first grade when Jane had actually been kind of cute in a serious-little-kid sort of way, all the way downhill to today. Irrefutable proof that she got dopier looking every year. But at least her mom was proud enough to put her face on the wall. It would be sad not to see yourself growing up in pictures, although Charley probably hadn't noticed.

Jane crawled to Charley. The row of cars made a boundary line between them.

"Charley, ya gotta help me. I'm bored to tears." Jane crossed her eyes, swooned and fell backward onto the carpet.

There was no response. Zip.

"Come *on*, I'm giving you my best material here!"

Sitting back up, she swiped her hair out of her eyes. Charley wasn't looking at her at all. His cars were already in line, so now he began moving the car at the far end of the parking lot to the first spot. Then he re-aligned all the other cars.

This was infuriating. What could she do to make him notice her? Jane put her index finger on the Match-Box ambulance and moved it forward half an inch. "There. I messed up your perfect world. Deal."

Charley immediately moved the ambulance back into position. His expression never changed.

Jane moved another car, this one a miniature red Corvette. Charley moved it back. Another car. And back. As Jane raised her hand and twirled her finger, scanning for her next target, she saw that Charley was looking at her, waiting. Not looking at her shirt, or even her finger, but at her face, for the first time. Jane brought her finger down until it almost touched the metallic blue convertible, then suddenly zipped her finger across the row and moved the black station wagon instead.

"Ha-ha!" she said. "Psych!"

Charley got up and left the living room.

Jane sat there, shaking her head. She'd actually thought he was enjoying this, as much as he'd enjoy anything. Stupid. She pushed herself off the carpet and started off down the hallway to look for him.

Charley emerged from his mother's room holding a pair of matted, fuzzy lilac half-slippers, the ones missing the heel. He walked back to the living room, staring straight ahead. Jane followed behind him, and when she entered the living room, Charley took her hand and pulled her to the couch.

"Shoes off," he said.

Jane was so astounded at hearing him speak that she forgot to listen to what he was saying. "What?"

"Shoes off." Charley began to tug at the shoelaces on Jane's stained and mud-spattered sneakers.

"Okay, okay! I get it!" Jane leaned over, untied her shoes, and slipped them off. "I hope my feet don't stink."

Charley placed the ratty slippers matter-of-factly over Jane's toes. Then, apparently satisfied, he sat back down on the floor and began to re-align his cars.

Jane searched Charley's face for anything that might indicate things had changed between them. But there was nothing. God, he was weird. And these slippers were at least a size too big. But at least he'd talked to her. That had to count for something.

At lunch, while Charley ate his peanut butter and jelly sandwich – cut on the diagonal – Jane tried to figure out how he looked different from other five-year-olds, how those boys would've known to pick on him. He was the same height as kids his age. He wore basic jeans and t-shirt, so his clothes didn't set him apart. He wasn't fat or too skinny. Maybe the hair. His haircut looked like his mom had put a bowl on top of his head, and while she cut around it, Charley kept moving. The edges were all uneven. But there was something besides the hair – something you couldn't see – some kind of invisible force field that rearranged his molecules, so that everyone just knew he was way different.

Jane wondered if she might be giving off some of that same vibe. She always felt like she had a neon sign attached to her sweater that read "Socially Deficient." She sat by herself at lunch. She wasn't a jock, or a prep, or a brain, or a girly-girl type. She wore baggy jeans and sweatshirts, not khakis and polo shirts or jeans jumpers.

Lunchtime was the worst, because that was where the whole school saw that she didn't have any friends. Jane usually brought her lunch specifically so she didn't have to go through the lunch line. That way, she could pick an empty table and let it fill up around her, rather than have to find a seat amongst the assorted cliques. Other kids thought she was a brain, because she brought a book to lunch with her, but that was just so she wouldn't look so pathetic, having no one to talk to.

Once, when she didn't know any better, she'd wandered into the girls' bathroom inhabited by all the punk smokers. The air was thick with nicotine and the smell of spearmint toothpaste. One of the girls – who was only a year older than Jane, but seemed like she was in her twenties – glanced at her from the mirror where she was reapplying stringy mascara. "What do you want," she said, but not in a question sort of way.

Jane had a million answers – a life, a friend, someplace to belong – but she wasn't about to say any of them. "I have to pee," was all she said aloud.

"Go somewhere else."

And Jane did.

She wished Meg hadn't gotten engaged. She felt like she'd lost the only real friend she'd had since her only other friend, Sam, had moved to Pittsburgh. Her parents had been friends with his, so it was one of those adult-arranged friendships. But having spent enough Saturdays with him, they'd reached a point where they enjoyed hanging out, even when he just wanted to practice his air guitar. And while there were a few other kids at school that Jane felt comfortable enough to say hi to, there wasn't anyone she felt like she had anything in common with. It was easier being alone.

She wondered if Sam sat alone in the cafeteria in his Pittsburgh school. Maybe Charley didn't have it so bad after all. Maybe the key to being different was not knowing or caring you were different.

After lunch, Charley stacked his dishes in the sink – he was a neatnik, all right – and then looked at Jane before walking toward his room. Was she supposed to follow him? She craned her head to see around the corner, down the hall. Charley stopped at his door, and turned. Jane still stood at the kitchen doorway. He walked back to her, tugged at her hand, and together, they walked back to his room.

Charley's room looked like the battleground between the forces of chaos and order. The books on his bookshelf were arranged alphabetically, their spines aligned just so. Of course. The Superman sheets on the bed were crumpled and shoved up against the wall. A teddy bear hung towards the floor: one leg wedged between the mattress and the headboard was all that kept it from plunging to its teddy death. Clothes were scattered on the floor, a trail of breadcrumbs to nowhere.

Jane pulled a picture book peeking out from under Charley's bed. "Can you read this?"

Charley looked at the cover of the book. "The-Run-a-way-Bun-ny," he read in a monotone, pronouncing each syllable with the same emphasis. "Mar-ga-ret-Wells." Taking the book from Jane, he walked it over to the bookshelf and filed it under "W."

"Cool. You really *can* read."

Charley grabbed a stack of papers from off his nightstand and handed them to Jane. "Bus."

They were the bus schedules for all the different local bus lines: Cleveland, Daedalus Falls, Tanglewood, Monroe Heights, Parkington. "Yup. These are bus schedules, all right. Are you a big bus traveler?"

Charley took the timetables back from Jane and stacked them on his nightstand. He grabbed a book of food stickers from his open toy chest, then started back to the living room.

Jane felt like she'd passed some sort of test. She pumped her arm in the air on the way out, feeling only seventy-five percent stupid.

Charley had switched on the television in the living room. "It's time for a pickle party."

Jane settled in on the couch. "God, who opened up the floodgates with you? I won't be able to get you to shut up from here on out, is that the deal?"

Charley was hypnotized by the television screen, so she had no idea if he was even listening to her. She smiled. He really wasn't so bad. Maybe she'd be the one to reach him, where no one else had been successful. It'd be just like that movie they'd had to watch in school about Helen Keller, where Annie Sullivan had signed "water" and Helen had finally gotten it. Jane would give lectures and write books, and wherever she went, people would look at her and nod and whisper, "She has a gift with those children, you know."

When Pam arrived home around four-thirty, Jane and Charley were making tall stacks of blocks on the floor. Jane scrambled to her feet to retrieve a drooping bag of groceries from Pam's arms.

"Thanks." Pam was breathless as she crossed the room and hoisted the other three bags onto the kitchen counter. She slid her purse off her shoulder and sank down onto a chair. "So how was your day? It looks like the two of you are having fun."

"We had a real good day, I think. Charley even talked to me."
Jane felt embarrassed about feeling so proud of this – it's not like she
cured him or anything – but she couldn't keep herself from telling.

Pam laughed. "That's wonderful, Jane. You should feel very
honored. It took Charley's speech therapist six weeks before he'd talk
to her, and even then, he only made animal noises and car sounds."
She glanced at Jane's feet. "He really has adopted you."

She was still wearing those ratty lavender slippers. Jane blushed.
"I figured if it made him happy, then what the heck?"

She took the slippers off and found her shoes. "He's smart, isn't
he? I mean, he can read and everything." She stopped and started
again. "Wait. You already knew that. Duh."

"Yes, our Charley has hidden depths, he does." Pam wiped her
eyes with the back of her hand, then walked over to Charley,
planting a kiss on top of his head. He held a block in the air for a
moment, looked up at his mother with that blank expression, and
resumed stacking. Pam moved to the kitchen and began unpacking
groceries.

Jane squatted down next to Charley. Out of the corner of her eye,
she could see Pam observing them from the kitchen. "Well, kiddo, I
guess I'll see you tomorrow, okay? You wanna walk me to the door?"

Charley stood up and followed Jane to the door. As she opened
the screen and stepped one foot outside, she extended her palm to
him like she'd seen Pam do every morning. He hesitated, then
pressed his palm to hers, a pressure firm and yet so giving that Jane
imagined layers of air sandwiched between. As she walked home,
she felt those layers of air beneath her sneakers, buoying her up,
making her believe she could take off and fly.

-5-
BONNIE

Whatever happened to sleeping in on weekends? Bonnie thought as she dropped Davey off at baseball practice. Saturdays and Sundays used to be so glorious, so lazy. She would daydream at work while alphabetizing files, about the key moment when the weekend began: the shutting off of the alarm clock on Friday night. The kids would wake up in the morning and plop in front of the television for marathons of Bugs Bunny and Scooby Doo, broken up by commercials like exclamation points for the latest obnoxious loud electronic toy or sugared-up cereal. Bonnie would have much of the morning to lie in bed, listening to NPR or reading one of her mysteries. Then she and the kids, and occasionally Meg, would take the afternoon and do something fun, something together, like a movie or bowling.

These days, Bonnie needed a color-coded diary just to keep everyone's activities straight. Today, for example, Jane had a swimming lesson, and Davey had practice and then was going for pizza with some of his teammates, so he wouldn't be back until mid-afternoon. Bonnie had to run out to the nursing home for a quick visit with her mother, then be back in time to complete the grocery shopping before picking Davey up. She wasn't too worried about Jane being home alone – she seemed to prefer it that way most days.

Before pulling out of the parking lot by the baseball field, she observed Davey for a minute. He and some friends were Indian wrestling, although it looked like they were laughing too hard to be very effective as they pushed, arms wrapped around one another's waists. Watching Davey, Bonnie was struck by the sudden rush of a mother's love, as potent as a narcotic. She used to wonder when Jane and Davey were babies if this feeling might be a little unhealthy, it was that strong. Certainly, her own mother could never have experienced this maternal rush.

At the nursing home, Bonnie walked down the hall, self-conscious about the squeak of her soft-soled shoes on the floor. She cradled a loaf of banana bread in her arms. Her mother was not in her room; she must be in the residents' lounge. Bonnie ambled past "apartments," really nothing more than glorified dorm rooms, with plastic flowers in sconces next to each door. From a distance, it looked like a nice touch, but when you got close, you could see the artifice of the blooms and the thin layer of dust matting the petals. As she neared the lounge, she saw Elizabeth in a rocking chair sitting companionably with another elderly woman. Bonnie didn't remember seeing her before.

She pulled up a chair. The old ladies stopped their conversation and stared at her as if she had just alit from another planet. Then Elizabeth leaned in close to the other woman, whispering something in her ear, casting a sidelong glance at Bonnie. They tittered and turned their chairs one hundred eighty degrees, so that they had their backs to her.

Bonnie shook her head in wonder. We have now reached the parallel universe where my mother and I are in high school together, and her clique is snubbing me. If I'm not careful, it won't be long before she Krazy Glues my locker shut.

While Elizabeth was behaving like an adolescent, Bonnie took in the goings-on of the lounge. A few residents were clustered around the big-screen television, staring hypnotically at the screen. While researching nursing homes, Bonnie had appreciated the fact that here, the television, while perpetually broadcasting CNN, was never blaring. The volume was kept low enough that you could hear yourself think. Several men were huddled over a checkers game, three of them providing back-seat strategizing. It never failed to amaze Bonnie that while most of these people could not remember the names of their wives or children, they all seemed to be able to recall the rules of checkers and card games with precision.

She decided to try again, since Elizabeth had probably already forgotten the snub. She stood and walked a half-circle over to her mother and her new friend. "Good afternoon, ladies."

Elizabeth looked up and smiled with genuine pleasure. "Why, hello! Please join us!" She motioned to a chair. Bonnie pulled it up to the women and sat.

"I'd like to introduce you to my friend, Eleanor," Elizabeth said to Bonnie. "Eleanor, this is my best friend, Camilla."

Hell's bells, who was Camilla? Bonnie patted her mother's knee. "I'm Bonnie, Mother, your daughter."

Elizabeth's face clouded over. Her smile dimmed, and she bit her lip.

Bonnie sighed. "Okay, fine, Mother, I'm Camilla. Whatever you want." She turned to face her mother's companion. "It's nice to meet you, Eleanor. Are you new here?"

The elderly woman blinked and smiled at Bonnie. "Aren't you sweet? Eleanor's my sister, or maybe my niece. Are you my niece?"

Oh, dear Jesus. She smiled pleasantly at Not-Eleanor and turned her attention back to her mother. "So, um, Elizabeth, how have you been?"

Elizabeth took Bonnie's hand and grasped it tightly. "*Are* you Camilla?" Tears welled up in her eyes. "I have missed you so much. I swear, I think of you all the time. Do you remember the times we had? Oh, the stories we could tell."

"We certainly could tell some stories about those times," Bonnie replied. "You could always tell them better than me, though. Why don't you tell Eleanor some of our stories?"

"Oh, Camilla. You haven't changed a bit." Elizabeth continued holding Bonnie's hand, stroking it with tremoring fingers. Turning to the woman she thought was Eleanor, she said, "Camilla was always the one who got me into the most trouble. We were roommates at Mary Margaret Atwood's College for Women, in Richmond. You have no idea how long and hard I had to fight to get to go there."

Bonnie forgot her role. "What was the fight about?"

Elizabeth gazed at her. "Stop being silly. In my hometown, women didn't go to college or take jobs. At least until the War, of course; everything changed then."

Bonnie nodded, fascinated. She did not know anything about Elizabeth's life before kids.

"My parents were completely baffled," Elizabeth continued. "I had no shortage of suitors, of course, so I'm sure they thought that after receiving my diploma, I would marry and that would be that. But I had bigger dreams. I was going to go to college, maybe someday run a company."

She patted Not-Eleanor on the knee. "You should've seen me marching into that building like I owned the place. The first person I saw when I walked into the women's dormitory was Mrs. Macknin, with her hair pulled back in a bun so tight you could bounce a coin off it. She tried to give me what-for since I was coming in after sign-in hours – completely unreasonable for women who'd had to travel by train, I might add. And I saw this girl grinning at me from behind Mrs. Macknin, making monkey faces and shaking her finger at me just like Mrs. Macknin. It like to have killed me, I was trying so hard not to laugh."

Elizabeth stopped and squeezed Bonnie's hand. She smiled in return, but said nothing, not wanting to break the spell. It didn't surprise her that her mother had wanted to run a company. She'd ruled her household and her children's lives with a micromanager's vise-like grip.

"Oh, I loved college. I loved the routine of it, the orderliness of my schedule, my classes. Especially math, in the bookkeeping classes. I liked the security of formulas, how you could isolate and control variables. I was in bliss. And then there was always you, Camilla, getting everyone all riled up. Remember that time you hid all the forks in the dining hall? I still don't know where you put them. But my, it was fun to watch the other girls try to eat their noodles with just spoons and knives. I liked routine, and you liked chaos, but we made a good team."

Not-Eleanor had fallen asleep, lightly snoring in her chair. Elizabeth did not seem to notice. Bonnie dared to ask Elizabeth a question, hoping that it was not out of character. "How did we lose touch? I regret it so much, but I can't remember why it happened."

Elizabeth's voice lost its softness, taking on the bitter tone that Bonnie knew so well. "Don't patronize me. You know perfectly well what that fight was about. I either had to marry Jonas before he shipped out or my parents would have made me pay my own way through school – as if I had any funds of my own. And then you wouldn't listen when I said I was trapped. You said there were always ways for a creative woman to make money." Her eyes filled with angry, frustrated tears. "You said I was just like all the rest of the girls, studying only until I found myself a man." She spat out the word "man" like she'd just tasted spoiled milk.

"I admit it, I was too proud to write to you afterward. Jonas had been hurt in the war, so I had to take care of him, and then when that seemed like it might be getting better, I was with child. Just one more thing to shackle me." Elizabeth harrumphed bitterly, then brightened again. "But now you're here, that's what's important. I'll go make arrangements to leave the baby with the nurse, and we can go."

"What baby?" Bonnie asked, trying to sound neutral. Where in time were they right now? She had been listening to Elizabeth as if she were relaying history. But with this sudden mention of a baby, it occurred to her that the entire story might be one vast delusion fabricated by the network of damaged neurons in her mother's mind.

"Vivian, of course." Elizabeth patted her non-existent lap with a wry smile. "There's not much we can do about this one, but I'm not showing yet - we'll just have to make the best of it."

Bonnie took a deep breath. "I would love to take you on a trip, Elizabeth, but I think you should rest. You're looking very tired. Should I get the nurse?"

Slumping against the cushions, Elizabeth muttered, "No. Just go." She sounded like a petulant child deprived of her favorite toy. "Go, like everyone else. I don't need you."

Bonnie leaned over and retrieved the banana bread she'd placed on the floor beside her chair. She laid it beside her mother. "I brought you some banana bread. It's homemade."

Elizabeth turned her head away and said nothing.

* * *

As she left, Bonnie tried to make sense of the story. Vivian was born in 1950, and Bonnie hadn't been born until 1958. Perhaps Elizabeth had had a miscarriage between the two. She'd have to ask Viv about it. Her mother had never talked about another pregnancy or another child, but then, she had never talked about her dreams for a career either. So much silence.

And still there lay the possibility that maybe none of this had really happened at all.

When Bonnie got home, she found Jane in the living room, curled up sideways on that ratty old wing chair with her legs hanging over the armrest. Her nose buried in *Alice in Wonderland,* she was so drawn into the story as to be oblivious to her mother's presence. She hoped she wasn't as much of a mystery to Jane as Elizabeth had always been to her. Although Jane herself was a mystery much of the time these days, offering little or no openings into her life, and answering questions mostly in monosyllables. This job of hers, for instance - she hadn't said a word about it, other than that it was going okay. Bonnie hoped so. She'd spoken with Pam Burke privately to see if Jane should take on something so serious. "Honestly?" Pam had replied. "If I had other options, I probably wouldn't have offered the job. But my husband and I have talked about it, and we're in a real bind, so if you tell me Jane's responsible and will do what I ask, the job's hers." So Bonnie had said yes, hoping that having a job would give Jane some self-esteem and confidence.

Jane looked up from her book, her eyes wary. "What do you need?"

Bonnie ignored the rudeness. "You know, that's a fine question. I think I need some ice cream. You want to walk uptown with me for a cone?"

Jane shot up from her chair. "Let me get my sandals."

They strolled in a comfortable silence toward the town square, meandering by the gingerbread Victorian houses with their brick walkways and clipped lawns. Bonnie enjoyed a love-hate relationship with the township of Daedalus Falls. The township was too twee, too quaint to be real. In the summers, you couldn't even park in the center of town, for all the tourists who'd decided to take in the antique shops. It was the kind of place where every other store used "Olde" as part of its name. But on days like today, with the sun peeking through the trees, and the town's intentional homage to a gentler, easier time, Bonnie couldn't imagine wanting to live anywhere else.

"Do you like it here?" she asked Jane.

"It's okay, I guess."

Bonnie had to smile at Jane's distrustful glance. She had receptive antennae for the precursors of any kind of heart-to-heart discussion. "There's not much diversity here. You don't get much of a chance to know anyone who's not white or upper-middle class."

"Mom, you're not going to ruin this by going all Martin-Luther-King-I-have-a-dream on me, are you?"

She lightly swatted her daughter on the shoulder. "Fine. I'll leave my bleeding heart leanings at the door – for now. What I meant to ask was, would you rather live somewhere else?"

"I don't know. I don't know what anyplace else is like."

Bonnie considered that for a moment. "Me neither, really. I always wanted to do that foreign study option when I was in school. I could have lived in Florence for a year."

"You're kidding!" Jane looked surprised and a little impressed.

Bonnie smiled. "It's true. I'd decided I wanted to be a chef. Not that you'd know it from the burgers and fries I make for dinner, but I've always loved cooking. Back then, I figured I'd go to Italy and find a culinary program."

"Wow. Italy. I'd love to go somewhere like that, where they speak a different language. That's actually pretty cool, Mom." Jane perked up, almost sounding animated. "What did Grams say? She didn't want you to go, right?"

"Actually, she was all for it. It may have been the only thing I ever did that she approved of, truthfully. But I ended up not going. I met your father a few months before I was supposed to go, and I didn't want to leave him, so I stayed."

Jane deflated. She looked back down at the sidewalk and shook her head slowly. "I'm never getting married. Falling in love screws up everything."

Bonnie stopped and turned to her daughter. "Boy. I don't really know how to respond to that. Certainly, you don't ever have to get married if you don't want. And yes, falling in love screwed up my chance to go to Italy. But if I hadn't met your dad, then I wouldn't have had you and Davey, now would I?"

Jane nodded once without looking at her, like she'd heard it all before.

"Honey, is this about Meg?"

She nodded again, eyes cast downward. Then suddenly, as if she couldn't stop herself, she burst out, "I just feel like she doesn't want me around anymore. I mean, I know Brady's going home soon and she's got to take care of him and all that, but she hasn't even called this week."

"Jane, this isn't about you. I'm sorry you haven't been able to get together with her, but you'll get your chance. Really."

"Whatever." She scuffed at the sidewalk with her sneaker and accelerated so that she could be several feet in front.

Bonnie deeply inhaled the scent of honeysuckle permeating the air and looked at the summer freckles beginning to blossom on Jane's shoulders. Bonnie couldn't help but be wistful of a time long ago when Jane hung on every word she uttered.

She jogged a couple steps, catching up, and nudged Jane's shoulder with her own. How had she gotten so tall already? Jane gave a return push to Bonnie's shoulder and gave a tepid smile, although it looked like it was given under duress.

Moments where Bonnie felt really connected to Jane were so rare now. When had it gotten so hard? Bonnie felt like she was bumbling her way through Jane's adolescence, casting out lines at random to see if anything would catch. "How's everything with Charley going?" she asked.

Jane nodded. "Okay, I think. He talks to me now." She shyly glanced up at Bonnie.

"Oh, Jane, that's wonderful!" Bonnie clasped Jane's hand and squeezed it. Smiling more broadly now, Jane let the contact linger a few seconds longer than Bonnie would have expected. She wished she could just give her daughter a full-out hug, but for today, this would be enough.

They reached Two Scoops, the ice cream palace/deluxe tourist attraction. The shop was situated on a bridge atop the famed Daedalus Falls. The waterfall itself was relatively tiny, only about thirty feet high. But it was full and picturesque, and the township had built a winding walkway down from Two Scoops to the base of the falls, even marking the spot on the landing with the best angle of the cascade. The falls was the township's main tourist attraction – its piece of New England in Ohio – and the ice cream parlor made a fine profit selling disposable cameras just inside the entrance.

Bonnie and Jane stood in line behind a group of women in Capri pants, jaunty bandanas tied around their ponytails. "Tourists," they mouthed to each other, and grinned.

Once served, they carried their cones down the stairs adjacent to the shop to watch the falls. Ducks paddled in place at the bottom of the falls, the avian version of a treadmill. Bonnie and Jane stood side by side, elbows perched on the railing.

Jane licked the chocolate that was looming at the edges of her cone. She seemed to be thinking about something, her brow furrowed. Finally she said, "Thanks for letting me take this babysitting job, Mom."

Bonnie bit part of her pistachio cone, touched that Jane's thanks seemed sincere. "My pleasure. I'm really proud of how well you're doing. And you know if you get stuck, I'm just a phone call away."

Jane wiped the ice cream goo off her fingers with a napkin. Sticking it in her pocket, she hugged herself tightly. Bonnie wasn't sure if her movement was brain-freeze from the ice cream or some more primal need. Standing side by side, the two watched the ducks swim against the river's flow.

~6~
MEG

Meg caught up to Brady at the foot of the stairwell of his apartment building. He stared up the Escher-like circle of steps with a defeated expression as he began to lever himself with his crutches, limping up onto the first step. She set his bag down on the floor and placed a hand on his shoulder from behind. "You big fool, why don't you take the elevator? That's what it's there for."

"I'm fine." Brady grunted a little as he hoisted himself up a step at a time.

"Seriously, honey, let's take the elevator."

"I said I'm fine!"

She extended her middle finger outward from her balled fist at her side, out of Brady's line of sight. "Yes, sir! You know best. I'll meet you at the top!" She scooted around to the other side of him, clutching his suitcase close to avoid banging into him.

He was so touchy since the mugging a week ago. Granted, he still probably felt like shit, but God, it was like living with her mother in her pre-menopausal PMS days, when a compliment about dinner could be taken by Vivian as a criticism of every other meal served in a lifetime.

And what was this "I am he-man" routine with the stairs? Take the damned elevator. God knows, it was just sitting there, waiting for someone to use it. The wrought-iron cage was a million years old, only wide enough for a single person, with a door that you closed by turning a crank. But it got you where you needed to go.

Reaching the landing, Meg dropped the suitcase with a solid thump next to Brady's door. It actually made the old flooring bounce a little. She leaned over the railing and saw him a floor below, steadfastly soldiering on. On the other side of the door, Barkley scratched wildly, knowing that someone was outside. "Cool it, Barks. Dad'll be up here in just a minute." She sat down on the floor to wait. Brady finally arrived at the apartment, winded and sweaty. He grinned at her. "Guess maybe I should've taken you up on that elevator thing, huh?"

Meg scrambled up to her feet and kissed him on the tip of his nose. "There's hope for you yet."

As they opened the door, Barkley sprang out and tried to give his best friend a Basset body-slam. Brady winced from the contact. Most of the swelling was gone, but his bruises were still impressively large and purple, and his cast and crutches kept him in an awkward stiffness.

Meg crouched and grabbed Barkley by the collar. "Careful, there." She patted the dog, holding him still while Brady made his way inside. Her moving boxes were stacked precariously in the center of the living room, a few nesting on the sofa.

Limping to an empty chair, Brady lowered himself with care. "I see you've moved in." Barkley waddled over and laid down at his feet.

She narrowed her eyes and mock-growled at him. "Ha-ha. I don't think you were under the influence when we talked about this." She adopted a lawyerly stance and began pacing as if in front of a jury. "Fact one: the court may remember you're going to need someone to keep you clean and fed until the cast comes off. Fact two: you can't move in with me because of my roommates. Fact three: I don't feel comfortable with the idea of a beautiful private nurse moving in and giving you sponge baths."

Brady raised his eyebrows. "I don't remember talking about that last one. It actually sounds pretty good."

Meg lightly swatted him on the shoulder. "So, if you recall, considering that we'll be living together with a license and everything in a couple months anyway, we agreed that I should move in early." She searched his face, suddenly not sure any of this was such a good idea. "Have you changed your mind? Do you want me to move back?"

"No, no. It's just that..." He sighed. "It's just that my place was clean when I was last here."

She grabbed a wadded sock lying in the box nearest her and threw it lightly at his shoulder, one of his only uninjured body parts. "I was trying to be considerate, you twerp! I didn't want to move my shit in and redecorate without you being here."

"Yeah, yeah, yeah, you're right, I'm wrong." Brady closed his eyes. "Let's just drop it, okay?"

Meg didn't really feel like dropping it. Brady had been grumpy ever since the doctors took him off the big painkillers, and she got it. Pain sucks. But would it kill him to temper it with a smile every now and then? This wasn't what she'd imagined for Brady's homecoming. In her head, he'd held her tight when they'd crossed the threshold, touched at the thought of them beginning a life together in this apartment, almost man and wife. She took a deep breath and shook these thoughts away. "How's your ankle? You should be elevating it."

"It hurts. I should probably go lie down."

"Here, lean on me and I'll help you over." They teetered over to the bedroom. Brady collapsed onto the bed with a moan. Crossing over to the other side, she lay down next to him and cuddled. She'd felt the loss of the steadfast heat and solidity of him next to her at night. "I'm glad you're home. I missed you, y'know?"

He put his arm around her. "Thanks for helping me, hon. I don't know what I would've done without you this last week."

There. That was what she wanted to hear. She nuzzled his neck. "I know how you could thank me."

Brady groaned. "Oh, honey, not now. My leg is killing me. Believe me, I'll let you know when I'm ready." He rolled to his side and reached for the remote. "Besides, it wouldn't surprise me if my parents stopped by soon to see how we've settled in."

Meg stood, harrumphing theatrically. "Well, I suppose I'll just take my poor rejected self and go unpack. Maybe I'll hang my Phish poster next to the Renoir. It *is* a print, right? Your mother didn't buy the original?"

"Rearrange whatever you want. And yes, it's a print, and you can leave my mother out of it." Brady stared at the middle of a *Seinfeld* episode, and his words had the tone of someone who was bored and only partly listening.

Meg bit her lip, trying to tamp down her rising annoyance. "I can seriously do whatever I want?"

He turned up the volume. "Meg, just leave me alone. Please."

She went into the living room, shaking her head. Maybe she should've just hired a nurse for him. God knows she certainly wasn't cut out for it.

Meg started unpacking her books, stacking them horizontally on Brady's bookshelves in front of his carefully organized groupings of mysteries, books on children and teaching, music. As long as he could see the titles, he couldn't get too bent out of shape, could he? Although in his current state, who knew what would set him off.

Bored with unpacking, Meg began leafing through Brady's CD collection. He'd always controlled the music selection during their evenings here, so she had never really given it much of a look before. The CDs were pretty eclectic, ranging from classic Squeeze to Richard Thompson, from Willie Nelson to the Clash. There were probably two hundred discs on the shelves next to the stereo, and they were all alphabetized within genre. God bless, he was a little anal.

Meg carried over a shoebox filled with her CDs. A couple fell from the open top, clattering on the hardwood floor. From his spot in front of the fireplace, Barkley thumped his tail.

"Sorry to wake you, Barks. Go back to sleep. I'm just going to teach your dad a little lesson in flexibility." She pulled out her Beatles' White Album and filed it in the country section, next to Johnny Cash. She interspersed six more of her CDs, placing them randomly throughout the collection. She knew it was childish, but at some base level, screwing with his sense of order pleased her. If he discovered what she'd done and thought it was funny, then they were meant to stay together. If he was pissed about it, then maybe they should re-think the whole marriage thing. Of course, who knows, maybe he wouldn't discover it until months after they'd been married.

Barkley went to the door and pawed at it, whining. Meg grabbed his leash, and the two of them went outside. It was a gorgeous day, the kind of day she and Brady would normally have spent window shopping, or taking a hike through one of the city's park trails. Instead, he was sleeping and she was walking his dog. And now she couldn't even enjoy walking the damn dog, because it would forever remind her of those boys who ought to be rotting in jail. As well as make her even more watchful for danger. Meg felt cheated, Brady's mugging having robbed her of her prior enjoyment of the neighborhood. But almost immediately, she felt pissed at herself. This was not his fault, she reminded herself. He did not ask to be mugged. Meg quickly shuttled Barkley around the perimeter of the building's courtyard and back inside.

Once in the apartment, Barkley resettled, and Meg sank down in Brady's recliner. She didn't want to unpack anymore. It only reminded her of how much she still didn't know about her fiancé. She might know his favorite restaurant or that he favored morning sex, but she had no idea who his favorite writer was in high school, or who the laughing people in Dr. Seuss hats were in that framed photo on the mantle. And what if this moodiness wasn't a phase? What if this was what Brady did in any kind of crisis? As a couple, before now they'd never experienced anything more traumatic than having to wait for a table. And look at his mother. Meg was certain Brady's mother would make sure he never had to work through obstacles on his own if she could help it. Meg glanced toward the bedroom, wondering if for once she was seeing her fiancé with clear eyes.

Meg squeezed her eyes shut and mouthed "Stop!" to herself. She stood and walked to the kitchenette to get a glass of water. She was being ridiculous. Brady was fine. This was just one more instance of her finding a way to bail on a guy when everything wasn't perfect.

Tired of dwelling on herself, Meg turned on the television. A rerun of *Cheers* was on. She relaxed into the comfortable predictability of Sam and Diane.

As the barroom trumpeted "Norm!," Brady limped into the living room. He lowered himself carefully onto the sofa and rubbed his eyes. "I think I must've fallen asleep. What time is it?"

Meg looked at her watch. "Close to five." She kissed him on the neck, feeling like she needed to make up with him. Taking his hand, she asked, "How're you feeling?"

"A little better, I think. Has Barkley been out for a pee?"

"I took him a little while ago."

"You stayed right in the yard, right? I don't know how I feel about you taking him for walks after what happened."

Meg took a deep breath. She wasn't crazy about the idea either at the moment, but right now he needed reassurance, not extra worry about her. "Brady, relax. I'm a big girl and can take care of myself, remember? Besides, you're out of commission for a while, so who's going to walk the dog, if not me?"

"I don't know. I could hire a service."

"Oh, honey." Meg shook her head. "That would be way too expensive. And why would it be any safer for someone from a service to walk him?"

"It would be safer for *you*." Brady took a breath like he was getting ready to say something else, and then swallowed it.

Meg stood and brought a hardback chair over, then sat so she could look him in the eyes. In as even a voice as she could muster, she said, "Here's the deal. I will walk the dog when he needs it. I will be street-smart about it. You can take over again when your foot is healed."

Brady didn't say anything.

Meg cocked her head with a questioning gaze. "Can we be done with this conversation now?"

She stared at him with eyes over-wide, refusing to blink, until he finally gave in and smiled. "Are you going to be this bossy when we're married?"

Meg grinned with relief. "Damn skippy, you bet." She kissed him on the nose.

"You know, I'm a little hungry." Brady stretched his arms back over his head. "You want to go out or something? I doubt there's anything in the fridge that isn't covered with green fuzz."

"That sounds great. But why don't we order in? That way you can rest your leg."

"No, I want to get out of here. I'm fine." Brady began pushing himself out of the chair. Beads of sweat dampened his forehead. "You up for Chinese or Indian?"

Before she could answer, the phone rang. He picked it up on the second ring and after saying hello, mouthed to Meg, "It's my mother."

She gave him a thumbs-up sign and went into the bathroom to get herself ready. Of course it was his mother. God forbid she should leave Brady alone now for more than twelve hours at a time.

She knew that she wasn't being fair, that Mona was only being the kind of doting mother Meg had sometimes wished she'd had, but oh, my God, it was stifling. Before the mugging, he'd barely seen his parents. But ever since, they – especially Mona – were around all the time, first at the hospital, and now apparently imposing by phone. Meg hoped that the frequency would fall back to its previous routine after the wedding.

*   *   *

Finally deciding on Indian, they found a table at their favorite tandoori restaurant. Meg tried to forge an unencumbered path for Brady, but it seemed that there were hazards everywhere – a table leg to trip over here, a purse on the floor there. Finally sinking onto a chair, he winced as he leaned his crutches on the table's lip. "I hope this gets easier," he said. She took his hand and squeezed it.

Over samosas, curry, and beer, some of the weight of the past week seemed to disappear from Brady's shoulders into the ether. They fell into a heavy debate over the upcoming Presidential elections, and Meg found herself starting to relax. At one point, she teased him about his "war wounds," and Brady even laughed. She felt like one of those plants that retracts into itself at the first touch, only to open itself up when it feels the warmth of the sun.

They lingered at the restaurant awhile, sitting at the patio table, sipping their beers and watching the passers-by. There was a pink tinge in the sky as they left, peoples' faces obscured by the approaching dusk. Brady was beginning to look fatigued again, his face tightening as he maneuvered himself into the passenger's seat.

When they reached his building, there were no parking spots close to the door. Meg slowed the car as they neared the entrance. "Do you want me to drop you off?"

"No, I'm okay. Let's just find a place and park."

Meg saw an open spot on the street a building down. "Oh, Lord, I'll have to parallel park."

She angled the car in, but her turn was too sharp, so she put the car in drive, brought it forward a few inches and slipped it into reverse again, finally fitting the car snugly in against the curb. "This is what you call parking like a fuck," she said as she flicked off the headlights. "In and out, in and out, in and out."

When Brady didn't laugh, she looked over at him. Following his gaze, she saw a group of teenaged boys walking slowly down the sidewalk, peering into car windows as they passed. In the looming night, Meg couldn't see what kind of expressions they wore. Brady, on the other hand, was so pale that she was afraid he might faint.

"Don't get out," he whispered. "Don't let them know we're here."

Meg squeezed his hand. "Yeah, that sounds like a good idea." She paused. "Do you recognize these boys? Are these the ones who mugged you?"

Brady pulled his hand away, tearing up. "I don't know." He took angry swipes at his eyes. "I'm never gonna know. Goddammit!" He punched the passenger side door and flinched.

"It's okay, baby. Look, they're gone now. It's safe. Come on, let's just go on inside." Meg spoke softly to Brady, like a feral cat she was trying to coax out from behind a bush.

"I need another minute."

"That's fine, babe. However long you need." She collapsed back against her seat, and stared at the sky as the last of the color faded to grey.

~ 7 ~
JANE

The laundromat was about a zillion degrees inside, and muggy. The brief rain shower that had just ended had done nothing to relieve the humidity in the air. Jane knew it was a coin flip, as likely to be sixty degrees and breezy in this part of June, but she felt it was somehow a personal attack that the weather had decided to go the steamy route. Meg was moving her laundry from the washer to the dryer, so Jane was saving their seats, alternately peeling her thighs off the molded canary-yellow plastic. Even though there were ten washers and ten dryers, the place only had room for six chairs, which were lined up against the window facing the street. The chairs could put your butt and legs to sleep in about twenty minutes, but there were always people, listlessly attempting to read books and magazines while leaning on a vibrating washer, who hungrily eyed the chairs like vultures circling over roadkill.

She and Meg had been coming here once a month for a couple years now. At least, they had until Meg had hooked up with Brady. She'd made the mistake of telling some girls at school about their practice once, and one girl between smacks of her gum asked, "Gawd. You mean your cousin only washes her clothes once a month?"

What a doofus. Jane had just looked at her like she was retarded and said, "Yeah." If she was going to be stupid about it, who was Jane to correct her?

Maybe some people would think the laundromat a weird choice for a special place. It suited Jane, though. Nobody here was worried about being fashionable or popular, or being "seen." They just wanted to get their clothes clean.

She'd been really surprised when Meg had called to schedule a date, and halfway wondered if her mom had asked her to do it. After all, Brady hadn't been home from the hospital very long, and from what Bonnie said, there was all that wedding stuff to plan. But in the end, Jane didn't care; she was just happy to be with her again.

Meg plopped herself down in the chair next to Jane. "All right. It's time."

Jane grinned. "I've been practicing."

"Yeah, talk's cheap. We'll see how good you're getting." Meg reached down into her tote bag and pulled out a bag of M&Ms. Tearing it open, she poured out a few and handed one to Jane. "All right. Make me proud."

Tossing a piece up in the air, she caught it in her mouth. She bowed in her chair with a flourish as Meg clapped.

"Well done." Meg scooted onto the floor, placing her bag on the chair to save her seat. She backed up a couple feet from Jane. "I think we're ready to try the two-person hand-off."

She lobbed an M&M to Jane in a lazy underhand arc. Jane tilted her head back and caught it easily, chomping down on the candy shell. "Is that all you got?" she taunted.

"Ooh, the girl has a mouth on her." Meg threw a couple pieces of candy in her mouth and looked at the dryers. "Crap. I need to throw another dime in. Don't move. I'll be right back."

At the dryers, Meg got roped into talking to a young mother who was folding clothes. Strapped to her chest was an infant who was waving his arms like he was directing traffic. The mother seemed not to even know he was there. Jane's attention was diverted to the opposite wall, where a stooped elderly woman had just kicked the soap dispensing machine.

Meg returned to her chair and hefted her tote to the floor. The way her muscles stood out, something heavy must be in it. "That woman I was just talking to is a scout for the U.S. M&M Olympic team. She thinks we have a shot. What was that noise just now?"

Jane swiveled her chair so she could look at Meg without getting a neck cramp. "Oh, it was Lucy," she whispered, not wanting the woman to hear they were talking about her. "She just kicked the soap machine and now she's talking to herself. I've been trying to read her lips, but I can't catch what she's saying."

"She's probably talking to Jimmy, who I think might be her invisible son. Once, I asked her if she wanted any help. But she just yelled at me to get lost, and then started telling Jimmy that someone was trying to mug her."

"God, that's so sad." Jane pulled a stray thread from her cut-offs. She felt depressed that the old lady was so alone. "Why does the world have to be so screwed up?"

Meg cocked her head. "Whoa. Way to bring down the mood. Okay, I'll bite." She put on a bad German accent. "Liebchen, come lay down on ze couch and tell me what troubles you."

Jane made a face at her. "I'm serious. I mean, it's not only her. It seems like there's horrible things happening all the time now, everywhere. Those guys who jumped your boyfriend – sorry, fiancé. Those morons who were throwing rocks at Charley..." She shook her head.

"Yeah, but it all turned out okay, right? And if it hadn't of been for those morons, you wouldn't have gotten a job."

"Maybe. But if that's the case, then what's the good part of Brady being mugged? And why are you here instead of home with him, anyway?"

Meg's eyes darkened. "Okay, you're right, I'm not sure there is anything good from his attack. It's pretty much sucked all around. And to answer your second question, he's being kind of a pain in the ass these days, and I needed some space away from him."

Jane raised her eyebrows. "Are you still getting married?"

"Hell, yeah. He may be driving me nuts, but I still love him. His mother, on the other hand ... but no fair turning tables on me. I was all set to ask you about your job. How's it going so far?"

"I like it. He's a smart little kid."

"So why were those jerks throwing rocks at him?"

"He's autistic. I mean, his mom told me that his actual thing is called PDD, but that it's basically like a kind of autism."

Meg sat back in her chair. "Jesus, Jane, that's a big deal. I mean, does he rock or bang his head on stuff?"

"He hasn't with me. It's like as long as Charley follows a general routine, things stay pretty mellow, and he's okay and it's no big deal."

"God. I can't believe she hired you to watch him, though. Doesn't this lady have anyone else she can hire to watch him, someone qualified?

"Thanks a bunch." She crumpled up the M&M wrapper and dropped it on the floor. She was doing a good job. Pam had even said so. "Besides, it keeps me away from Davey, which might extend his life span, you never know."

Meg laughed. "You know, one day you might actually want to be friends with Davey. He's not a bad brother. I wish I had a brother like him."

"Ugh. Change topic, please, before I puke."

"Charming." Meg bent down and retrieved her tote bag from under her chair. She fingered a ragged etching on the chair– "Deadalus Falls Class of '92 ROCKS!" "Geez. You'd think they could spell the name right after all this time."

"What are you talking about?"

She gestured to the chair's markings. "Do they at least teach you who Daedalus is, I hope?"

"Yes, Professor Newman," Jane intoned, rolling her eyes. "Geez. You're not the only one who knows these things. Icarus, the Minotaur, blah blah blah."

Meg pulled a face. "Point taken." She drew a wedding magazine called *Today's Bride* out of her tote.

"Holy crap," Jane said. "That thing's two inches thick. How much does it weigh?"

"It ain't light, that's for sure. You could probably incorporate this into a pre-wedding workout routine, buff up the arms."

Jane didn't want to talk about the wedding. She didn't want to talk about Brady, or getting married, or any more changes. But at the same time, she knew she wasn't being fair. She could hear her mother saying something dorky like "If you want to have friends, you have to be a friend back." It sucked, but it was probably true. So she would try.

They huddled close as Meg opened the magazine and flipped through page after page of advertisements. They all seemed to be showing versions of the same wedding dress, in endless variations of satin, sequins, and pearls. This had to be the dumbest excuse for a magazine, ever.

Jane rolled her eyes. "Gag. It's disgusting. And please tell me why a bride is supposed to be wider than she is tall in these stupid dresses? So the groom can't get too close to her?"

Meg snorted. "It's as good a theory as any. I'll bet that this is probably the kind of dress Mona has in mind for me to wear."

"So? She already got married. You should get to pick what you want if it's your wedding."

"It's complicated, Jane. His parents are paying for almost all of the wedding. And between you and me, she's a little scary. I probably need to pick my battles. I'll have a better idea after I meet her designer this week."

Jane stared at Meg. "Are you high? Why should his mother get to pick the dress just because she's rich? Why don't you stand up to them? What happened to your principles?"

Meg drew the magazine back into her lap and closed it. "For Christ's sake, Jane. Principles are what you have when you stand up to racism or harassment. I mean, you showed principles when you chased those boys off of Charley. Principles don't even enter into the equation when you're talking about keeping your prospective mother-in-law happy over a wedding that'll be over with in a matter of hours."

"Fine." She stared at the washers. God, if being in love turned a person into such a wuss, she would make sure it never happened to her.

She slid her chair back so she wasn't facing Meg anymore. Meg continued leafing through the magazine. Puh-leeze. Jane knew that she wasn't really looking at the magazine. She pretended she was interested in observing a stressed-looking woman move her clothes from the washer to dryer, keeping one hand on a frisky toddler intent on escape, *and* rocking an infant carrier with her foot.

"Hey, Jane. Look, I don't want to argue with you. We're supposed to be having fun together, remember?"

Jane eyed Meg. She didn't usually back down so easily. What did she want?

"You're my favorite cousin for a reason. So I have a question for you. Would you be one of my bridesmaids?"

Jane turned and stared at her cousin. "Are you serious?"

"Of course, I'm serious. Do you want to or not?"

Before she could stop herself, Jane heard herself say, "God, no." As she said it, all she could see was herself, up at the front of a church in some awful pink froufy dress with ruffles. Everyone would be looking at her, thinking couldn't she do *something* with that hair? It's so stringy and flat. And you'd think she'd be starting to develop some kind of figure by now, but no, she still looks like a sausage. It would just be beyond humiliating.

Meg tucked the magazine back in her tote bag.

Jane started to apologize: "I –"

"Y'know, I don't know why you're being so pissy about this wedding. I thought maybe you were worried that I wouldn't want to spend time with you anymore, but here we are, and you're still being rude, so clearly, that's not it. Brady's wigging out on me, and I've got people on my back about the wedding. It would've been nice to have a little support from you, but hey, I guess I was asking too much."

Meg was really mad. Her voice was even trembling a little. Jane felt a little bit powerful to be able to get her to respond like that. And that made her feel a little bit better. Even if Meg was right, and she really should be feeling guilty. She was about to say something, but Meg had apparently paused only to catch a breath.

"What really gets me, though, is that you haven't even met Brady. You haven't even given yourself a chance to like him. I mean, right now, he's trying to get over this thing, and he's not himself. But normally, he is the nicest guy in the whole world. He's the kind of guy who would take one look at you, Jane, and know you are worth getting to know. He'd be interested in who you are. But you've already written him off. So I give up. I'm going to go fold my clothes." She stalked off without giving Jane the chance to apologize.

Jane stared at the cracked linoleum. She cast a quick look around to see if anyone had been listening in. How could they not have heard? Sure enough, the woman who was sitting a couple chairs down was staring right at her. Stupid old cow. Jane stuck her tongue out, knowing she was acting like a five-year-old but not caring. Great. Now she'd never be able to come here again, not that Meg would want to have anything to do with her anyway.

She stood up and walked outside. Sitting down cross-legged on the damp concrete walk, she faced the anonymous sea of the parking lot. Jane wished she had an ice cream, a popsicle, anything to cool off a little. She wished she could've explained herself better to Meg. She dreaded the ride home. Stupid old summer, she thought. Stupid old me.

~ 8 ~
BONNIE

"You've got to be kidding me." Bonnie surveyed Vivian's living room, its floor covered in a foamy sea of lavender mesh net. "What on earth are you doing?"

"You mean, what are *we* doing?" Vivian grabbed a pair of scissors off the dining room table. "I figured as long as you were coming over, I'd enlist your help in making sachets for the wedding."

She took a deep breath. "Vivian," she said softly, trying to remain cool, "I need to talk to you about Mother. I told you that on the phone."

"I know we need to talk about Mother." Vivian mimicked her tone. "But I don't see why you can't give me a hand as long as you're here."

Bonnie sighed, conceding defeat. "If I'm going to be drafted in this sweatshop, I need coffee."

Vivian headed back to the ribbon and mesh. "Go ahead and make some if you want. I'll take a cup too, while you're at it." As Bonnie went into the kitchen, she saw Vivian scrutinizing her ribbon choices.

Searching the cupboards, she finally found the coffee and filters. This had to be a new record. Vivian didn't usually reach critical irk levels for at least half an hour. She might be forty-two, but honestly, sometimes she acted more self-obsessed than Jane did at fourteen. Every time they saw each other, Bonnie came away from the visit feeling prickly and wanting a stiff drink. She'd reached a point where she dealt with her sister only when absolutely necessary.

When the coffee had brewed, Bonnie carried two cups out to the living room and handed one to Vivian. "You're looking fit," she said, thinking privately that her sister's sinewy tautness made her look hard and tough, like a stringy chicken.

"Thanks. I'm training for the 25 K that's coming up next month. We'll see if I beat my time from last year."

"It amazes me that you still run marathons at your age." Bonnie sat down on the couch. "I feel like a lump of overcooked pasta next to you."

Vivian sipped her coffee delicately. "I'll let the crack about my age pass – and yes, you are a lump of overcooked pasta next to me. You're not too old to take up running. I first took it up when I was your age, in my naïve attempt to spend some time with Meg when she was on the cross-country team in high school." She laughed mirthlessly. "You remember, that short period when Meg actually wanted to do anything with me. It was good while it lasted."

Bonnie looked down into her coffee. Vivian didn't know what Meg had told her – that she'd stopped running after her mother had entered them in a 10 K together and then beaten her. Meg had thought she wanted them to run the race together. It hadn't bothered her until Vivian treated it like a big competition. She gloated about the win for weeks, giving Meg "constructive criticism" on improving her form. Bonnie resolved then and there not to take up any sport Jane went for, in the unlikely event *that* would ever happen.

Bonnie switched tactics. "Have you talked to Meg this week? How's Brady doing?"

"Not well. I've been calling Meg every day for reports. He's still on painkillers and emotionally a wreck. I mean, Meg doesn't say that, but it seems pretty clear. That poor boy." Vivian clucked her tongue sympathetically.

"I know. You always think it could never happen to you."
"Exactly! It's like when Pastor Magnuson had that heart attack on the

golf course and died. It's so shocking. You feel like your world is spinning off its axis."

Bonnie let the reference to Vivian's pastor slide away. Vivian had been trying to "save" Bonnie and her children, bring them into her church, for years now. Bonnie possessed a mental switch that now shut off her hearing at any mention of Vivian's church or its members. She suggested, "Meg and Brady should postpone the wedding. Give themselves a chance to catch their breath. Certainly no one would blame them if they wanted to change the date to later in the fall."

Vivian set her coffee cup down on its saucer, the porcelain dishes scraping against each other like fork against teeth. "Don't you dare say that to Meg."

"I'm not saying that they cancel the wedding. I just think it might be good for Brady to have a little extra time to heal."

"Yes, but I know Meg. She cuts and runs at the first sign of trouble. Remember Dan? Remember Chris? They were such nice young men."

Bonnie nodded, but mentally rolled her eyes. Dan had looked like a pretty good thing for a month – until an old girlfriend called him out of the blue to ask for a loan. Chris, who was apparently much too possessive, hadn't lasted much over a few weeks. But still. There had been some other guys Meg had dated who disappeared for no apparent reason. She wasn't certain whether Meg's snappy breakups were a sign of immaturity or just the opposite. Wasn't it better to be picky early on than fall in love, be committed in a relationship, only to have your heart broken?

Vivian rose and gathered the mugs, despite the fact that Bonnie hadn't finished her coffee yet. "If this wedding is postponed, do you really think it'll ever happen? Of course not. Meg will be gone as fast as lightning. Which would be a real shame. I think Brady could be really good for her."

She took the coffee cups back into the kitchen; even agitated, her posture was perfect, as if she had a book balanced on top of her head.

Bonnie sat quietly while her sister was in the kitchen, stroking the leather sofa like the fur of a cat. It annoyed her that Vivian had a point. She had to agree that if Meg were forced to wait for this wedding, she'd lose faith that it would ever happen.

When Vivian returned, she handed Bonnie a pair of scissors and a wad of mesh, and instructed her to begin cutting out six-inch squares of netting for the sachets. "We're going to need a bunch. The Campbells are inviting practically all of Cleveland. Don't worry about perfect. It'll just slow you down."

Bonnie smoothed out the fabric. "Do you know where they're going to live once they're married? I can't imagine them staying in that apartment, given what's happened."

"Meg has not seen fit to give me that information. Frankly, I'm amazed I know anything at all." Vivian watched Bonnie cutting out squares. "Oh, for goodness' sake! Why are you cutting each square out individually? You cut out rows, and then cut the squares. It's much more efficient."

Gritting her teeth, Bonnie continued cutting the squares just as she had been. She didn't give a damn about being efficient.

Vivian lasted about ten seconds. "Just stop. Give it to me, I'll do it." She snatched the netting from Bonnie's lap and gave her a roll of scalloped ribbon and a yardstick. "Here. You think you can manage cutting lengths of this? Eighteen inches each."

Bonnie smiled at her, the same smile she used at work with the annoying little old ladies who came up to the desk and told her every thirty seconds that they *really* needed to see the doctor and could not wait any longer. "Of course, Vivian."

They worked in silence for a few minutes. Vivian appeared to be trying not to talk, but glanced sharply up at Bonnie every thirty seconds or so. When she did not respond, Vivian heaved a heavy sigh and sliced another row of netting.

Bonnie cut ribbon automatically, finding peace in the repetition. It was always so draining coming out here. Everything was such a drama.

Eventually laying down the ribbon and scissors, she stretched her arms high over her head, and shifted position on the sofa. Her leg was asleep, with miniature fireworks exploding everywhere beneath her hip. "So about Mother ..."

"Yes, fill me in. By the by, I've been meaning to tell you that my prayer group has her on their list. We pray for her every night. There're twenty of us, so we've got a good block going."

"Well, pray harder, because she's getting worse."

Vivian frowned. "I'll bet the nurses are ignoring her. I've heard that these places get shut down sometimes because of neglecting the patients."

Bonnie felt like a twig flexed beyond its breaking point. "Damn it, it's not the nurses, or the orderlies, it's Mother. Don't you dare cast aspersions when you can't even manage a visit. It's not like your all-holy prayer group absolves you of the responsibility to go see her once in a while." She paused to inhale.

Vivian set her scissors down on the table in a tightly controlled fury. She glared at Bonnie but said nothing.

"What's with you and her, anyway? For God's sake, you were the 'rebel,' but you were also the one Mother liked. How is it that I'm the one who's always taking care of her?"

Although she expected her sister to be upset at being called out, Bonnie was still taken aback by the strength of Vivian's reaction. Her face became splotchy and her breathing exaggerated, as if she were trying not to cry. "You think Mother *liked* me? That's rich." She clenched her hands into fists and ground them into the chair cushion.

"Then what?"

Vivian sat up straighter, unballed her fists and slowly, deliberately laid them in her lap. "Why should I go visit? She doesn't know who I am, and you obviously have things under control."

"The point is that Mother is getting worse." Trying to make her understand, Bonnie gave the words equal emphasis. "She's losing weight. I think she's not eating much, if anything, and if you don't go see her soon, she will be dead." She enunciated the word *dead*.

Tears coursed down Vivian's face, racing to the finish line of her jaw. "I feel like she's been dead for a year now." She wiped her cheeks with a tissue.

"Trust me, even if she doesn't know you, you'd never mistake her for dead." Bonnie laid her head against the back of the sofa. The sun dipped low enough to blaze into the window. She closed her eyes. "Just let go of what's between you two and visit her soon, okay?"

"I'll do what I can." Vivian noisily blew her nose.

Bonnie continued to rest her eyes. It felt good to feel the sun's warmth, but she still had business to complete. She opened her eyes.

"I wanted to ask you something that Mom's been talking about recently. Did she have a baby after you? A miscarriage or something?"

Vivian visibly blanched. "No, nothing like that."

"What the hell?" Seeing Vivian's wince, Bonnie frowned. "Pardon me. What the heck? You're lying."

"Oh, no," Vivian shook her head with such vigor that a hank of hair escaped from her ponytail. "I can't talk about this." She rose and quickly walked out of the room.

Bonnie followed her. Viv wasn't going to get out of this. "Why not? It won't make any difference to Mother. Viv, ninety-five percent of the time, Mother doesn't know who you are, or who I am."

"I can't talk to you about this." Vivian refused to look at Bonnie.

Oh, for God's sake. Bonnie thought of a new tack. "You know, it's a sin to tell a lie."

Vivian took a step toward Bonnie as if she was going to charge at her. "I'm not telling you a lie. I'm not telling you anything."

Bonnie sighed. If Viv didn't want to say anything, no amount of pressure would get it out of her. "Fine. But I'm going to find out what the big mystery is eventually, one way or another."

Vivian strode back into the living room, knelt and started to reorganize her scattered materials. She picked up the scissors and set them on the table. She gathered the cut mesh squares one at a time, aligning them just so. All this time, Bonnie tried to catch her gaze, but she refused to play.

Eventually, Vivian asked, "How bad does she look?"

"Frail and skinny. You could probably fit your fingers around her wrist with some overlap now. But she's still acting like herself, like she's too good to pass gas."

Vivian's mouth twitched upward into a smile. She started to giggle, putting her fingers to her mouth.

Good God, she was as crazy as Mother. "What is so funny?"

Vivian was chuckling harder. "Something you just said. Think way back, let's see, you must have been about eight, and I was sixteen. Mother was driving me and one of my girlfriends to the movies in our old Studebaker. Remember how those vinyl seats always stuck to your legs in the summer? I think it was fall, because all the windows were up, and we were in the back seat, when all of a sudden there was this awful smell, like rotten eggs."

Bonnie started to giggle. Of course, they all knew that someone had farted, and Vivian had hit her on the shoulder and said, "Say 'excuse me' next time, sheesh." Bonnie had insisted that it wasn't her. The smell was so bad. Frantically, they rolled down their windows. And the back of Elizabeth's neck got redder and redder. She rolled down her window as well. But she never admitted that she farted.

Vivian continued to laugh, guffaws that had her bending at the waist and wiping tears. As her mirth subsided, she said, "Oh, my. I haven't thought of that in years. Poor Mother, her ears must be burning right now."

Bonnie grinned. "Yeah, maybe we can put it on her gravestone – 'Here she lies, dearly departed; may have had gas, but never farted.'"

Vivian's face turned tragic. "She's really going to die, isn't she?"

"Looks that way." Bonnie tried to sound stern, but her voice shook with the weight of the words.

*   *   *

Bonnie's fingers ached as she drove home. It was those damned scissors. Maybe she'd sue Vivian for giving her carpal tunnel syndrome.

It was so funny how people turned out. Take the summer of '66 that she'd brought up, for example. Vivian had been an absolute hellcat that year. Blatantly broke curfews, ran around with lots of boys. Bonnie would watch her in the back seat as they traveled in the car. Vivian would apply a deep, blood-red lipstick, dragging it across her lips as she pouted prettily. She had Elizabeth's thin, angular frame. Clothes draped on her as if she were Twiggy, and she wore her hair long, clipping a tortoiseshell barrette low on one side, like she couldn't care less about its placement. It, of course, looked drop-dead sophisticated.

She openly defied the rules that their mother set up, and the odd thing was, Elizabeth never seemed to care. In fact, their mother seemed to relish Vivian's rebellions, often nodding with satisfaction as the screen door slammed after her wayward daughter. She'd sit down next to Bonnie, coloring at the table, and say, "Good riddance to bad rubbish. Although you could do with a little more of that independent spirit, Miss Priss."

Bonnie never felt like she had the right answer for her mother, so she just said, "Yes, ma'am."

Elizabeth would throw her arms up dramatically."Oh, Lord! I give up on you."

And then Vivian had found the Lord. She was just nineteen; her birthday had been not even a month earlier. She'd been arrested for shoplifting aviator sunglasses and a transistor radio from Woolworth's. At the time, Bonnie had wondered what the connection was between the sunglasses and the radio – she probably should have asked, but never had the nerve to bring up the topic with Elizabeth.

This upward shift of Vivian's rebellion level annoyed Elizabeth, finally. After she bailed Vivian out, Bonnie was banished to her room. Like that had ever stopped her from eavesdropping.

Elizabeth's voice was low, menacing: "You do what you want. My only rules are that you don't get pregnant and that you don't get arrested. Do you think you can abide by that?"

Bonnie could hear the sneer in Vivian's response, and cast out a fervent wish to the universe that her sister wouldn't abandon her, leave her alone with Elizabeth's silent rage.

A few weeks after that incident, Vivian started attending a Bible study group set up by one of her old high school teachers. Bonnie was impressed. She was fairly certain this was just the newest ploy to outrage their mother, but it was a brilliant move: Elizabeth hated all things religious. But Vivian started to change. First, Bonnie noticed her carrying around a Bible everywhere she went. Then she stopped wearing lipstick and eye shadow. Her friends would call and ask where she'd been, because she'd abandoned their old haunts. But worst of all, Vivian began staying home – a lot – studying the Bible and bowing her head in prayer at all times of the day, not just before meals.

While Bonnie didn't exactly miss the old Vivian, she couldn't help but wish this new Vivian would be more attentive to her. Or at least give her some tips on how to not care about Elizabeth's ever-present disapproval. But her sister failed her. And although Bonnie expected Elizabeth to be crazed by Vivian's transformation, it did little to dent Elizabeth's shield of indifference toward her older daughter. She said only one sentence on the topic, after Vivian had prayed in front of them: "Jesus Christ, if you're going to end up some spineless God-puppet, then just go live in a commune or something."

Vivian *had* changed. Instead of launching into her trademark hysterics, she leaned forward so that she was not five inches away from their mother's face. With a deadly calm, she said, "You need some serious help, Mother. I will pray for your soul every night as I lay down to bed, because you are surely going to hell without Jesus' salvation. Praise God I found Him when I did, because He has released me from you."

She turned to Bonnie, who was trying to melt into the couch. "I'll be praying for you too, Bonnie. Blessings be on you."

Vivian picked her Bible up off the table, turned, and walked out the front door. For good.

The next time they heard from her, it was a year later, and she'd just given birth to Meg. When Bonnie and her mother got the news, Elizabeth shook her head. "Another casualty," she said.

Bonnie wasn't sure if she meant Vivian or the new baby.

Her wrist throbbing as she pulled into her driveway, Bonnie sat quietly and massaged the sore joint. Never again. It was too hard to maintain the level of anger at Vivian that she deserved. She'd run away from Elizabeth all those years ago, leaving Bonnie to handle the resulting mess. And Bonnie had been handling it ever since.

~9~
MEG

Meg squirmed in the passenger seat of Mona's BMW. Not that she was averse to traveling in comfort – the leather seat had just the right amount of suppleness to it, that distinctive smell of saddles and the outdoors. But riding alone in a car with her future mother-in-law was not her idea of a relaxing outing. More like a game of chess, with Meg unsure of when to give up a pawn or attack with the queen.

Opera played softly on the stereo, surrounding them in a shower of falling notes. Meg knew nothing about opera, but she liked what she heard, even if it was so soft as to be barely audible. Mona would never be so crass as to blast. Still, she wasn't used to being so quiet in a car. When she was with Brady, even if she wasn't talking, she was singing with the radio, intentionally screwing up song lyrics. Mona probably wouldn't appreciate that kind of wit. She wished Brady were here.

"I'm surprised you felt comfortable leaving Brady on his own," Meg said.

Mona's eyes never strayed from the road. "I'm not, entirely. Certainly, having me or Arthur there while you've been at work has helped Brady recuperate. But he's been home more than a week now, long enough for him to know what he can and can't manage. There is still a good deal of wedding planning to be done. Unless you and he would be willing to postpone it until next summer, when we can take the time to plan it properly." Her voice raised on the last word, a verbal ellipsis.

This wasn't the first time she'd insinuated doubt about managing to plan the wedding in such a short time. Too bad for her. "We talked about it a little, and we think we can still pull it off."

"Then we have work to do. Arthur will be there by lunch. I think they'll be able to get by until we return. You did bring photos or sketches of the dresses you're interested in?"

Meg held up the cluttered portfolio and sighed. "Too many, I'm afraid. They all have elements of what I want, but none of them is perfect."

"Well, we'll put Lydia to work. She's designed for me for years. She'll put something wonderful together. I'd rely on her judgment, if I were you."

What had she meant by that? Was it some sort of backhanded insult about Meg's taste – or lack thereof? She mentally checked herself. She needed to stop rooting for hidden meaning in Mona's words and give her the benefit of the doubt. Just because her own mother twisted threads of criticism into all comments pertaining to Meg's life– "This apartment could be so quaint if you'd only pick up a little" – didn't mean that Mona would as well.

A soprano's aria swirled around the car while Meg thanked Mona for arranging the meeting with the designer. The pure high song lifted and fell like an eagle swooping through the air. She closed her eyes to let the music wash over her in waves.

"That was amazing," she said as the piece ended. "What are we listening to?"

Mona smiled, wide and genuine this time, not the tasteful purse of lips with which Meg was more familiar. "It's one of Mozart's operas – *Idomeneo*. Arthur and I saw it at the Met the last time we were in New York. It's one of Mozart's first mature *opera seria*, and while it isn't perfect, I still love it."

Meg bit her lip. Should she try to bullshit her way through a conversation about opera, or plead ignorance? She wished she actually knew about the subject. It would've been nice to be able to converse about a topic Mona actually was passionate about. "I saw the movie about him. Great costumes, although a lot of the music seemed slightly hysterical to me. I've never heard any of his operas before."

Staring at the windshield, Mona nodded as if she wasn't surprised. Her smile had disappeared. "The sum of the man is much more than a film could ever portray."

Dear God, dealing with the woman was exhausting. "I meant no disrespect to Mozart, Mona. I'm sure his music is incredible. I mean, I love what we're listening to now. Maybe you could recommend some recordings?"

"Certainly, but you might want to check Brady's collection first. He may already have some. Some of the better recordings can be rather expensive."

Meg knew every CD in Brady's apartment. If his tastes ran to classical, he kept it a secret from her. But Meg was starting to rile. That comment about recordings being expensive–was that some kind of innuendo about Meg being low class, like she couldn't afford a damn CD? She was not going to lose her temper with this woman. First, Meg had set out today truly intending to try to find some common ground with Mona, get a fresh start. Second, if she blew up, Mona would win whatever this was they were playing. "Perhaps," she said. "Maybe we could attend an opera together sometime. I've heard the Cleveland Opera is really good."

Smoothly, Mona pulled in front of an upscale-looking building. As a valet rushed over to open their doors, she patted Meg's knee lightly twice. "Let's take things one step at a time, dear. No need to rush into anything." She handed the keys to the valet and gracefully exited the car, gliding into the foyer without a glance back to see if Meg were following.

Suddenly, Meg couldn't find her portfolio. Mona had already entered the building before she found it, slipped under the passenger seat. Scrambling out of the car, she tripped. The valet grabbed her elbow, steadying her.

She felt like she was seven again, with the same shame burning in her cheeks as when her second grade teacher, Mrs. Rockwell, suggested in front of the whole class that she might be better off in the remedial reading group. *One step at a time, my ass.* She climbed the stairs, maneuvering them carefully so that she didn't trip yet again.

* * *

Mona looked cool and crisp in her linen dress as they rode up in the elevator. Meg wished she had sweat stains or wrinkles across the waist, or anything that might reveal a more human fallibility. She'd bet this Lydia person was just as bad. She probably didn't perspire either, and she'd doubtless be showcasing gigantic silver jewelry of her own design set against an all-black ensemble. She and Mona would drop names of friends and stories of summer houses, and Meg would be left trying to look as if it didn't bother her at all.

Trying to navigate through the manners of the rich without causing an extreme breach of etiquette felt pointless. Seriously, with kids getting shot over sneakers, did it really matter whether she had her dress designed or bought it off the rack? God, she wanted to confront Mona about that opera rebuff. But even if Mona were profiling her as ignorant, it would be a fatal move to force her to admit it, to say explicitly the words from which there could be no retreat.

A gorgeous young man dressed for a corner office ushered them into Lydia's suite and offered them coffee. They settled themselves in on creamy leather wing chairs. Without saying a word to Meg, Mona appropriated an issue of *W* sitting on the glassy coffee table and began to leaf through it. *Fine. I don't want to talk to you anyway.*

Unsure what to do with herself, she idly took in the décor of the office. The lobby area was sparsely furnished, but what there was looked expensive. The good-looking boy complemented the cherry wood desk that he sat behind. A faint smell of lavender wafted around them, intermingling with the soft classical music being piped through a speaker on the ceiling. Meg hoped it wasn't Mozart.

Heavy, off-white drapery curving in a wide arc separated the lobby from another area, presumably Lydia's workspace.

With a dramatic swish, a short, plump woman pulled aside the curtain and bustled through. Cream-colored leggings bound her lower half like two sausages, and a diaphanous silk tunic swayed as she sashayed in. She embraced Mona – who withdrew slightly, much to Meg's interest.

She floated her way toward Meg, extending both hands to her. Grasping her fingers in pudgy, childlike hands, she said, "You must be the bride. Forgive my entrance. I like to imagine myself as the Great Oz, you know?" She giggled and settled herself in the chair next to Meg.

Meg stammered a hello. *This* was Lydia? This woman was the love child of a garden gnome and Miss Marple.

Lydia's eyes crinkled mischievously. "Are you always this shy, my dear?"

"I'm sorry. I don't know why, but I was expecting you to look different."

"And how is that, exactly?"

"I don't know. More New York-ish, I suppose. Dressed all in black, that sort of thing. You know, like a model." Meg hoped she wasn't insulting her. Mona sat in silence, her face an impassive mask.

Lydia chortled. "Oh, my. Maybe twenty years and thirty pounds ago." She leaned in close as if disclosing a juicy secret. "And that's being conservative." She gave an exaggerated shudder. "Although I've always detested black. So funereal. Shame on you, Min. You set her up."

Mona waved off the reprimand with raised hands. "You know I hate that nickname. I didn't think I needed to discuss your *appearance*. Your skill is what matters."

"Oh, please." Lydia rolled her eyes. She shook her head at Meg, elongating her face into a caricature as if to say, "Get a load of *her*."

Meg was stymied. She did not seem to be the type Mona would tolerate, let alone typically associate with, but Lydia's ease gave the impression of a long history. "Have you and Mona been friends a long time?"

"Mona's had to put up with me since we were both toddlers. Our families go way back. Unfortunately, I'm loaded – even more so than she, if you can believe it – so she's had no choice but to endure me and pretend she enjoys it."

Mona stood abruptly. "Don't be absurd, Lydia. I doubt Meg is interested in your garbled memories of our youth." She strode over to the window and peered out.

"Actually, Mona, I'm fascinated," Meg replied. "Lydia, if you don't need to support yourself, why do you design?"

"Please, child. I was bored to death until I started this business. Besides, I need slender young bodies to wear my inspirations. They require a sleeker silhouette than my Rubenesque figure." She groped her bosom lustily, then called over to the young man at the desk. "Ethan, bring my portfolio and sketchpad over to the table like a good boy, won't you? And run to the back and fetch us some tea and cookies as well. Those lemon drops, I think. Thank you, darling."

As Ethan disappeared behind the curtain, Lydia said conspiratorially, "He's lovely to look at, but slower than syrup. While we're waiting, tell me a little bit about yourself, my dear."

Meg began telling her about Yesteryears. It turned out Lydia had been in there to browse several times. But she was more fascinated with the particulars of Meg's romance with Brady.

"I love a speedy courtship. It makes me swoon. How did he propose to you? I'll bet it was astounding."

Mona nodded thoughtfully, cocking an eyebrow. "Yes, I'd like to hear this as well."

Lydia's eyes grew wide. "You mean you haven't heard the details? Why ever not?"

Lacing her fingers together, index fingers extended, Mona placed the tips to her lips. Her facial expression was serene, but her eyes were guarded. "Brady's been rather secretive about this relationship. We must be a terrible embarrassment to him, I'm afraid."

Meg winced. Mona's tone had a faux-light quality to it, as if the entire scenario were terribly amusing. But frankly, Mona was right to be angry. Hadn't she been herself? One morning, after more than two weeks of dating, when she had practically moved in, Brady's mother had phoned. He'd made vague comments about hanging out that implied he was alone. She'd had to grip the arms of the chair to keep herself from grabbing the phone and introducing herself.

She was used to not being meet-the-parents material – her purple spikes leant themselves to a bad girl persona, after all. But she'd thought Brady had seen through all that. She'd thought he knew her. When she confronted him about it, he made noises about it being "complicated," explaining how his parents thought no one was good enough for him, particularly if it wasn't someone from their country club. The few times he'd brought girlfriends home, his mother had actually made them cry. "I don't want that to happen to you," he'd said.

After she'd threatened to kick his ass if he was lying, and he in turn had sworn on his posterior's life that this was the truth, and that he would tell his parents when the time was right, Meg had let the issue drop. But he'd never explained to his parents why they'd never been told about her until the engagement. And now she was left to try and maneuver through this muck.

She realized that both Mona and Lydia were gazing at her expectantly. She shook her head. "I wish I could explain the reason for the secrecy, but honestly, I can't. And I feel awkward talking about it without Brady here. It was not my decision."

"I see." Mona looked thoughtful.

Meg had no idea whether she'd won points for refusing to blame Brady in absentia or whether she'd simply dug herself a deeper hole.

But Lydia rushed over to Meg and squeezed her, then flung herself at Mona, who sat rigid. "Family dramas can be so tiresome. You simply must let it go and be friends." Despite the words, she had a sharp little smile on her face, a miser who'd just discovered a secret stash of gold. "But what about the story of your proposal, Meg?"

Biting into a lemon drop, Meg started at its too-sour tang. "It was beyond charming. I went to meet Brady on the last day of school, and he'd coached his class to ask if I would please be Mr. Campbell's wife. Eighteen little kids all shouting in unison. It was a little embarrassing, but sweet." She smiled at the memory.

Lydia clasped her hands. "I love it. We must make you a dress worthy of such a proposal."

Mona cleared her throat. "Now, Lydia, time is of the essence. With the wedding in August, we'll need something with classic, simple lines. Nothing too ornate."

The designer pushed her reading glasses down her nose. "Last time I checked, Min, you're not the bride. But feel free to offer your opinion when it's time to discuss the mothers' dresses."

Meg brought her fingertips to her lips to hide the smile that fought to emerge. This was getting fun. "I'm afraid she's right. There really isn't time to get terribly fancy with my dress."

"Fiddlesticks. Let me worry about that." Lydia opened her sketchpad to a blank page. "Now, what did you have in mind?"

Pulling the photos from her portfolio, Meg spread them all out on the tabletop, explaining the elements she liked in each. Lydia's pencil flew across the page.

Watching her work, Meg wished she had some artistic ability. It must be incredible to be able to translate people's thoughts and words into pictures. She'd tried sketching once when she was a kid. All the sizes and proportions were off; her portraits looked as if all her subjects had hydrocephaly.

After what seemed like a long time, Lydia tucked her pencil behind her ear "What do you think of this?"

Meg and Mona drew near. It was simple, elegant, fitted. The neck was high, with a gathered bustline. Nothing too showy or tacky. Meg was thrilled to have such a close representation of what she knew she wanted, but had not been able to visualize until that moment. "I like the train a lot. And the neckline is what I was imagining. But the arms are too pouffy."

But Mona's face had grown dark. God, now what? What possibly could displease her about this dress?

A devilish grin played on Lydia's face. "Mona, what do you think? This dress remind you of anything?"

"No." She said the word quietly, but with absolute power. It did not sound like the answer to the question, but a statement of fact.

"Tut tut. You heard her describe the dress as well as I did."

"Her description could fit a hundred dresses, and you know it." Mona glared at her. "I never would have brought her here if I'd known you were going to pull this stunt."

Mystified, Meg waved a hand in front of them. "Pardon me. What are you two talking about?"

"Go on, Min." Lydia took a delicate sip of tea. "Fill your new daughter in."

Mona took a deep breath. "This is *my* wedding dress."

"Which her own mother wore at her wedding," Lydia practically sang the words, "and which has been preserved lo, these many years, just waiting for the next generation."

"That's enough, Lydia!" Mona snapped, her composure slipping.

Meg examined the drawing more closely, her irritation with Mona expanding further. Not only did she not believe her to be well-bred enough to take to the opera, she apparently would rather eat glass than offer her wedding dress. "It's really a beautiful dress, Mona."

"And may I just add," trilled Lydia, "it would be far easier to alter the existing piece than to assemble a new one. You did say that time is of the essence, didn't you?"

Mona set her empty teacup on its saucer. "Your tea was a little bitter, Lydia. You should be watchful of that with your clients." She twisted her wedding ring round, her head bowed.

"What's your decision, Min? I need to know now whether I'm going to alter the original or make a replica." Lydia's voice was forceful.

Mona lifted her head with a weary smile. "Of course you shall wear the dress, Meg. My dress is yours." Her words were even and modulated. Only the whiteness around the periphery of her lips betrayed the lie.

Meg felt like a pawn in this battle, two harpies fighting over the same scrap of meat. She had no idea of the history between the two, but she felt something close to pity for Mona, a sympathy akin to watching a lioness cornered and brought down. She wasn't sure if she was being a fool or not, but she wanted no part of this. She'd let Mona off the hook. "I appreciate the offer, Mona, but I think I'd like to find a dress where I'm its beginning, not its end."

"I understand." While Mona gave no overt expression of emotion, her breath caught once, so quickly that Meg almost missed it.

She shook Lydia's hand. "Thank you for your time, but I'm going to keep looking."

Her apple cheeks crinkling so much that they almost obscured her eyes, Lydia embraced her. "You'll be a fine addition to that family. Won't she, Min?"

Mona nodded contemplatively. "She may, at that."

-10-
JANE

Jane arrived at the door as Charley opened it to let her in. "Thanks, man." She briefly pressed her fingertips against his.

"Shoes off," Charley said.

"Already on my way." As Jane slipped off her shoes and put the slippers on, Charley, apparently satisfied, walked back into the living room and returned to his blocks.

Pam walked out of the bathroom, clipping an earring to her lobe. "Looks like you and Charley have fallen into a decent routine."

A smile crept onto Jane's face. "He kind of grows on you, doesn't he?"

Pam laughed. "Yeah, that's a good way to put it." She opened the refrigerator door and grabbed her lunch. "Oh, by the way, I'll be a little late getting home today. I have to stop at the bakery to pick up Charley's cake."

"I didn't know he liked cake."

"He could take it or leave it, to tell the truth. But since it's his birthday, hopefully, he'll take it."

Jane stopped picking at a loose thread on the heel of her sock. Silly, but she'd never imagined Charley being older, or younger, or anything but the way he was right now. "Wow, I wish I'd known. I would've gotten him a present or something–"

Pam stopped her, shaking her head. "Jane, it's just another day in this house. We don't do anything outside the normal routine. Well, except for the cake. It's best for Charley that way."

Jane was horrified. "But that sucks! I mean ... ." She groped for the words to explain why this was so unfair. "Are you sure Charley wouldn't want to have more of a big deal made on his birthday? After all, it's only once a year."

Pam smiled that little half smile that Jane interpreted as thinking she was sweet but a little dim. "It's what's best for him right now, Jane."

After Pam left, Jane took her wallet from her purse. She had a few bucks on her, enough to maybe buy Charley a couple new Matchbox cars from the toy section in the drugstore. She knew Pam meant well, but for Pete's sake, he was still a kid. Yeah, he was a little weird, but he wasn't dangerous or anything. Jane had even taken him on some walks around the block over the last week, when the weather was just too pretty to stay indoors, and nothing bad had happened. Okay, it was a route he was accustomed to, but let's face it, outside was outside. Charley was fine – he held her hand and took tiny steps next to her like an obedient dog. The only time he'd looked "different" was when he held his Ninja Turtles wristwatch up in front of his face and twisted it back and forth to catch the light glinting from the sun. Jane had yanked his hand back down when she saw someone else walking on the sidewalk, and that had been the end of that.

Jane sat down on the living room floor facing Charley. He was studying the bus schedule. "So it's buses today. Okay, what bus do I have to take to go downtown?"

Charley studied the schedule for a moment, then pointed to one of the black circles on the route map. Jane checked the number listed with the key under the map. He was right. "Well done, Chuck. What if I wanted to go to the hardware store?"

Charley paused, then pointed to another circle with an arrow pointing in the direction of Daedalus Falls' business route. "You're very good at this, Charley," Jane said. "Have you ever ridden on a bus?"

"Time to win some beaucoup bucks," Charley used the exact intonation as that idiot Pierre Miller that he loved to watch.

"Right." One of these days she would figure out his code, what he meant when he said different things. Probably not today, though.

They played with Charley's cars long enough for Jane to get a little bored with just moving his cars out of their line. She started to hide them to see if Charley could find them. She made the hiding places really lame, like halfway sticking the ambulance out of her pocket. When they'd first started this game, Charley had needed a lot of help finding his cars – he couldn't even find it if she told him where it was – but today he was doing pretty well. He'd probably let her hide cars all day. But too bad. It was his birthday. Time to get the party started. "Hey, Charley, let's go for a walk!"

Jane grabbed her backpack. "We're going to celebrate your birthday today, buddy. We'll show your mom what a big boy you are now. She'll see they should celebrate with you a little." Charley took her hand, totally normal.

As she and Charlie walked down the porch steps to the sidewalk, he turned left to walk the route they usually took. Jane put her hand on his shoulder to stop him. "We're going to go the other way today, Charley – to the store, okay?"

He looked at her without expression as he turned around, but he gripped Jane's hand more tightly as they began to walk. The two began to stroll down Oak Street to the corner. Since they were on a fairly steep hill, Jane expected Charley to move faster, maybe be forced into a jog. But no. He planted one foot in front of the other, stopping at each step to steady himself. She felt almost hypnotized watching him.

Still, even going at a snail's pace, the corner was nearing. Jane figured it might be a good idea to tell Charley about what he'd see next, so that nothing would come as a surprise. If there *were* going to be trouble, which there wouldn't.

First, she told him about the crosswalk, because she didn't know whether he'd ever crossed the street with his parents. Then, she told him about the stores they would pass on their way to the drugstore. "Really, Charley, most of the stores here are so boring – old furniture or clothes for rich old ladies who like pink tweed. My cousin's store is in the square as well, but again – old clothes – so we'll skip everything but the drugstore." She felt like she was jabbering, but Charley didn't seem to care one way or another.

As they passed the bus stop, he stopped and cocked his head, looking at the sign. Jane nodded, proud that he was observing so much.

As they reached the intersection, she reminded him that he was not to let go of her hand while they were crossing the street. The green walking man flashed. Jane tugged on his arm. Charley was staring at the flashing light, but at least he was moving. At the halfway point, the red stop light blinked and he stopped.

"Charley, c'mon!" Jane swiveled her head to see if anyone driving was paying attention to them. She didn't want them to think she couldn't handle a little kid.

Charley stood planted like a tree in the middle of the road. Jane pulled at his arm, but he didn't budge. The stop signal glared its solid light at them.

"Please, Charley! We can't stand here!" She didn't think anyone would try to run them down, but what if someone came around the corner too quickly? What if the police had to come? She would be in so much trouble. Her breathing quickened.

A red station wagon beeped at them, and Charley jerked as if he were a marionette who'd had his strings yanked. Jane tugged again on his arm. This time, he moved his legs in a jerky walk, his mouth open in a perfect round "O."

When they reached the curb, Jane walked Charley to a park bench and half-guided, half-pushed him onto the bench. "Just sit there a minute."

Breathe, Jane thought. Maybe this was a mistake. But it was too late to turn back. The drugstore was right there, and if they turned around now, they'd still have to cross the street again. She looked at Charley, who was sitting on the bench as straight as a Ken doll, staring directly ahead. He shook his head back and forth, back and forth.

"Okay, Charley, that adventure's done, and you did good." Jane tried to sound perky and optimistic. "Let's go get you that present now."

They walked into the drugstore together, Charley gripping her hand so hard that it hurt. As soon as the door closed, he looked up at the lights on the ceiling and began to hum a single note quietly. Jane looked at him sharply. He looked calm enough, but she'd never heard him do this before. They'd better get this done with and get back to the house.

Jane steered Charley into the toy aisle and showed him the Matchbox cars, all snug behind their shrink-wrap plastic.

"Which would you like, Chuck?" Jane held out two models, a flashy green roadster and a black Stingray with red stripes. Charley pointed to the roadster, still humming and every few seconds looking up at the fluorescent lights. He was rocking back and forth now on his heels, too.

Please, please, God, just let him keep it together, Jane prayed. Don't let him freak out or start screaming or anything. And even though this is really selfish, God, please, don't let him embarrass me.

As they paid for the car, the cashier looked at Charley. "Is he okay? He seems a little… stressed."

"It's okay." Jane was firm, hoping that Charley was listening, too. "We're going home now, anyway."

After they left the store, the spooky hum stopped. But now they were at the intersection again. When the walk signal flashed, Jane didn't want to risk his stopping in the middle again. "Sorry, Charley, but I gotta do this." She picked him up and carried him across the road. He went limp in her arms, his arms and legs flopping against her in time with her steps. Oh my God, he was heavy, like trying to tote about four bags of groceries at the same time. Jane wasn't sure she could even make it across the road. She squeezed his middle and, with her elbows, hoisted him up a little higher, walking as fast as she could.

She stumbled as she reached the curb, dropping him as she fell hard, right on her knees. He landed on his butt on the sidewalk. A car beeped. Jane picked herself up off the road and scrambled onto the sidewalk. There were gray spots floating in front of her eyes, and she shook her head, clearing her eyes to see. Charley jerked as the horn sounded, stood and began to run uphill in the direction of his house. He had a goofy run, arms and legs stiff and robotic. But he was fast. He was already a house length's ahead of her by the time she stood.

"Charley, stop!" Jane began to jog, limping from the pain in her knees. As long as she could keep him in her sight, she figured he was okay, and his house wasn't that far up the street. But still, this was Charley. For all she knew, he might wander off the sidewalk into the road following a stupid bug. God, she was so screwed. "Charley!"

He was now several houses ahead of her. A gray bus lumbered up to the bus stop that he had just passed. Charley stopped momentarily and looked at the bus. Oh, crap, Jane thought. He wouldn't dare get on, would he? She'd kill him. He'd better not even think about getting on.

She ran faster, even though on the hill, it felt like walking. Her heart pounded in her chest from the unaccustomed exertion, and her shirt felt like a wet washcloth under her armpits and across her back. The bus pulled away. Thank God. Charley was still running toward his house, so she guessed she'd dodged that bullet. Man, for a kid who looked like a lump, he was in pretty good shape. They hadn't locked the door when they left – nobody did in this town – and Jane watched as Charley ran up the stairs and flung open the door.

Panting, she finally reached the house. Jane paused inside the door, trying to catch her breath. She was torn between a desire to giggle hysterically or burst into tears, her relief that nothing bad had happened was so great. Tears tried to win, itching at her eyes, but she squinted until the feeling passed.

Okay, where was he? She wanted to hug him, if she didn't murder him first for scaring the crap out of her. Jane called out to him in a breathy voice between exhalations. "Hey, Charley, everything's okay. We're home, and you're safe."

He wasn't in the living room. Poor kid. She hoped he wasn't still freaked. He'd probably gone to his bedroom. Jane started down the hall, talking in a loud voice so he'd hear her coming. She opened his bedroom door. He wasn't in here, either.

Jane started to feel new seeds of panic swell inside her chest. He had to be in the house. She'd seen him come in. But the house wasn't that big, so where the heck was he?

"Charley, this isn't funny. Come out right now!" Jane yelled as loud as she could.

Nothing. Deafening silence.

Dammit, dammit, dammit. Way to go, Jane. Traumatize the kid on his birthday. She wanted to find a corner and curl up in it and cry. Of course she would screw up the one thing in her life that was going right.

"Please, Charley..." She stood in the doorway of his room, her eyes darting from shadow to shadow, even stupid places like under the dresser.

The damp on her shirt had cooled and felt clammy to her now, like a ghost's hand resting on her back. As she glanced past his closet door, she stopped. Had she heard something?

She gently opened the closet door. The closet itself was completely empty of toys, outgrown shoes, clothes. Not even cobwebs. There was only Charley, sitting on the floor in the dark, hugging his knees to his chest and rocking to and fro. He shook his head back and forth, like he was saying "no, no, no" to some unseen monster.

Jane bent down and put her hand on his kneecap. "Hey, Chuck. I'm so sorry. But it's okay now. Come on out, and I'll get you some milk."

The rocking and head shakes grew more frantic. Charley started to beat his head against the wall.

"Charley, please don't do that. Stop. Stop!" She tried to grab his shoulders, but he wriggled away. The thump on the closet wall grew stronger. Jane stood up and backed away, afraid that *she* might be what was causing him to bang his head like that. Maybe her stupidity had broken him. She wasn't special. She wasn't good with these kids. She was dangerous.

She had no choice in what to do next. She picked up the phone and dialed the number to the office where Pam worked. "Pam, Charley's in his closet and he's banging his head and I can't get him to stop. It's all my fault–"

Pam interrupted her. "I'll be home in ten minutes." She hung up.

Jane hovered in the hall while she waited for Pam to get home. She figured she was fired, but she hoped there wouldn't be yelling when it happened.

Judging by the sound coming from Charley's room, the banging seemed to be a little slower. But each thump still brought a vibration that traveled through Jane's toes to her spine.

When Pam finally walked in the door – it seemed like hours since Jane had called – she nodded briefly at Jane as she passed her in the hall heading to Charley's room. Jane shuffled from foot to foot. She hooked her thumbs in her belt loops, then took them out. She figured she shouldn't go in, afraid to set Charley off into something worse than what he was already doing.

After a few minutes, Pam came out. "He's calming down. He stopped banging his head, but he's going to stay in the closet for a while. Which is okay. That's his safe zone. Why don't we go into the kitchen and talk?"

She didn't sound mad, but Jane figured that had to be an act. Sometimes, when her mom sounded calm, that was when she was actually the most pissed off.

Pam put on some water for tea, then sat down. She folded her hands, but the skin around her knuckles was so tight it looked like she was trying to pull the skin off. "Tell me what happened."

Jane went through the whole day, watching Pam closely to see when the calm would pass and anger would erupt. All she could see, though, was Pam chewing on her lip a little.

The kettle burbled, then let out a wet shriek. Pam poured hot water into two mugs. The water dragged the threads from the tea bag into the cup with it, leaving the little paper tag floating on the top like a leaf.

When Pam finally spoke, she sounded sad. "Jane, I don't even know what to say. I told you this morning not to make a fuss or do anything out of the routine. You did hear me tell you this, right?"

Jane flushed. "Yes, but, I mean, Charley's been doing so well this summer. I just thought...."

"You thought what? You thought he was fixed?"

"No. Well, not really, but maybe a little." Jane picked at her fingers. How could she be honest? It sounded so lame. Finally, she said, "I just thought that, I don't know, maybe you had, I guess, underestimated him a little."

Pam quietly snorted. "Underestimated him. That's a good one." She took a deep breath, then sipped her tea. She had a little tic in her eyelid that she rubbed at. "Okay, I take responsibility for some of this, because I probably should've given you a lot more background on Charley's disability.

"Jane, the reason Charley's done so well this summer is because he's had a routine, a predictable schedule that stays the same, day to day to day. That routine, which would be boring to death to anyone else, makes him feel safe. When Charley leaves his routine, he can't predict what's going to happen next, and he gets scared. And when he gets scared, he does all the things you saw today – he rocks and bangs his head, and sometimes he gets aggressive and hits people. For a little kid, he's pretty strong. He's given me and his therapist black eyes."

"So none of the good things that have happened this summer have been me?" Jane felt so humiliated. She stared at her tea, not wanting Pam to see her embarrassment.

"Maybe a little of it has been you." Jane peeked up. Pam wore a sad, pitying smile. "It's pretty clear Charley has bonded with you as much as he can. But Jane–" Here, Pam lost her smile and her voice took on a hard edge. "You are not his teacher and you are not his therapist. You are fourteen, for goodness' sake. The stuff that you tried with him today, he might not be ready to do for years yet. We pay you to babysit, to sit here in the house, and maybe be bored, and make sure that Charley gets to follow his routine."

Jane gripped her left thumb tight under the table, her portable security blanket. "I'm so sorry." Almost as an afterthought, she added, "Are you going to fire me?"

Pam waved her hands helplessly in the air. "I probably should. Certainly, Charley's dad will want that. You might just be too young for this much responsibility."

She felt afraid to breathe, as if to alter the air in any way might shatter the newfound possibility that she might still be able to come here. Words tumbling out in a rush, she babbled, "I swear I'm not. Please, Pam, give me another chance. I'll do just what you want. I promise I won't do anything else but Charley's routine from here on out." She heard herself pleading; she sounded desperate, and hated herself for it.

Pam stood and turned her back to Jane as she put the dishes in the sink. The cups clattered onto the porcelain, as if she had lost her grip on them. She spoke to the wall. "Let me think about it. I can't promise anything." She sounded tired and sad. "I'll give you a call tonight and let you know what we've decided. You can go on home now; there's no reason for you to stay."

Jane retrieved her backpack and walked back to Charley's room. It was quiet in there now. She opened the closet door and knelt down. She could smell pee, and she felt like she would never be able to wash the odor out.

She held her hand out for Charley to touch her fingers. "Charley, I'm leaving now, okay?" She prayed that he would answer her. If he said "goodbye" to her like any other day, then it would be an omen that everything would turn out all right. But he made no movement toward her, and after waiting, Jane withdrew her hand, untouched.

~ 11 ~
BONNIE

Bonnie looked at her kids as they dutifully plodded into the kitchen for breakfast. Davey was a morning person, one of those naturally sunny kids who could pop open his eyes after a night's sleep and be fully alert. Jane was neither a morning nor a night person. She woke up grumpy and went to bed depressed. Maybe she was a noon person. She usually had at least a few good hours mid-day, where she was civil, and occasionally smiled. Bonnie always felt like if she got a smile from Jane, she must be doing something right. This morning, Jane entered the kitchen with her hair snarled and hanging in her face, obscuring her eyes. She had taken a vow of silence after coming home from Charley's house the other day. The only details Bonnie knew were from Pam's phone call yesterday. She'd explained to Bonnie what had happened, and then told Jane that she still had a job, but would be on probation. Bonnie had tried to talk to Jane about it afterward, but it was like talking to a stone. She'd hoped maybe a night's rest would make Jane feel better, but you certainly couldn't tell it by looking at her.

"Pancakes okay with you two?"

Davey nodded with vigor as he bounded over to the refrigerator to get the orange juice. Jane sat quietly at the table.

Bonnie mixed up the pancake batter, cracking eggs one-handed into the bowl. After ladling the first pancake onto the griddle, she paused, waving the coated spoon in the direction of the table. "I hope you guys don't have any big plans for the day. I want you to go with me to see Grams."

Jane swiped her hair behind her ears; she and Davey shot each other a look. Bonnie didn't know whether to be irritated or pleased that they'd found solidarity on at least this one topic. Still, it didn't matter. They were going. With Elizabeth teetering on the brink of that scary precipice where she didn't even remember how to eat, Bonnie wanted the diversion of extra people to take her own mind off of all the ugly possibilities.

Davey tested the waters first, with the same wheedling tone he used to ask for an advance on his allowance. "But Mom, it's the fourth of July."

"What, pray tell, is the relevance of that statement?" Bonnie turned back to the griddle. She flipped the first batch and began pouring out more batter. "It's a holiday, therefore we should be able to ignore our relatives?"

Jane stepped in. "I think Davey just meant that with the picnic and fireworks, wouldn't it be kind of a rush for us all to go today, as well as overwhelming for Grams?"

"Nice try. I want us all to go visit today, specifically because it *is* a holiday. The last time you went to see her was Christmas. We'll still have plenty of time to get to the picnic, since I plan to have us go right after breakfast." She flipped the pancake like an exclamation point.

Jane muttered under her breath, "Like she'll even know we're there."

"I heard that," Bonnie said, a warning edge to her voice.

"I'm sorry, Mom, but it's just that it's creepy, going to see her and talking like nothing is wrong when she has no idea who we are. And geez, you go almost every day. How do you keep doing it all the time?"

A wave of weariness rolled over Bonnie with such force that she laid down the spatula and leaned against the counter. "I know," she said, so quiet it was almost inaudible. Taking a deep breath, she forced herself to stand up straight. "I don't expect you to understand completely. But she's family. And this is what you do for family. Besides, she can be lucid at times. Sometimes she's totally with it, and when she is, she always asks about the two of you."

Jane grimaced. "Like that's better." She started to mimic her grandmother, in a startlingly accurate facsimile of her tone. "'Jane, stand up straight. Quit slouching! Why must you always dress like you're trying to hide? When I was young, girls knew how to dress...'"

Davey, in a falsetto voice, chimed in. "'David, you need to be the man of the house now and take care of your mother and sister. You need to be responsible, and it won't be fun.'"

Bonnie winced as she plated the pancakes. Not for the first time, she wished her children could possess the kind of normal grandmother who would sneak them candy and always take their side.

She set their plates on the table with a little more force than necessary. "This needs to stop right now."

The kids stopped and looked at her with the wide-eyed, innocent gazes of born liars.

Bonnie sat down at the table, softening her tone. "Look, I may have issues with Grams. You may have issues with Grams. Grams may have issues with us. I don't care how crotchety and senile she is, I don't care if she's mean as a snake, she is your grandmother, and you will treat her with respect. Do I make myself clear?"

Jane's face flushed with embarrassment, and Davey looked like he'd been slapped. But they both nodded.

Bonnie sighed. "Let's eat. Can we please just try to have a nice day?"

They arrived at the nursing home, having endured the marathon commercials of the soft rock station during the car ride. Both children looked sullen and tense. *Welcome to my world*, Bonnie thought.

In the lobby, she held up her hand. "Listen, you guys, I know it's hard for you to see Grams like this. Geez, it was hard to see her *before* she had Alzheimer's. But we need to do this."

When Jane gave a short nod, Bonnie squeezed Davey's shoulder. "It's probably a little much to bombard Grams with all of us. Let's play it like we did at Christmas. Jane, you and I will go in first, and Davey, you go over to the lounge. You can watch TV or see if you can start up a game of Hearts. We'll come get you in a few minutes, and you and Jane can switch."

Davey nodded and loped off. Bonnie marveled that she'd ended up with a child so amiable, so ready to accept the world as it is. He actually loved it in the lounge. She would watch him on the few visits he made: cracking jokes with the elderly gentlemen, flirting with the ladies, grinning as they all pressed quarters into his hand as if he were their favorite grandson. Jane, on the other hand, always seemed like she was afraid she was going to drop a cup or accidentally touch someone.

Bonnie turned to Jane, trying to make her tone light. "Do I look okay?"

Jane sighed. "Yeah. I bet Grams won't be real happy with those cinnamon rolls, though."

Bonnie peeked inside the wilted bag and shrugged. "Yeah, I know. But I didn't have time to bake, so she'll just have to make do. She actually hasn't been eating a lot of what I've brought recently, but she still seems to want the gesture made."

They made their way to Elizabeth's room and rapped lightly on the door, which stood ajar a couple inches.

"Come in. Don't expect me to answer it."

Bonnie was surprised her mother had even responded to the knock. Hopefully, she was having a good day.

"Hello, Mother. Happy Fourth of July. Look who I brought to visit."

"Hello, Grams." Jane's voice was tentative. "It's Jane."

"Of course it's Jane." Elizabeth's voice was soft but raspy. "Do you think I'm stupid? I know your name."

Bonnie had told the kids her mother might be lucid, but she hadn't really expected it. She hadn't remembered who Bonnie was in months now.

"Sorry, Grams," Jane said. "That was silly of me."

Elizabeth snorted from her chair. "Did you bring me a treat today?"

Bonnie handed her mother the bag of cinnamon rolls. Elizabeth opened it and took a deep sniff. She curled her nose with disdain. "These smell artificial. They're not homemade."

Bonnie stifled a grin. Score another one for Jane. "Mother, even if I bought them in a store, a baker still made them. They're not mass-produced."

"That's not the point." She closed the sack and set it on the floor. "I'm not hungry, anyway." As Elizabeth shifted position in the chair, Bonnie could see the outline of her mother's hipbone jutting through her housedress, and was alarmed to note how thin she'd become.

"I wish I could tempt you to eat more, Mother. Is there anything in particular you're craving? I could make it and bring it by tomorrow."

Elizabeth glowered. "Don't put yourself out."

Jane said, "You should at least try a cinnamon roll, Grams." She perched herself on the edge of one of the wooden chairs.

Elizabeth smiled like a coquette. "I have to keep my figure, you know. People used to compare me to Katherine Hepburn. You have to be thin for clothes to drape right." She cast a scanning eye at Jane with a raised eyebrow and pursed lips.

Jane flushed and tugged at her camp shirt, which she'd ironed in deference to her grandmother. Bonnie changed the subject, trying to keep the peace. "Mother, do you know Jane has a job this summer? She's been extremely busy lately."

Elizabeth smiled tightly at Jane. "Good. Maybe you'll be able to buy some clothes that fit." She glared at Bonnie as if to note that she didn't have to change the subject if she didn't want to. She turned back to Jane. "Actually, I like to hear about keeping an independent spirit. What is it you're doing?"

"I watch a boy who has autism."

"What's that?"

Jane furrowed her brow. "Um. It's kind of like he's in his own world. It's a condition."

Elizabeth pressed her lips into a sharp frown of disapproval. "Absolutely not. You should quit tomorrow. My God, I would rather you beg money on the street."

Jane stared at her grandmother. "What do you mean? I have a lot of responsibility."

Bonnie knew she ought to jump in and tell her mother to back off. But even as she opened her mouth to speak, the words jammed in the back of her throat, choking her.

"Watching children is bad enough. It casts you in that stereotypical mold that women are only good to cook and have babies. Next thing you know, you'll be pregnant yourself. But even worse, watching a retarded child – it's beneath you." Elizabeth's hands tremored in her lap.

The invisible ropes tying her tongue loosened and Bonnie tried to intervene. "Mother, that's inappropriate—"

"It's okay, Mom, I can stand up for myself." The desperation had left Jane's voice. She sat up straighter on the bed. "First of all, Grams, I said he has autism. He's not retarded. He can read and follow a bus schedule and is probably as smart as you or me."

Elizabeth harrumphed.

"And you don't have to worry about me. I don't ever want to be married or have children. I'm going to have a career and be important."

Bonnie stared at her daughter. This was new. Jane had never said a word about what she wanted for the future. She flashed back to herself at Jane's age. She'd had only amorphous dreams about escaping Elizabeth's tyranny, with no idea of how to go about doing it.

Elizabeth closed her eyes, as if she were dismissing the entire conversation. When she spoke, her voice was weary. "You say that and maybe you even mean it. But you'll meet a boy and spread your legs and get knocked up. Just like your mother." She opened her eyes and smiled sweetly at Bonnie.

Bonnie glared at Elizabeth. A bubble of hatred rose in her chest, tried to burst out of the pores of her skin. That old witch had to ruin whatever semblance of a relationship she had with her daughter.

Before she could say anything, though, Jane had stood up and walked over to her grandmother. She knelt down so that she was looking at Elizabeth straight in the eyes. "You know, Grams, you can be a real bitch sometimes."

Elizabeth laughed, a deep belly laugh, as Bonnie simultaneously grimaced.

Peeking at Bonnie with questioning eyes, Jane stood up. "I think I'll let Davey come in now."

Bonnie nodded, worrying if she said a word, whatever slim thread of composure she was clinging to would vanish without a trace. Hell. She'd known Jane would figure out one day that her birthday was remarkably close to what had been Bonnie's wedding anniversary. But since she didn't celebrate an anniversary anymore, she'd thought maybe she'd dodged that bullet.

Once Jane had gone, she turned to Elizabeth, who was gazing at the open door with a savage grin.

The demon wrath, that had lain quiet as she listened to Jane defending her, returned to rattle her body, but was not strong enough to allow her to speak without restraint. "Mother, you were completely out of line. I know Jane had no right to call you that, but–"

"Hah. She had every right. I was provoking her, wasn't I? Finally spoke her mind, which makes me respect her more than anyone else in this mousy family. Kind of reminds me of me, to tell the truth."

Bonnie thought, *I wouldn't wish that on her in a million years.*

"I wish I understood you, Mother."

"I wish you did too." Elizabeth leaned back in the chair and closed her eyes again. "I'm tired. Be quiet now, and let me rest a minute."

Far from being annoyed at the brush-off, Bonnie was relieved at the temporary reprieve. She padded around the room, straightening the few knick-knacks – a worn copy of *Atlas Shrugged*, a collection of tortoise-shell hair clips, a sepia-tinted photo of Elizabeth in her twenties. She really had looked like Katherine Hepburn. No pictures of her children or grandchildren, although Bonnie made sure to give every year's school pictures to her. God knew what she did with them. Probably tossed them aside like so much junk mail. She opened the drawers to make sure all of Elizabeth's clothes were there. In the past, other Alzheimer's patients had wandered into Elizabeth's room and set up camp, or gone through her drawers, believing them to be their own.

"What are you doing?" Elizabeth had her eyes open now.

Good Lord, she couldn't even leave Bonnie in peace when she was supposed to be sleeping. "Mother, I'm just making sure all your clothes are present and accounted for."

Elizabeth gripped her cane, pointing it accusingly at Bonnie. "I don't know you. Thief! Nurse!"

Davey opened the door. "Hey, Mom. Hey, Grams. Is everything okay? Do you need a nurse?"

Bonnie clenched and unclenched her hands. "No, honey, it's okay. Grams got a little confused."

Elizabeth gave a high little hiccup of a sob. Her hands to her lips, she stared at Davey with a mixture of fear and wonder.

"Is she okay?" he whispered to Bonnie.

"Pete, is that you? Oh my Lord, come here and let me look at you." Elizabeth reached for him from her chair, her voice tender, caressing.

Bonnie looked sharply at her. Her mother had never used that tone of voice, ever.

"Mother, this is Davey, your grandson."

Elizabeth waved her words away. She cupped Davey's face in her hands. "I knew you would come back to me, my baby," she crooned. "I've missed you so much. And you've grown so. I knew you would come back."

Davey tried to pull away, but Elizabeth had grasped his hands and would not let go. "I'm Davey, Grams, I'm Davey! Mom?" He sounded slightly hysterical.

Bonnie extricated Davey, holding her arm protectively around his waist. "Mother, you've made a mistake. This is Davey. My son. And I'm Bonnie. Your daughter. It's okay, you got a little confused."

Elizabeth stared at him, her forehead wrinkled with doubt. Her voice broke. "You're not Pete?"

Davey still looked a little scared, but his voice was full of compassion. "I'm Davey, Grams."

Bonnie put a hand on his shoulder. "Davey, why don't you go out and wait in the lounge with your sister. I'll be along in a minute." When he left, she knelt down on the floor in front of Elizabeth, her face turned into the upholstered wing of her chair. Tears rolled down the worn tracks of her face. "Mother? Are you okay? Is there anything I can do? Anything I can get for you?"

"No, just go. I don't want to see anyone anymore." Elizabeth clutched her lap blanket tightly.

Bonnie gazed at her, her anger forgotten. The desire to know whatever this piece of her mother was overrode her usual caution. "Mother, who's Pete? Why can't you talk to me about him?"

"It's none of your business. Please go now. I want to rest. I'm tired." Elizabeth sounded more snappish than tired, but Bonnie didn't doubt that when she left, her mother would sleep for hours.

"Let me help you into bed, then." She gripped Elizabeth's arm and together they walked over to the bed. Bonnie smoothed the chenille spread over her mother as though she were a child home sick with the flu. "I'll come back tomorrow, okay, Mother?"

Elizabeth didn't answer.

Before heading to the lounge, she ducked into the Ladies' Room. Locking herself into a stall, she sat. The enormity of all the emotions that had been flung around that bedroom like so much confetti settled over Bonnie. Feeling dizzy, she slumped against the side partition, forcing herself to breathe in, breathe out, until the room stopped spinning.

In the lounge, she saw Davey and Jane sitting on one of the couches, watching the Indians game. Davey had recovered quickly: he was leaning forward, talking to the pitcher on the set. He didn't appear any the worse for wear. Jane, on the other hand, sat with her arms wrapped around her knees. She looked like someone awaiting a certain guilty verdict.

"Let's go, guys." Bonnie tried to sound perky. "We don't want to get to Aunt Viv's too late, or we'll miss all the good food and get left with the stale chips and that nasty fudge her neighbor brings every year."

"We're still going?" Jane asked.

"I guess we could skip it." She realized that she didn't want to have to face any more of her family.

"No, I totally want to go," Jane said.

"Me, too," Davey chimed in.

Oh, well. "Then it's set."

Jane face shifted. Bonnie could see the realization dawn in her face that she wasn't in trouble, that her sentence had been commuted. As the three of them left the building, Bonnie felt like the clouds had parted and the sun broken through. She sandwiched herself between Davey and Jane and pulled them close in an impromptu hug. Uncharacteristically, both her children accepted the public display of affection and even reciprocated.

As Bonnie buckled her seat belt, she looked in the rear view mirror at her daughter. "Hey, Janey?"

Jane lifted her head, catching her mother's gaze. "Yeah?"

"I appreciate that you stuck up for me in there."

Jane wrinkled her nose. "Yeah, whatever."

Bonnie could still see a tiny smile lingering on her daughter's face as they pulled away from the nursing home. It was barely visible, but somehow, it was enough.

-12-
MEG

Meg stood at the kitchen counter, twisting the stems off strawberries and throwing them into the garbage disposal. Brady was cutting up some pineapple next to her. It was a small kitchen, and he wasn't but a foot and a half away. It felt like more. In the two weeks he'd been home from the hospital, he'd been silent as air, speaking only when spoken to. Meg tried to joke with him, saying, "You *are* planning on leaving this apartment to attend our wedding, correct?"

He only answered with a derisive "Very funny."

Brady had also become quite proficient at fine-tuning the nuances of the exhale. Meg could immediately tell whether the sigh was one of stoic self-pity ("I guess I can do this myself") or patient self-righteousness ("You can't possibly understand what I'm going through, so I won't bother to try to tell you.") All of the sighs made her want to kick him in his bad leg.

She tried to think positively. That Brady was even helping her with the fruit salad was a baby step in the right direction. He'd gotten her to wait on him since he came home from the hospital, and her general rejoinder to female servitude of, "Why? Is your leg broken?" didn't exactly show her sensitive side in this instance.

"Wait 'til you see who shows up to this picnic," she told him.

Brady grunted.

"It's this mishmash of neighbors from the development, kids from Mom's youth group, friends from her church, and Bonnie and Jane and Davey. The fun part is predicting when someone's going to get drunk and say something they shouldn't. It's generally someone from the women's guild, historically. I don't know why."

Brady chuckled. "I'm a little surprised your mother even allows beer."

"That's a concession to Dad, I'm sure." Meg grinned. "Some of the early ones were dry, but someone always ended sneaking some in."

The pineapple completed, Brady moved to the sink and began washing the knife. Meg figured she drove him crazy with her habit of leaving dirty dishes in the sink for days. But at least she rinsed them.

"After our next-door neighbor passed out in Mom's begonias, it was decided that if Mom and Dad provided the beer, they had grounds to supervise intake."

"I guess taking pot brownies is out, though." Brady's voice was sincere, but his eyes were crinkled with mischief.

Meg swatted him with a dishtowel on the behind. "Like you've ever been high in your life, Mr. Eagle Scout. Although it might get Mom to loosen up a little." She grinned. "You'll like Bonnie. She's about the nicest person alive. And you'll love Jane and Davey. They make me wish I had siblings to fight with."

"It'll be fun." Brady leaned over in her direction and pecked her on the cheek. Then, as if the cheek had proven not enough, he began nuzzling her neck.

Meg backed up so that she was spooning into him and pulled his arms around her, letting herself be supported by his steady frame. Just as she was getting comfortable, the phone rang. "Let the machine pick it up," Meg said. But as the tone squawked, and they heard Mona saying, "This message is for Brady ... ," the spell was broken. He picked up the kitchen receiver. "Hey, Mom, I'm here ... wait a sec and I'll get on the other phone?" He gave Meg a "What can I do?" look and limped out.

Meg hung up when Brady picked up the other line, but continued to watch him through the cutaway. She'd tried to keep the books and *Newsweeks* picked up so that there was less to sabotage Brady as he moved around the living room. But there was still way too much furniture – all heavy, dark antiques – for this tight an apartment space. It was like trying to wind through a maze, and that was with two good legs.

She eavesdropped on his side of the conversation as she carved up the watermelon, more than a little annoyed. This was the first time that she and Brady had connected, had any kind of physical intimacy at all, since he'd been home. Mona must have some maternal antenna that alerted her to any foreplay by her son. It was practically superhuman.

He was apologizing to his mother for something. He seemed to sink into himself a little, hanging his head as he feebly protested some unknown wrong. Not at all like he'd been when Meg had first met his parents at their house – more accurately, their estate, with its stunning, but intimidating, Georgian-style manor and English garden full of irises and topiaries. During lunch, when Brady had mentioned they were getting married in August, Mona had peered at Brady, then Meg, as if between them she could sniff out the truth, and asked if such a fast engagement was really necessary.

Meg could feel Mona choking on the unasked question. Arthur stared at his champagne fixedly, refusing to meet anyone's eye. Meg considered patting her flat belly, just to see the reaction, but stifled the urge. There was no need to be sadistic.

Instead, Meg began explaining their reasons for choosing such a close date, but Brady interrupted. "I know it seems like a huge amount to do in a short period of time, Mother. But frankly, we want a simple wedding. Just family. Not one of these three-ring circuses like the Franks' threw for Eileen last year – just a quiet, small wedding, with a nice meal following. That should be easy enough to accomplish, I would think."

Mona smiled at Brady, but her lips were pinched and her eyes contained no humor. "I don't think you realize how difficult it is to pull off 'simple,' darling. Is this date negotiable at all?"

"No, Mother, it's a deal-breaker."

Meg had not heard sarcasm from Brady before. Mona must have been unused to it as well, for she winced.

He sighed. "Of course it's negotiable. Do you really have to talk to me like an attorney?"

"Of course, forgive me. I see. Well, we will simply do the best with what we have." Mona paused and rose stiffly from the table. "If you'll excuse me, I'll go see if dessert is ready."

The cool stickiness of a dropped watermelon ball on her instep brought Meg's attention back to the present phone call. It now seemed so odd to her that Brady had been so assertive, even aggressive, with his mother that first meeting. Which was the real mother-son relationship?

Meg heard Brady say, "Well, Meg's not going to be happy about it." This couldn't be good. "No problem, Mom. I'll see you this afternoon." He stayed seated on the couch, his back to Meg, long enough that she knew he was trying to avoid telling her what she'd just overheard.

Warily, she walked into the living room and sat facing him. "Spill it."

Brady wouldn't look her in the eyes. "I can't go to the party."

"Can't go, or won't go?" Meg heard a hard edge coming into her voice and tried to quell it. Maybe she could still avoid a fight.

Brady sighed. "Does it really matter, Meg? I'm not going."

Meg attempted to sound reasonable, the perfect fiancée. "Okay, just tell me what your mom said. I promise I won't get mad."

"Look, I always do the Fourth of July at my parents'. At least, I have up to now. Well, I guess it was a set thing to Mom. She called to ask what time they should expect us today."

"Your mom's a big girl. She'll get over it. It's not like you can drive all the way to your parents' anyway, with your foot." Sheesh.

"I know. I told her that. So she and Dad are coming here for the day."

Meg didn't say anything. She blinked a few times. But she didn't trust herself to speak. She didn't want to speak ill of Mona in front of Brady – that would be tacky – but honestly, she could wring her prospective mother-in-law's neck for being so rigid. And she began to wonder if in the accident, his spine had been damaged along with his ankle.

"Look," he said, talking faster, "I tried. I told her about the party. But she was getting pissed. You haven't seen my mother pissed. Believe me, you don't want to."

Disgusted, Meg said, "And I'm supposed to just … ?"

"You should definitely still go to your mom's. No one expects you to stay."

She felt her face flush, the uncomfortable rush of blood pounding in her cheeks. "I'm being dismissed, in other words. You have got to be fucking kidding me."

Brady hoisted himself up from the couch. "I knew you'd do this." He grabbed his crutches and started hobbling away.

Meg reached him in two quick steps. "Don't you walk – hop – away from me."

His face was mottled with anger. "Why? What's the point of talking?"

"Because I'm not done, that's why." Meg stepped around Brady so that she was blocking the door to the bedroom, her arms on either side of the door jamb.

Brady heaved a sigh – his patronizing "I'm so much more mature than you" sigh. "Move. Please."

"Are you always going to cave to your mother? Am I always going to come second?"

"Don't be stupid. It's just one day, one party. Get over it." Brady was breathing hard, even though he was standing still. He tried to nudge Meg with his crutch to get her to move.

"Right. But you conveniently get to avoid contact with the outside world this way."

Shaking his head, Brady stared at the rug. Then, with a deep inhalation, he made a fist and punched the wall with a resounding smack.

"Fuck!" he said, massaging his knuckles. He fixed his eyes square on Meg. "I said I was sorry, all right? I don't want to talk to you right now." He limped into the bedroom, still holding his wrist, and turned on the television, louder than necessary.

"Asshole!" Meg slammed the door behind him, kicking it for good measure. Shit, hell, and damn. She could feel tears starting to well up. She almost never ever cried, and certainly not over a guy.

She spied one of Barkley's babies – a drool-matted, stuffed, chew toy – picked it up, and threw it at the china cabinet. Having minimal heft, the doll bounced off the hutch, rendering the act grossly unsatisfying. Its sole effect was to make Barkley run for cover, cowering under the end table.

"Fuck it, I'm outta here." Meg grabbed the half-completed fruit salad and left.

The Cure, usually a good band to bring her out of a funk, blasted from the car stereo while wind whipped through her hair. One thing was clear: she couldn't let her mom know anything about this fight. God, that'd be a disaster. She'd probably close up the party, send everyone home, and lock Meg and Brady in a room with the pastor while Vivian and her friends held an emergency prayer vigil outside. So that was out. Which meant telling her dad was out, too, because he'd just tell Vivian. She wished Carla had accepted her invitation, but she had her own plans.

The line of cars was parked like a stationary parade at the side of her parents' street. "Showtime," she mumbled as she walked up the sidewalk.

As she moved around to the back of the house, the party atmosphere jolted her like a dunk tank of ice water. She'd been around Brady and his sighs so long that it was making her morose as well. It wasn't even three o'clock yet, but the backyard was filled with people in varying designs of red, white and blue. Her high school biology teacher's makeshift bluegrass band was already playing over at the far end of the backyard – her dad played mandolin. They played every year and were actually pretty good.

Her dad saw Meg as she walked toward them and raised his mandolin in greeting. Meg blew a kiss and walked on. A train of picnic tables lined the back wall of the house, crammed with cold cuts, jello molds, potato salads, hot dogs and hamburgers. Meg felt a little nauseated looking at all the excess. It reminded her of when she was a kid, and snuck an entire plate of brownies out under the oak tree to eat in secret. She'd missed the fireworks that night because she felt so awful.

She made a space for her fruit salad and went off in search of her mother. She finally found her inside the house, unpacking screened dish covers that would keep the flies and gnats off the food. "Hey, Mom, I made it."

Vivian crossed over to give her a dry kiss on the cheek. "You're earlier than usual. I'll take that as a compliment." She craned her neck to see behind Meg. "Where's Brady? Is he checking out the band?"

Meg focused her gaze at her mother, knowing that if she avoided eye contact, Vivian would catch the lie she was about to tell. "He had to back out at the last minute, Mom. He sends his apologies. His leg was cramping up on him pretty bad."

Vivian narrowed her eyes and scrutinized Meg's face, probing for the chink that would give her falsehood away. Meg held back a blink. She could practically hear the whistle from *The Good, The Bad and The Ugly* as the blink face-off went down. And then, like that, the moment passed, and her mother switched back into her supercilious self. "Oh, that poor baby. You should've stayed home with him, Meg."

"I tried, Mom, but he wouldn't let me." Meg shifted from one foot to the other, feeling a growing urge to flee.

"Well, here, make yourself useful and take some of these out to the picnic tables."

"Gladly." Meg gathered up the screens in her arms and hid her sigh of relief behind the gray domes.

Back out at the picnic table, she was trying to prioritize which dishes most needed covering when someone grabbed her around the waist from behind. Meg whirled around and there stood Davey, grinning. "You're it."

"You'd better watch yourself." Meg ruffled his hair. "One of these days, I'm going to mistake you for a thug, and do one of my patented kung fu moves on you." She rearranged air molecules in a complicated zig-zag to illustrate.

Davey giggled and struck a pose like Bruce Lee, then gave a high side kick, knocking into the table.

Meg smoothed the tablecloth. "Okay, enough fun, my friend. Is your mom around anywhere?"

Davey grabbed a brownie. While he shoved it in his mouth, he pointed to the far corner of the yard.

"Thanks, dude." Meg blew him a kiss and took off.

Bonnie was talking with a couple women from her parents' church, so Meg stopped a few feet shy. She looked clean and smart in a sleeveless peach madras blouse, but not especially patriotic. Giving a little wave, she raised her eyebrows as if to say, "Don't go anywhere." She finished up her conversation, patting forearms as she left. She squeezed Meg around the shoulder. "What's wrong? You look like you could burst into tears."

Meg felt a balloon deflate in her chest. "Hell's bells, Bonnie, I don't know. I don't even know where to begin."

"Let's go sit." Bonnie led her to a pair of mismatched benches, currently unoccupied. "Stay there," she ordered. "I'll be right back."

She returned with two tall goblets filled with something garnet-colored. "Sangria. I don't know who brought it, but your mom must be keeping better company at the church." She sipped it and gave an approving sigh. "So, what's going on?"

Meg recounted the fight with Brady, then backtracked to include the episode with the panic attack. "I swear to you, he has not stepped foot out of that apartment since."

"Haven't you guys had to meet with the priest?"

"Came to the apartment."

"Has it occurred to either of you that Brady might need some help getting over this?"

Meg snorted. "Uh, yeah. I've been trying for the last week to get him to agree to talk to a shrink or something. He promises to think about it, and then apologizes for being a jerk. But it's just words. He doesn't really feel bad about what he's doing, or think about what it's doing to us."

"What about the wedding? Are you going to postpone it?"

Meg shrugged. "Honestly, Bonnie, I don't know. At the moment, everything is still set for August twenty-eighth, mostly because Mona had to pull strings with her club to get the reception set. But it's not like we've really even talked about it. And frankly, I'm beginning to wonder if the whole thing is a good idea in the first place." She ran her fingers through her hair. "Help me. Tell me what I should do."

Bonnie laughed. "That's a first. I don't think you've ever asked me for advice before."

"Desperate times call for desperate measures."

"Put your drink down and come sit by me," Bonnie commanded. Meg complied.

Bonnie pulled her close. Meg laid her head on Bonnie's shoulder and closed her eyes, feeling like she was about eight years old. It wasn't a bad feeling.

"Are you sure you're not my real mother?" she asked contentedly.

"Considering I was ten when you were born, I'd venture it's certain." Bonnie sat up straight and faced Meg. "As for Brady, I really can't tell you what you should do. Is it possible this is all just a variation of normal cold feet?"

Meg shook her head. "I don't know."

Bonnie smiled. "Well, I can tell you I had cold feet about my own wedding. I didn't really feel like I had a lot of choice, though, all things considered."

"What do you mean?"

A flush flooded Bonnie's face. "Well, I guess if Jane knows, it's not really a secret anymore. I was four months pregnant when I got married."

Meg stared at her, dumbfounded. "You never told me that!"

Bonnie sighed. "The subject never came up. Anyway, it was a stressful time. I had major cold feet. Joe was so excited, though. Every time I was convinced getting married was the wrong thing, Joe would turn around and buy His and Hers toilet seat covers, or a football for the baby, or something so nerdy yet outrageously sweet that I'd forget my reservations. This was *before* he became a no-good cheating asshole, of course."

Wow. Meg almost couldn't get her head around all this. She'd known how Bonnie's marriage ended; Bonnie had shared that herself in bitter, matter-of-fact tones when she'd told her family that she was getting a divorce. But Meg had never known about Jane.

"Wait a minute," Meg said. "You said Jane knows? How?"

Bonnie shook her head slowly. "Funny you should ask." She told her the events of the morning at the nursing home.

"Damn. Elizabeth really knows how to twist that knife, doesn't she?"

Bonnie scowled. She opened her mouth like she was about to say something, then abruptly closed it.

"What?"

"Nothing. I had something I wanted to say, but it's off the subject. We were talking about Brady."

Meg shook her head. "Don't worry about it. Frankly, I'd rather talk about other people for a while. What were you going to say?"

"It's just that I wish you wouldn't call your grandmother 'Elizabeth.'"

Meg was perplexed. "Why?"

"It seems so callous, somehow," Bonnie said with a sadness to her voice.

"Bonnie, I don't have a relationship with her. What I know of her I've gotten from half-forgotten memories when I was a kid, and Mom's ramblings when she's on her third rum and coke. I don't have any reason to call her 'Grandmother.'" Meg felt annoyed having to justify herself.

"Still, I wish you'd go out to see her. I wish anyone would go out to see her. She's got no one but me – which is no fun for me, let me just say – and I think she's losing ground. Let bygones be bygones. I've probably gotten to know her more during the times when she doesn't recognize me than the times when she does."

Meg nodded, unsure what to say. Out of the corner of her eye, she saw her mother walking towards them with purposeful strides. It never failed that if Vivian were in the general proximity, and Meg and Bonnie were together, she tried to insinuate herself into the conversation. Meg didn't know whether it was that she was jealous of the relationship between Meg and Bonnie, or whether she was so insecure that she needed to intrude, just to be a part of something. She nudged Bonnie. "Gotta go."

Bonnie nodded with a knowing roll of the eyes. Meg gave her a quick kiss on the cheek, grabbed her sangria and wove her way through pockets of partygoers with tilting plates. She saw her mother throw up her hands in exasperation as Meg walked away. She looked around. Despite the crowd, she could not see anyone she really wanted to talk to. None of her crowd was here. But everyone was going to want to know about Brady, and Meg couldn't stomach lying on such a grand scale. Finally, she spotted Jane over at the corner of the yard, sitting in a lawn chair by herself, dangling her feet in the wading pool that Vivian set up every year just for the party.

Meg pulled up a chair next to her, slipped off her sandals and stuck her feet in the pool. "I can't believe this thing still holds water. My parents bought this pool when I was, I don't know, four or five. You'd think it would be a sieve by now." The water was toasty warm and she lifted and lowered her feet, letting the water swirl between her toes.

Jane looked downward and scrunched her eyes up tight. Then, as if coming to some sort of resolution, she asked, "Are you still mad at me for not wanting to be in your wedding?"

God, it sucked to be fourteen. "Oh, wow, no. Has this been bothering you the whole time?"

Jane wouldn't look at her. "Well, you haven't talked to me since then. I just figured …"

Meg grimaced. She'd been so preoccupied with herself that she'd neglected to remember how Jane obsessed about not only actions, but omissions. "Hey, Janeling, I'm not mad. Carla will be my maid of honor and that's all I need. And I apologize for not calling. I can be kind of an ass these days. Tell you what. Before the summer ends, let's go see the Indians. It'll be fun."

Jane's lips upturned the smallest degree. Meg knew baseball was more her thing than Jane's, but she might still have fun. "Maybe. Will Brady come? Where is he? Did he come with you today?"

"No." Meg shifted in her chair. "We had a fight."

Much to Jane's credit, she did not ask for details. Meg was grateful.

"I called Grams a bitch today."

"I heard. Did she deserve it?"

"Oh, yeah. She thinks I'm stupid for watching Charley."

Meg gave Vivian mental points for having kept her away from Elizabeth while she was a kid. "Have you ever really cared about what she thought?"

Jane didn't answer for several seconds. "No and yes. I mean, according to her, nothing I do is good enough, so why should this be any different? But I keep thinking that just maybe I can do one thing that Grams will like." She peered at Meg with questioning eyes. "Can I tell you a secret?"

Meg eyed Jane's face, which was drawn with worry. "I don't know. How bad is it?"

"Sometimes I just want Grams to die already so that Mom can stop being stressed out all the time. And maybe leave us some money, too."

Meg smiled. Boy, did she love this kid. "Don't lose any sleep over that, Jane. I'll bet your mom feels that way too sometimes."

"Yeah, Grams was such a total bitch today, especially to Mom. She told me not to get myself knocked up like my mother."

"That's kind of a bombshell, don't you think?"

Jane raised her foot out of the water, waggling her toes to let the water drip off. "It's no big deal. I knew a couple years ago when I was looking through some old photo albums. What I don't get is why anyone would think that because Mom got pregnant before she got married, I will too. I don't even want a boyfriend yet. And I don't want to have sex. I think it's overrated."

"Trust me. It's not."

Jane groaned and mock-gagged. She seemed so much younger than Meg had been at that age. She hoped Jane wouldn't lose all of her innocence these next few years. Jane scissored her feet back and forth in the pool, smiling and silent. This was one of Meg's favorite things about her: that she didn't feel like she had to maintain a conversation, but was able to sit in a comfortable quiet. She had, for just a short time, once felt this with Brady. Meg mentally chastened herself – no. She'd deal with Brady later. But not right now. Feeling Jane's presence beside her, as comforting as flannel, Meg watched the sunlight glint off the water, prisms refracting like diamonds.

~13~
JANE

It was all going okay until Charley threw up. In the two weeks since Jane had been on probation, things had gotten mostly back to normal. She and Charley were back on "shoes off" basis, even if he refused to go on walks with her anymore. Not that he said "no" – he just backed up into the hallway anytime she approached the door.

This morning, Charley had been sorting the coins his mom had left for him, making neat stacks of ten on the coffee table. Jane left him alone, thinking about her latest idea. She had brought her Polaroid camera with her, after checking with Pam about making Charley a book of things he liked. Pam liked the proposal, so Jane had, to date, taken pictures of his bedroom and his cars. She figured maybe when she was finished, she could write a sentence on each page to match the picture. She didn't have any clue whether he would like it or just ignore it, but it was something to do.

Jane heard the chinkety rain of coins being knocked over, and glanced up from her list of "To Get" photographs. Charley didn't tip over his stacks – ever. He was staring at the table, rocking back and forth; his foot tapped against the table rapidly, like a thumping rabbit's paw.

She felt the burning lava of fear start to bubble in her stomach, but tried to keep her voice calm. "What's up, Charley?"

He didn't answer, but started shaking his head no, no, no. It seemed like there was no part of him that wasn't swinging now. It made Jane dizzy. He was really pale, too.

"Charley, stop! What's wrong?"

He opened his mouth as if he were going to say something and vomit sprayed out of his mouth onto the coffee table and the rug. It was exactly like that scene in *The Exorcist* that Jane had seen on TV, even though her mom had told her she wasn't allowed to watch it yet.

Jane stared in horror at Charley, now sitting in the middle of this puddle of stink. God, it smelled terrible. She felt a stirring of panic. She knew she had a bunch of jobs to do – call Pam; get Charley away from the mess and cleaned up; clean up the barf – oh, God, she didn't want to have to clean that up! But she didn't know what she should do first.

She scrambled to her feet. "Charley, get up. You can't sit there." Grabbing the scruff of his shirt, she pulled him to his feet. She guided him to his room at arm's length, rummaged through his dresser, and found him a clean shirt and pair of pants. He stood in the doorway like a statue, eyes on nothing.

"Here. Wear these." But before she could help him remove his shirt, he started the throw-up dance again, and sure enough, blew like Old Faithful.

"Oh, my GOD!" Jane yelled. She clamped a hand on his shoulder. "Stay here. Do not move. And try not to throw up anymore. I'll go call your mom."

Pam groaned when she heard the news. "I can't come home right now. I'm the only one here in the office, and I have to handle the phones."

Oh, perfect. Jane stifled a groan. "So what do I do?"

"Stay calm. I'll call his dad. Jim doesn't have classes this summer, so he should be able to leave. Just sit tight and try to keep Charley comfortable, okay?"

"Okay." Jane would've preferred Pam – she was pretty sure that Mr. Burke had wanted her fired after Charley's birthday – but it was better than nothing. She screwed up her face, trying to find the right way to ask the next question and not sound like a moron. "Um, Pam?"

"Yes?"

"Should I clean up the throw-up?"

"Um, yeah, Jane, I think you should. Probably a good idea. Sorry." Jane could almost see the amusement on Pam's face.

She laid the phone back in its cradle and covered her face with her hands. She so did not want to mop up barf. The smell alone made her nauseated. If she started, she wasn't sure she wouldn't be adding a second layer of vomit. She was convinced she was the only kid alive who'd ever had to do this, and it just wasn't right. It defied the laws of the universe to make her do a job so foul.

Charley walked into the kitchen. He looked so pathetic in his stained clothes, damp with perspiration, that Jane forgot about feeling sorry for herself.

"C'mere, kiddo." She led him back to his bedroom, maneuvering him safely around the puddles to the bed. She wet a washcloth and wiped his face with the cool terry cloth. He raised his arms above his head, and Jane helped him take his sick clothes off and put his pajamas on. After he'd climbed into bed, Jane went to the kitchen and brought a bowl in. "If you need to throw up again," she said, "try to aim for this."

With Charley taken care of, there was no way to stall. Jane really couldn't stand looking at the puddle. The thought that the disgusting mass on the floor had been the contents of Charley's stomach made her gag. Breathing through her mouth, Jane threw pages from the morning's newspaper over the lakes in the living room and bedroom. Charley was curled up in a fetal position on his bed. She stopped what she was doing long enough to put her hand on his cheek. He did not avoid her touch, but closed his eyes.

Once everything was covered up, Jane felt the tiniest smidge better. What she couldn't see could be handled. She found some dish gloves under the sink and began stuffing the soaked newspaper into the garbage, then wiped up the rest with thick wads of balled paper towels. She wiped sweat from her forehead. Was she hot? She'd better not get sick from this.

As she threw open windows and sprayed Lysol around the room, trying to mask the stink, Jane tried to imagine what Charley's dad would be like. She'd never met him, and there were no pictures around, so she mostly imagined a version of her own dad blurred around the edges. She figured he'd be kind of handsome in a denim shirt and khakis kind of way, with graying hair, and he'd be stern but nice, a lot like Pam.

She glanced up as the latch clicked on the front door and Mr. Burke arrived. He grunted – she supposed it was a hello – and nodded, dropping his briefcase and jacket on the floor and heading to Charley's room.

He didn't resemble her imaginary Mr. Burke at all. He was chubby, for one, not in the "merry Santa" way but more in the sinking fat way. His hair was thinning, and he had a bald spot developing at the back of his head. Jane couldn't figure out how he and Pam, who was so pretty, had ever gotten together, except that Mr. Burke had absolutely gorgeous eyes, green with brown flecks. They looked like they belonged on another person, maybe a male model.

After checking on his son, Mr. Burke came out of Charley's bedroom and sat down on the couch. Jane settled on the upholstered chair, ready to give him a detailed report and show him how responsible she could be.

"Well, he's asleep for now, so I guess I'll take him to the doctor if he throws up much more." He paused. "We've never been introduced. I'm Jim." He looked at her directly with those eyes, no blinking, as if he were trying to memorize her. It was a little freaky to have a grown-up peer at her so intently.

Jane mumbled her name and focused on her feet. Didn't anyone ever tell him that it was rude to stare? Fishing for anything to break the silence, she said, "So what do you teach?"

"College algebra. Do you like math?" Mr. Burke's voice became a little more animated, as if maybe if Jane said yes, he and she could have something to talk about.

She felt awkward telling him the truth. "No. I took Algebra this year and did okay, but I don't really see the point, to be honest."

"Oh." He said the word like it was a curse, flat and disgusted. Apparently losing interest in Jane, his eyes rested on a water stain on the wall. At least he wasn't staring at her anymore.

She had no idea what to do. Did he even want to know about Charley? Should she ask if she could leave? Clearly, he wasn't going to tell her. Maybe Charley wasn't the only "special" one in the family.

The suddenness of his nasal voice jolted her like a glass breaking. "So. What do you think of Charley?"

Jane was relieved to have a question she could actually answer. "Oh, wow, he's a great little kid once you get to know him and he gets to know you."

"That's not what I mean," Mr. Burke's tone sounded like he thought she was not very bright. "Do you think he's smart?"

"Well, sure." Jane answered, not really sure what he was asking. "I mean, he reads, and he can figure out those bus schedules like nobody's business. I bet he'll be good at math, too, in a few years."

He nodded, but since he wasn't looking at her, it seemed like it was more to himself. "See, I've been telling Pam that he's smart and capable of a lot more than we're having him do, but she continues to baby him."

No way was she going to get drawn into a squabble about how to raise Charley. Jane reached down and started to straighten up some magazines. "I should probably pick up a little now. Then, unless you need me for something, I guess I'll go."

"Fine." He dismissed her with a hand wave, staring into space as if Jane had already left. Charley appeared in the doorway, his eyes trained on the television across the room.

"Hi, Charley," Jane said with a forced perkiness. "How're you feeling, buddy?"

"Hey, sport!" Mr. Burke's voice boomed like a sit-com father's. "Come give your dad a hug."

Charley crossed the room and stood next to him, but his eyes never left the blank television screen over in the corner of the room. He was like the reverse of one of those paintings whose eyes follow you wherever you go.

Mr. Burke pulled him into an awkward hug, made especially so since Charley was facing away from him. "Charley, look at me when I talk to you," he said loudly.

Jane was annoyed. He was autistic, not deaf.

Charley moved away from him and walked to the front of the television. "Beaucoup bucks," he said.

"I think he thinks it's time for his show," Jane said.

"That's exactly what I'm talking about." Mr. Burke slammed his hand on the table. It made Jane jump, but Charley didn't flinch. "He's been watching that stupid show since he was three years old. He's too old now. If he has to watch TV, let it be Bugs Bunny or something normal, for Christmas' sake." He blushed, as if even this lame substitution for cursing was more emotion than he cared to display.

"Beaucoup bucks," Charley repeated.

"You can forget it, Charley," Mr. Burke said. "Keep asking for that show and you'll get a spanking."

Jane had knelt next to Charley, but now she tilted her head up to see his dad. A spanking?

She positioned herself so that she was gazing right into his eyes. "Charley, it's not time for *Food Frenzy* yet. See the clock? It's only 11:30; you have to wait until 3:00, when the hands get to here."

Charley looked at Jane with no expression. But he sat down on the carpet and began to line up his cars.

Mr. Burke had opened his briefcase and was examining some papers.

Jane cleared her throat, then hesitated. "Maybe I should stay a little longer."

Mr. Burke laid down his papers and leveled those eyes at Jane. "I think I can manage, thank you."

Jane fumed as she walked home, huffing and puffing, picking at her nails with a vengeance. What a pinhead jerk. Charley might as well have been invisible. Jane hoped he would throw up in his dad's lap, or over his shoes, or in his briefcase. Someplace where Jim Burke might actually have to see him for once.

By the time she reached home, she was simply tired of it all. She didn't want to think about Charley, didn't want to think about his dad. She plopped down on the couch and flipped on the television – since she was home early, no one else was around, and she could watch all day if she wanted. But even with the TV on, she couldn't stop thinking about Mr. Burke. He didn't know Charley at all. He probably brought him a basketball on his birthday, just like Jane's dad had bought her Barbies for every Christmas and birthday from the time she was four. Thinking back, maybe it should have been a hint that her parents' marriage was shaky that they didn't buy joint presents like most families.

Jane had never played with Barbies, never even wanted to. They were too perky, too happy, their boobs too pointy, and their hair too blonde. Even as a little kid, Jane knew enough not to trust them. And yet she continued to receive them from her dad, on every gift occasion: Malibu Barbie, Veterinarian Barbie, Skateboard Barbie, Olympic gymnast Barbie.

Every time she opened a present from her dad, Jane held onto a small spark of hope that maybe, this time, he'd figured out that it wasn't Davey who was tearing the heads off the dolls and leaving the corpses in between the couch cushions – that maybe, just maybe, she might want something different for a change. And she'd tear open the corner of the package and see a skinny white arm waving through the clear plastic, and she'd know that once again, a stupid doll was going to have achieved more than Jane ever would.

Her dad hadn't even put it together after the divorce. Jane didn't know why she'd thought he would – she wasn't silly enough to think it had been part of the separation agreement. But it had seemed like a good time to stop with the Barbies.

Jane had finally told her dad on their last visit: enough was enough.

"Well, honey," he'd said, his face sincere and troubled, "Why didn't you ever tell me this before?"

She wanted to scream in frustration. "I guess I thought you'd figure it out, Daddy. Didn't you ever notice you never saw a doll after you gave it to me?"

He pursed his lips. "Now that you mention it, yes. I just thought all girls liked those kinds of dolls."

Jane bit her bottom lip. When she felt like she could look at her dad, she said, "I'm not all girls."

He squeezed her hand. "I'm sorry, Janebug. You're right, you're not all girls. You're better than all girls." He paused. "If you don't want Barbies anymore, what do you want?"

Jane was stymied. She hadn't thought about that. Besides, if he really knew her, he'd be able to pick something on his own. "I don't really know. But anything else will be great."

This last birthday, he'd gotten it exactly right. A big package had been delivered to the door. It was the right size to be a Barbie mansion, and for a second, Jane was afraid to open it. But then she did, and it was a guitar – a beautiful nylon string guitar. When she'd called her dad to thank him, he'd said that he played a little in high school and college, and that maybe Jane might have an ear for it.

Of course, when she sat down to play it, she didn't know how to tune it or do anything but plunk the strings, and it sounded really bad. She'd tried to practice on her own, even bought a book on teaching yourself to play guitar, but still the thing sounded like monkeys were grabbing the strings at random. It was hidden away in her closet now.

Maybe Mr. Burke had some moments like that, too, where you could tell he was trying, even if he got things wrong. Jane hoped so. She nestled herself deeper into the sofa, finally able to concentrate on the hypnotizing images of the stream of mid-day commercials. She closed her eyes and dreamed of guitars played by Barbies.

-14-
BONNIE

Bonnie arrived at the nursing home with the beginnings of a world-class headache stirring behind her eyes. Right now, it was just an ominous presence lodged behind sight, but it worried her nonetheless. She always felt as if she had to be in peak condition, like an Olympic athlete, to deal with her mother. Anything less and Elizabeth would sense the weakness and swoop in like hawk to mouse. She briefly rubbed her temple, inhaled deeply, tucked the Tupperware holding the homemade strudel under her arm, and left the sanctuary of her Nissan hatchback.

Elizabeth's room was closed tight. The door, barren of photographs and other signs of personalization, loomed anonymously but imposing all the same. She had tried to put a flowered wreath on the door one day to at least make it seem more homey to people walking in the hallway. She figured her mother probably wouldn't even be aware of something on the outside of her room. But it was gone the next day, and Elizabeth remembered enough to tell her that some moron had thought she was dead and was putting up memorial wreaths already.

Bonnie knocked on the door, but received no reply. Elizabeth frequently ignored social niceties such as this. She cracked the door. "Mother, it's Bonnie. May I come in?"

When she received no response, a pebble of concern lodged itself in her gut. She was supposed to be in her room for the afternoon.

"Mother?" Bonnie scanned the room quickly. She even walked around the bed to check the floor on the opposite side of the room, just in case Elizabeth had fallen. She was relieved not to find a body, but still perplexed.

"Boo!" Elizabeth cried, popping out from behind the bathroom door. She cackled happily as Bonnie jumped.

"Christ, Mother, you scared the life out of me. What are you doing?"

"I'm not 'Mother,' silly. I'm Lizzie." Elizabeth stuck her index finger in her mouth and rocked back and forth on her heels.

Bonnie raised her eyebrows. This was a new one. "Well, hello, Lizzie. How old are you?"

"I'm four years old and ten months," Elizabeth said. "You're not very pretty. Do I know you?"

"Not yet." Bonnie noticed the dark circular stain deepening the hue of Elizabeth's brown slacks. Looking back toward the bathroom, she saw a puddle on the tile floor. "Lizzie, did you have an accident?"

Elizabeth flushed. "Please don't tell. I'm not supposed to wet myself now that I'm a big girl."

Bonnie started to put her hand on her toddler mother's shoulder, then pulled back. Elizabeth had never liked physical contact from her; who was to say she had been any different as a child? "Let me get someone to help us clean you up, okay?" She unsnapped the waistband to Elizabeth's slacks. "Go ahead and slip these wet pants off, and I'll be right back, okay?"

* * *

She saw her favorite orderly sitting in the charting room. "Hey, Rodney, I need you."

"Sure, Ms. Stanton." Rodney leapt to his feet, surprisingly graceful for his linebacker's frame. "What can I do you for?"

"Mother's wet herself, and the bathroom is wrecked. I can get her cleaned up, I think, but if you could help, I'd really appreciate it."

In the few moments it took them to reach Elizabeth's room, she'd taken off her pants and underpants, and was now standing at her window, completely oblivious to her own nakedness.

Grabbing a towel, Bonnie rushed to her side, embarrassed both for her mother and for Rodney, as bearer and witness to this loss of dignity. As she draped the towel around her mother's waist, she apologized.

"Oh, ain't no big thing, Ms. Stanton," Rodney's low voice rumbled quietly, like an idling truck. "I see worse than this ten times a day." He stepped into the bathroom and returned with a wet cloth, handing it to Bonnie and then turning away as she cleaned Elizabeth and helped her step into clean underpants.

As Rodney pantomimed mopping and moved in the direction of the door, Elizabeth blinked several times and narrowly gazed at Bonnie. "Helen, who the hell have you brought with you this time? Is this another one of your pet projects, reforming wayward coloreds?"

Bonnie groaned inwardly. As if Elizabeth hadn't alienated enough people in her life. She was about to scold her, but stopped when she heard Rodney chuckle.

"Mrs. M., this here's your daughter, Bonnie. And you know me – I'm your favorite helper. Rodney's the name."

He glanced toward Bonnie with a grin. "She finds some way to bring 'the coloreds' up every time I'm in here."

Bonnie groaned. "I am so sorry about that, Rodney. Where she grew up–"

"Forget it, Ms. Stanton. Your ma has way more suffering than I do right now."

She wanted to let the topic die, but couldn't. "It still doesn't make it right."

Rodney began to look towards the door. Time to let it drop. Making an attempt at a graceful segue, Bonnie said, "But I feel a lot better knowing that she's got you in her corner."

"Helen, I'm right here, and I'm not deaf, you know," Elizabeth snapped. "It's extraordinarily rude to be talking to your protegé about me as if I'm not even here."

Rodney nodded to Elizabeth and Bonnie and strode out of the room. Bonnie watched him go. How was it that even when she was trying *not* to be racist, she felt like the effort itself classified her as one?

As Elizabeth poked her, Bonnie turned and murmured an apology. She preferred the Lizzie version.

Rodney returned with a towel and bucket. "Who's Helen?" he asked in a low voice as he set them down and Bonnie helped her mother slide on some dry slacks.

Bonnie answered at a normal volume. "I think she must mean Helen Goodacre. When I was ten, she helped Mother for a few months after she broke her ankle. Helen was married to the pharmacist she did bookkeeping for." Bonnie paused. "Do you think she could be flashing back to this time in her life because she needed our help now?"

"Seems as good a theory as any." Rodney found Elizabeth's shoes and brought them to her. "Who knows where these poor folks end up in time or why?"

Elizabeth poked Bonnie forcefully with her index finger. "Again, I'm right here."

"Sorry. Stop poking me." Bonnie steered Elizabeth with a light touch to her recliner and eased her down into it. As Rodney moved into the bathroom, Bonnie smiled and hoped he could see the gratitude in her face.

She sat down on the Shaker stool opposite the recliner. "You ought to feel better now, with dry clothes. I brought you some homemade strudel."

"You always were a homebody, Helen." Elizabeth snatched a piece of the proffered strudel and took a small bite, but spit it out into a napkin after a couple chews. "Too dry. You're losing your touch, Helen." Bonnie took the rest away and set it on the carpet. She allowed herself a single moment of resentment, then shook her head, as if the feelings were gnats that could be swatted away.

Elizabeth peered at her. "You seem different to me. More serious."

"I'm the same as usual. Really."

"No. You're different. You were so perky, so damned optimistic, that time when you came to help with the baby. I wanted to kick you sometimes, except that you were the only one who could calm her down. I'd pick her up, and she'd scream and scream until I thought I'd have to smother her to get her to quiet. And then you would come and just ... jiggle her, and she'd stop screaming and smile."

Who the hell was she talking about? "Which baby was this, Elizabeth? I don't recall."

Elizabeth barked a humorless laugh. "Hell, I suppose it was both the girls, wasn't it? All they did was mewl and try to suck me dry. Vivian had that colic, and Bonnie was like a vampire, wanting to stay on the nipple for hours and still seeming like she never got enough. If they'd have been kittens, I suppose I could've put them in a sack and drowned them in the river and nobody would've looked twice."

Bonnie felt her chest tighten. No matter how her head expected the insult, she still felt like a child receiving that first stinging slap on the cheek. All the worse because Elizabeth didn't realize she was saying anything horrible: she was just being honest.

"Pete was never that way. He was the only easy one of the bunch. He'd just grin and burble at me the whole time, like I was giving him straight cream. You could get the girls to love you, Helen, but he was the only one who ever loved me." A lone tear escaped from the corner of Elizabeth's eye and rambled down her cheek. She shook her head violently, as if she was coming out of a trance. "Heh. Got me to forget my own rule, did you? Tricky."

Bonnie raised her face to heaven. "I don't know what you're talking about," she said wearily.

Elizabeth chortled. "Yes, Miss Sweet and Innocent. You are such a godsend, helping me with this ankle during my time of need."

She put her hand on Elizabeth's knee. "Mother–" she started.

Elizabeth slapped her hand away. Her voice grew shrill, sawing at Bonnie's eardrums. "Are you aware, as you so kindly assist me through my convalescence, that your husband has been sticking that pathetic excuse of a penis into me for the last two years, has been cornering me in my office and taking out his ... worm ... and putting it into me?"

Bonnie raised her palms skyward in shock and frustration. "Dammit, Mother, I'm not Helen. And you can't blame her anyway–"

In a sudden snakelike thrust, Elizabeth slapped her. The clap of skin on skin resonated in the still air of the room like a thunder strike.

Rodney bolted out of the bathroom at a pace surprising for one of his heft. Inserting himself between Bonnie, who was already backing away, and Elizabeth, he grabbed her wrists as she started a second back swing. Holding her arms gently but firmly against the arms of the chair, he began crooning to her: "Ms. Elizabeth, that's enough now. You need to calm down. No need to be riling yourself up. Take a few big breaths."

Elizabeth shuddered, her gaze darting back and forth from Bonnie to Rodney. After what was probably only a minute, Elizabeth seemed to tire, and she blinked, regarding a spot on the wall. Rodney eased his grasp, then released her.

Still staring at the wall, Elizabeth began to speak, her voice dead of inflection. "Stupid man, running his own business into the ground. Liked the ponies, too. Account books don't lie. I could've run that store blindfolded and hog-tied, made it into a real moneymaker. But he just laughed at me. And then he said he'd start making some of my changes if I'd do something for him. And you know who I thought of, Helen? I thought of you, being more of a mother to my own blood than I would ever be, with this degenerate for a husband, and I thought, well, what's the use of it all? He's going to poke me or fire me. The thought of making a fool of you was what tipped the scales for me, to tell you the truth. That's how much I despise you."

Elizabeth turned to face Bonnie and smiled beatifically, as though being able to express this level of hatred to her target gave her immense pleasure. Bonnie felt incapable of speech. The level of horror, for both her mother and Helen, paralyzed her vocal cords. But with that incandescent smile, the gorge rose in her throat, and she stumbled to the bathroom and released all the bile in racking spasms.

As she stepped out of the bathroom, Rodney was helping Elizabeth back into bed. The thin cotton weave of the blanket molded itself over the sharp angles of Elizabeth's hips and knees, throwing her thinness into sharp relief and spinning Bonnie's emotional Roulette wheel back to worry.

"I think she's done and got herself tuckered out, Ms. Stanton. She'll be asleep not ten seconds after we leave the room."

Bonnie bent forward to kiss her mother on the forehead, and realized she couldn't. She made do with finger-brushing her hair back from her face. Elizabeth pushed her hair back as it had been, just as the four-year-old Lizzie would've done.

Rodney stopped in the hallway. "You wanna go get a Coke? You don't mind me sayin', you look like you could use it."

In the dining room, Bonnie cracked open the Coke and drew a long, sweet sip. Cupping both hands around the can, she closed her eyes to better feel its wet coolness. When she opened her eyes, Rodney was watching her with concern, his jowly cheeks drooping from the absence of his usual amiable grin.

"I'm okay," she said. "I promise, you won't have to call 911 on me."

"I'm glad to hear that, Ms. Stanton." He continued to keep an eye on her, but didn't say anything.

The silence was vaguely unnerving. "I mean, I'm physically okay. I think my headache finally got the best of me today. Emotionally, I'm not so sure. I mean, that was pretty hateful stuff in there."

Rodney nodded slowly. "Lotta hateful stuff in the world out there, ma'am."

"Yeah, but you don't expect to hear it coming from your own mother." She forced a laugh out, trying to make herself sound less shaken. "I mean, I had no idea that she'd been sexually abused. But does that justify so much loathing?"

Rodney ran his short stubs of fingers over the gray on his chin. "You want my opinion?"

"Yes. Help me make some sense of this."

He sighed. "I think that all of us gonna have some reckoning to do when it's our time to go to Jesus. Some people got more to do than others, but all of us got hate in our hearts sometime. I don't think your mama's got a lot of time left, and I think that maybe she's doing what she has to so she can right herself with Jesus before she goes. You know, comin' clean before her Maker so that He can forgive."

She smiled briefly. "Rodney, my mother's been an atheist since before I was born."

His face broke into a grin so wide his eyes almost disappeared. "Maybe she don't remember that right now."

Bonnie started to smile back. "You're bad."

"Yes, ma'am."

When she reached home late that afternoon, she felt as though she hadn't slept in a week. Jane was slouched on the sofa, one leg slung over the back cushion, watching television. Davey was spending the night at Robbie's house.

Bonnie sat down on the sofa with a sigh. Her shoulders sagged with fatigue.

Jane hoisted herself into a sitting position. "Rough day with Grams?"

"You could say that." She smiled at the understatement. Jane seemed slightly less miserable this afternoon than her usual; her hair was brushed, at least. "How about you? Everything going okay?"

Jane nodded. "Yeah."

"You want to talk about anything that's been bothering you recently?"

She shook her head vigorously. "Not really. I mean, things are okay right now."

Bonnie regarded her daughter, trying to gauge the truth of her words. The memory of her mother's hateful smile floated to the surface. "Okay, honey. But please, don't hold it inside when something upsets you. It's not good for you."

Jane lowered her eyes, saying nothing.

Bonnie patted her knee and stood, yawning. "I'm going to go lie down, 'kay?"

In her bedroom, she sank onto the old mattress, spooning herself into its holes and divots, but couldn't relax the tension in her body. Pictures kept cluttering her mind: her ten-year-old self carrying cups of coffee to Mr. and Mrs. Goodacre in the living room, the good one that was just for company, and being so careful not to spill any on the saucers. They had always seemed so friendly to her. Mother had always been so cordial to them, even warm – Bonnie had been grateful there was at least someone she liked, who could tease her out of her dark moods. She felt revolted thinking about Mr. Goodacre now, as if he'd exposed himself. How horrible it had to have been for Mother to have to entertain the man who was sexually abusing her on a weekly basis.

And what was that business about Pete? She drifted off to sleep as she tried to put a face on this boy, the brother she'd never met.

The next day, during a quiet time at work, Bonnie called Information and asked for the number for Public Records in MacArthur County. She dialed the long-distance number, feeling like a sneak, even though it was her own family history she was investigating.

"Public Records," said a voice with a slow drawl.

"Hello. I don't know if I've got the right number. I'm trying to find the birth records for someone who ..."

"Let me connect you with Birth and Death Records. One moment."

The phone clicked rhythmically, the sound eventually replaced by another woman's voice. "Birth and Death Records. This is Mrs. Bissell."

Her voice creaked and shook as though she might have personally witnessed every birth and death on record in the place. Bonnie wondered how long this woman had worked there.

"My name is Bonnie Stanton, and I'm trying to obtain some birth records for my brother, Peter MacKenzie. I believe he would've been born at William Howard Taft Memorial Hospital - that's where I was born, too - in 1958."

"Oh, that was a lovely hospital. I was so sorry to see it close down."

"I didn't realize it had closed."

"Oh my, yes. It must've been going on twenty years now. Progress, you know. Those new hospitals they put up, they're so impersonal. Patients are just bodies to fill beds. When I had my hip replacement last year, nurses rushed in and out like it was a race. No one had time to sit and chat with an old lady."

"I'm so sorry to hear that," Bonnie murmured. She tried to stifle her impatience, recalling that nothing in her childhood home, near the Ohio-Kentucky border, could be hurried.

"Well, that's just the way with most places now, don't you think? Everybody's more efficient, but nobody talks to anybody anymore."

Realizing that if she cut this lady off, Bonnie would be committing the same sin as Mrs. Bissell was elaborating upon, she let the woman talk on, interjecting neutral asides when appropriate. Finally, running out of steam, Mrs. Bissell said, "I sure appreciate the chance to talk to you. You seem like a nice young lady. Now, what was the name you said you were looking for?"

"Peter MacKenzie."

"And when was he born, dear?"

Bonnie felt like an impostor, not to have this information at hand. "I don't know, ma'am. That's actually why I'm calling, to see if I can get the information."

"Well, of course, dear. It was just that you said he was your brother. I assumed you knew his birthday."

Bonnie apologized. She knew how bizarre this must sound. "It's a complicated story, Mrs. Bissell."

After a pause, as if waiting for the saga that didn't come, the old woman said, "It must be." Her words were clipped, perhaps offended that after sharing her own medical history, Bonnie didn't trust her enough to share the tale. "Well, dear, with just a name, it'll take several weeks to get this information out to you. Give me your address, and I'll see what I can do."

Bonnie hung up, doodling Pete's name on her notepad, working the letters over and over with her ballpoint. It was only when the paper tore, worn thin from repetition, that she realized what she was doing and laid the pen to rest.

~15~
MEG

Meg stood in line at the Italian bakery, behind a portly man whose dark jacket bore such a dusting of dandruff snowflakes that he looked as if a powdered donut had attacked his neck. In the display case before her, pastries and sweet rolls and cookies revolved on automated trays. Too sweet – she licked her teeth, as though she could feel the sugar granules eating away at her enamel just by examining the array.

"May I help you?" The guy at the counter was new. All the rest of the staff knew Meg at least by face now, if not by name, and would yell out her order – two maple twists, two butter croissants, two coffees – before they even said good morning to her. Still, while he might be new, he was certainly hot. As Meg recited her order, she took in his deep, black eyes, bookends to a long, aquiline nose, and sighed with satisfaction. This was way better than pouring flakes into a bowl.

As he handed the bag to her, he held her gaze just long enough that she felt herself begin to color. But she didn't break the eye contact, and when their fingers brushed as Meg accepted her change, she felt an electric charge, like she'd just hit her funny bone. She smiled and murmured a thank-you, then left without glancing back to sneak a peek.

"I'm practically married," she said out loud while walking home, hoping that no one was watching her. Of course, there was no harm in looking. Really, the episode had simply been a harmless flirtation. She'd never actually do anything about it. So why did she feel guilty?

Brady was sitting at the dining room table reading the paper. He took the coffee from her. "Manna from heaven. Thanks, hon."

Meg sat down opposite him, and reached for a croissant from the bag, darkened with butter and oil. "Pass me the comics?"

He handed the Life section to her. "You should really take more of an interest in the world around you."

"Hey, I take plenty of interest. Garfield is fighting with Odie again. That crazy cat!"

Brady raised one eyebrow, then went back to his Local News section. Meg surreptitiously observed him as he read and ate and drank. She wondered if this is what their married life would be like. The Fourth of July fight had never been mentioned since: it just lay between them like an ugly rug they weren't willing to pull up. But conversations were brisk and businesslike, a perfunctory morning conference around the breakfast table:

"Did you look at your mother's seating plan for the reception?"

"I need a check for the DJ's deposit today."

"Barkley's due for his yearly shots; you should check your schedule and call the vet."

Truth be told, Brady had actually made it out of the house a few times since the Fourth of July, always for follow-up visits for his ankle. But Mona had been the one to take him. Meg was always working during his appointment times – in her less charitable moments, she thought he scheduled them that way on purpose – so she didn't know how he had fared on these short field trips outside the apartment.

She had to admit, the current state of their union was not all Brady's fault. He had tried to reach out to Meg a few times. She could recognize the signs – he'd lay a hand on her shoulder and say her name in a quiet voice full of uncertainty. And she would shut him down, using some lame excuse like having to finish the dishes, or work on the store's books.

She'd found herself at times wondering if Brady might've contributed in some manner to his mugging, might've advertised in some way that he was a victim ripe for beating the shit out of. The idea was clearly insane; she knew she needed to jerk herself out of this "blame the victim" mentality. It was this knowledge of her own failings that kept Meg civil, kept her continuing to plan a wedding that she had no certainty would come to pass, kept her in the mundane routine of commitment.

Brady brushed the crumbs from his mouth. "I can't remember. Are you working today?"

Meg shook her head. "I took the weekend, so I've got today off. Why?"

"Well, if you're available, you could take me to the doctor's. I get my walking cast today." Brady reached down and scratched Barkley's ears.

"That'd be great. I'd love to." Meg had been hoping for something other than chauffeur duty. She pumped enthusiasm she did not feel into her voice. "Will your mother mind my taking you?"

"Why should she mind?" Brady cocked his head.

"Never mind," Meg said. "Forget it." Mona probably *would* resent being usurped in one of her many helper roles. If she wasn't calling to see how he was, she was dropping off clothes and books and food. Nothing they ever actually needed – just a variety of excuses to keep from having to let her son rely on himself or Meg. But if Brady chose not to see that, she knew it would do no good to voice her opinion on the topic.

Brady scrutinized Meg's face, but didn't say anything. She purposefully buried her head in the comics, scanning "Family Circus" and "Marmaduke" for their buried sociological subtexts.

Meg realized, as she witnessed Brady traverse the steps down the apartment, nimbly hopping on one foot down the stairs, that he did seem a lot better. She observed him as if he were a stranger as she followed him down the stairs: the taper of his back down into a trim waist, and that gorgeous butt. She felt a pulse stirring in her groin. Meg caught up to him at the landing and cupped the curve of his ass. "You're looking pretty good for a gimp there."

Brady didn't say anything, but pulled her to him tightly. As she gazed up at him from the confines of the hug, she thought his eyes might be a little wet. It would be too romance novel, however, to think that the moisture was anything other than allergies.

*   *   *

The visit was innocuous enough. The doctor complimented Brady on the state of his ankle. Still, when he cut the cast off, his atrophied leg, withered and fish-belly white, made her feel slightly queasy. Juxtaposed next to Brady's left calf, tanned and toned from the sports he'd done all his life, his weak leg seemed like a cripple's. Meg was moderately ashamed of the repulsion she felt, as well as the relief when the doctor encased his leg in the new walking cast.

She smiled at Brady. "Nice cast. Now you can walk like a penguin."

"Look Ma, no hands." He weaved around the office, demonstrating his prowess with his arms held out at his sides.

Coming out of the doctor's office, Brady put a hand on her arm. "Let's not go home yet, okay?"

Meg threaded her fingers through his and squeezed. Her heart clutched with gratitude at this apparent reversion back to his old self. "You got it. Name your dream date."

They ended up at the library. Brady picked up some old Ellery Queens, while Meg leafed through back issues of *Spin* magazine. Afterward, they stopped at the grocery store and stocked up on wine, curry spices, and basmati rice. When Brady started to droop in the bread aisle, his limp becoming more pronounced, Meg suggested a glass of lemonade at the cafe around the corner, followed by a nap at home.

"Sounds great." He squeezed her waist. "Maybe we can take Barkley to the park after I've had some sleep."

Meg nodded with a neutral smile. She'd drop in a dead faint if Brady followed through with that promise. Since the accident, she had taken over every aspect of Barkley's care – feeding, walking, scooping the poop. Brady hadn't so much as stepped foot out into the hallway with the dog. In fact, he'd had one of his buddies deliver a remnant of sod the size of a welcome mat, and with as dramatic a flourish as a man on crutches could have, placed it on their sliver of a balcony, announcing that this was where Barkley could pee once it got dark. Meg could swear the dog looked embarrassed, having to pee on the porch. She called it "the goddamned litter box" out of earshot, feeling like Brady had somehow emasculated the poor canine. Of course, she could be projecting her resentment that despite her taking over the care of Barkley, he stuck to Brady's side like a growth.

Still, if he was truly considering going out with Barkley this afternoon, maybe the litter box was just another temporary setback. Maybe this was the turnaround point she'd been seeking.

At the café, they sat under the blue and white-striped Campari umbrella. The slightest hint of breeze undercut the humidity. The lemonade was tart and sweet at the same time. Meg felt like a golden cloud of contentment had settled around the two of them as they laughed at stupid details about the wedding, like whether she should be wearing white or, let's be honest, burnt sienna, and whether Brady's ushers would even know what a cummerbund was, much less what direction it went in.

The train wheezed into the depot across the town circle, and they watched as its occupants straggled off at the Circle stop. Meg was just about to jokingly suggest that they use the train to get everyone from the wedding to the reception, when a stocky woman fell clumsily to the ground and began to yell after a teenager sprinting away from her, clutching a large brown tote bag.

Meg winced. She turned away from the scene to Brady. He was staring fixedly at the gingham-checks on the vinyl tablecloth, but considering that he'd lost the majority of color in his face, she knew he'd seen what had just happened.

"Should we go to her, you think? Or at least call the cops?"

He shook his head no. He began to rub his eyes with his fingertips.

"Seriously, hon, what if she needs help? It looks like she might've fallen hard."

Brady stopped rubbing his eyes, raising his head with a dead expression. "Don't get involved."

Meg wanted to cry, both for the pain he was suffering, and selfishly, for the loss of their closeness. She took his hands in hers. "Look, Brady, I get it. But it wasn't the same guys. This kid was even white. It's just a purse snatch."

He cocked one eyebrow and softly snorted. "You 'get it.' Good for you." Slowly, deliberately, he removed his hands from hers.

"Enlighten me, then." She kept her voice low to keep him from noticing her growing frustration. Didn't she get points for at least trying?

Brady stared at his glass of lemonade. "I can't ever get away from it. It follows me everywhere." He started picking at his fingernails without seeming aware of it, tearing tiny bits of dead flesh from the corners of his cuticles.

"I'm trying to get on with things, to drop this … event, or whatever you want to call it. But every fucking day, there is something that makes me live through it all over again."

"Like what?"

"Sometimes it's seeing a group of kids on a corner. Sometimes it's just peering out the door into the empty hallway, and wondering what might be waiting out there."

While she knew this was excruciating for him, Meg could not understand how he could not take steps to lessen this hell. "So talk to someone about it," she said with impatience.

"You don't get it. A shrink is not going to help me forget. He's going to want me to re-experience it, to process it. And I just can't."

Meg took a sip of her lemonade. It had lost its taste. "What about Barkley? Does he remind you of it, too?"

"It's weird, but no. He's a fellow victim. Maybe that's why we stick together so much. He's the only one who understands, who was there, who wasn't trying to kill me."

Meg felt it might be unkind to remind him that Barkley was a dog, and not a very bright one at that. Her head felt like it weighed a hundred pounds. She cradled her chin in her palm. "So what do we do?"

"I wish I knew." Brady sounded defeated. He continued to pick at his cuticles. "I don't think we should live here anymore."

This was news Meg hadn't expected. "Wow," she said. "Is this something you've been thinking about for a while?"

"Yeah. What do you think?"

What *did* she think? She wasn't averse to finding a safer neighborhood, but there was something about the idea that bothered her, the timing, perhaps. Like they'd just be running away from a problem that hadn't been dealt with. She traced the path of condensation on her lemonade glass with her finger while she tried to think of a way to say this without Brady getting defensive. "I'm not sure how I feel about it. Is there someplace you have in mind?"

"I don't know. But I don't feel safe here anymore, and when I think about something happening to you, or to our kids down the line, I can't breathe. Literally. It gives me a panic attack."

Meg sighed. "Honey, I'll move if you really want to or need to. But you know that we can't live in a bubble, right? There's no guarantee anywhere we go that we'll always be safe."

"That's such a platitude, Meg, and you know it. You can look at the crime stats of this city and Daedalus Falls, and know for a fact that we would be ten times safer there than here."

Oh, God. They'd also be ten times closer to his mother, and all the people in that town who were just like her. "I am so not moving to Daedalus Falls, bucko. You can kiss that train goodbye."

"Why? What's wrong with it?"

"It might be safer in a physical sense, but it's ten times more dangerous in an intangible, *Stepford Wives* kind of way. There's a right-wing, wing-tip, buttoned down Christianity there, the kind that judges you to burn in hell if you hold any views other than the official ones sanctioned by the village elders. I think it's probably a more dangerous environment to be raising kids in than here."

He shook his head dismissively. "You're being ridiculous."

"Damn it, Brady, I'm not. You know what it's like there. You want our kids to grow up in a town where they draw school district lines so that the black kids in the subsidized housing get shunted off to the adjacent district, rather than sully the virgin whiteness of Daedalus Falls? I don't. "

Brady wiped his hands with the napkin, but continued twisting the corners. "This isn't some abstract political discussion we're having, Meg. You may hate Daedalus Falls, but you can't deny that it's safer than here." He paused like he was trying to decide whether to say something. Finally he took a deep breath. "Does it even bother you that I got mugged, that I could've died? What if I had died? Would you still have wanted to live here? I feel like – like you don't really care."

Meg felt her face go hot. How could he have misunderstood her so badly? Quietly, she said, "I'm sorry you feel that way. Because I could not have borne it if you'd died. But I thought you knew that."

Brady said nothing, just glared at the table. Meg watched him and hung her head. Words were useless now. And she felt so tired, too tired to even know what to do next. She threw a couple bills on the table in defeat. "We're both tired and stressed out. You've had a lot more activity this morning than you've had recently. Let's just go home."

Wordlessly, they traveled back to the apartment. Once inside, Brady asked if Meg could take Barkley out for a short walk. She nodded, grateful to have any excuse to get out of the apartment. She clipped Barkley to his leash, and stood in the empty hallway, unsure which way to go.

~16~
JANE

Jane awoke with a vague sense of dread, the kind that could only come from the prospect of a day of forced shopping with Mom. She endured it twice a year – when school was about to start, and when she needed new shorts for summer. But once she was in the doors of a department store, Jane liked to operate on a speed model. What was the point of browsing? She knew what she wanted: sweats, plain rugby shirts, baggy t-shirts. She and Bonnie had come to an unspoken pact: Mom would drop her at the Juniors' section with the promise that Jane would at least consider the clothes there. But that area was full of close-fitting jerseys with sequined butterflies or daisies, shirts only an anti-Jane would wear. So she would sneak over to the Boys' section to find her clothes, where the biggest decision was stripes vs. solids.

Today was going to include an extra exercise in torture endurance, since not only did Jane have to go shopping, she needed to buy a dress. For Meg's wedding. Meg knew how she felt about these things – she looked like a kielbasa in dresses, and they were always too tight in the waist. Why couldn't the invitation, which had just arrived last week, have specified "casual dress allowed?"

And to top it all off, her back was aching. She must have pulled a muscle doing one of her workouts, such as reaching down for her shoes. She stretched and tried to massage the sore spot right above her butt as she walked to the bathroom.

As she sat down on the toilet, she inhaled sharply. In the center of her underpants was a dark brown smear, a painted road stripe. It was too dark to be blood, so she didn't think it could be her first period. It had to be Number Two.

How humiliating. She must've had an accident while she was sleeping. But what kind of doofus wouldn't realize *that* first thing? What a loser. She bit her bottom lip to distract herself from the lump in her throat that forecast imminent tears.

When she wiped herself, more brown came off on the toilet paper. Oh God, it was still happening. What if there was something really wrong with her? She took off her panties, wadded them up in a ball, and hid them in the trashcan under an empty shampoo bottle and some crumpled tissue. Jane pulled off a few sheets of toilet paper and stuffed them between her legs, then pulled her pajama pants back up until she could get back to her room and figure out what she was going to do.

As she was shuffling back to her room, taking teeny, mincing steps so that the toilet paper wouldn't become unwedged, she noticed her mom eyeing her with raised eyebrows.

"What in God's name are you doing?"

Crap. "Nothing."

"Right, nothing. Come on, Jane, spill it. What's wrong?"

Jane was torn between being too mortified to ever tell anyone, and desperately wanting to get advice so that she could fix this. "Come here." She walked back into the bathroom with Bonnie following, reached down into the trashcan, and retrieved the underpants.

"I think there might be something wrong with me, Mom. I must have pooped in my pants overnight, and it's still leaking out."

Bonnie bit her lip, obviously trying to hide a smile that was playing around the corners of her lips. "Oh, honey. That's blood. You got your period. I know we talked about it eons ago, but didn't it also get covered in health class?"

"Well, yeah." She knew Mom hated that tone of voice, the one that sounded like Jane thought her mother was a moron, but hello, of course she'd learned about her period. Luckily for her, Mom let it pass.

Bonnie began a long-winded explanation of dried versus new blood. When she paused, Jane stared in horror at her, as if she had just punished her with a month of changing diapers. "So I have this to look forward to for the rest of my life?"

"I'm afraid so, Janie. Until you hit menopause, which won't happen for a long time yet, or until you get pregnant, which also better not happen for a long time."

"Gross. I wish I were a boy."

"Welcome to the club. But we'll stop and pick up some tampons on the way to the mall, and you'll be all set. Until then, I can probably find a Maxipad around here somewhere for you to use."

Jane was repulsed. "You really don't expect me to stick something up into myself, do you?"

"It's your call, kiddo. Most girls your age use pads, but trust me on this one, you'll be happier and feel less gross with a tampon. It's not that hard to do."

Jane put her hands over her ears and started to drone "La la la la la" to drown out her mother's voice.

Bonnie grinned. "I'll just go get you that pad now," she said, leaving the bathroom.

In her bedroom, Jane pulled off her pajamas and tossed them in the corner. As she pulled on a t-shirt, Bonnie knocked, then entered.

"Here you go." She handed a minipad to Jane and surveyed her t-shirt, worn enough to feel like she was wearing a security blanket. "You're not going to wear that, are you?"

She didn't still expect them to go to the mall, did she? "Mom, do we still have to go? I mean, this isn't exactly a great time."

"You'll feel better if you're out walking around. Trust me."

Didn't Mom know by now that Jane took nothing on faith? "I think I know how I feel, Mother."

"Fine. You won't feel better. We're still going. Change your shirt." With a whispered mutter, Bonnie stalked out. Jane waited until the door was closed and stuck her tongue out.

* * *

In the car, Bonnie hummed, her good humor apparently restored. At the stoplight, she looked at Jane. "This is a milestone, you know. You're not a child anymore."

"Oh my GOD, Mom, let it go, okay?" Jane could swear Mom was enjoying how uncomfortable all this made her. Sicko. "It's just a period, not some Afterschool Special. Can it just be what it is?"

Bonnie smiled. "Point taken. I will try to restrain myself from any further unseemly acts."

At the store, Jane avoided entering the aisle with the feminine hygiene products, pacing around a panty hose display while Mom examined the various brands. Some workmen were hanging a large banner – *Food Frenzy* was going to be filming an episode here in a couple weeks. She shuddered at the idea of all those crazy women hurling themselves over one another at the prospect of being picked for the frozen foods relay.

Bonnie walked up behind her and, following her gaze, said, "Isn't that Charley's show?"

She nodded. She was still annoyed, so she decided to punish her mother by giving her the silent treatment for a while.

"You should tell Charley's folks. Maybe they'd bring him up to watch."

Jane shrugged. Her last field trip idea hadn't turned out to be so brilliant. She doubted she'd be suggesting another trip for him anytime soon.

When they got to the mall, Bonnie turned to her as she released her seat belt. "Truce?"

"Okay, I guess." Jane rubbed at a muddy spot on the floor mat with the toe of her sneaker. She guessed it wouldn't hurt to at least be civil, even if she wasn't ever going to be enthusiastic about the day.

They reached the door of Zimbel's. The store was shiny and bright, with crayon colors spilling onto dresses, and sequined sweaters for fall sparkling like water. Shoppers lingered over items, fingering a silk shawl here, examining a brocade pattern there. The glitz of the foyer, the women shopping in heels and skirts, instead of jeans and sneakers, made Jane feel small and poor, a mutt in an arena full of purebreds.

Her voice dropped to a whisper. "Maybe we should go somewhere else."

"It's fine," Bonnie said. "Just relax. Have a little fun. And stop whispering, for goodness' sake."

Fun? Fun was bumper cars at a carnival. Fun was giggling with Meg over Monty Python reruns. Shopping for a dress that she didn't even want did not show up on the "Fun" map. Maybe if she bled on something they'd have to leave.

They walked toward the Junior Dresses section. A blond woman suddenly appeared from behind the racks. "Can I help you find something?" she asked with a perkiness that made Jane want to pop a balloon next to her ear, just to see her lose the act.

"We're just looking," Bonnie told her. Jane looked down at her sneakers.

"No problem. Find me if you need anything." Just as suddenly as she had appeared, she flitted away.

"She's a pretty girl," Bonnie said. "Too much makeup, though." She studied Jane. "You know, I'm not a big fan of makeup on girls your age, but we might be able to find you a nice, subtle blush and some nail polish for the wedding. If you'd let me."

Oh, God, makeup. This just got worse and worse. Not only would she have to worry about sitting with her knees together and not busting a zipper, she'd also have to make sure she didn't look like a stupid clown.

They wandered the maze of dress racks. Most of the dresses looked like prom night gone bad, an overdose of ruffles and burnt velvet. Jane pulled out two of the least-awful dresses and showed them to her mother. "What do you think?"

Bonnie examined the dresses with pursed lips, glancing at the dresses, then Jane, then back to the dresses. She looked doubtful. "They seem a little … I don't know." As Jane made a move to put them back, she quickly said, "No, you're good. Go ahead and try them on. Maybe they'll look better off the hanger. Do you want me to come into the dressing room with you?"

Geez. She wanted her to look older, but still treated her like she was five. "Mom!"

"Just asking. But I want to see them, okay? Don't just put them on, hate them, and then take them off. Give me a chance to hate them too, is all I'm asking."

"Fine." Jane escaped into the dressing room. She knew her mom didn't understand her aversion to shopping. Mom loved to browse, looking in windows, analyzing what made a quality piece. She always talked about how she couldn't wear this or that because of her tummy or thighs, but it was ridiculous. Bonnie could wear anything from jeans to an evening gown and look as if she wore that all the time. She didn't understand that in order for shopping to be fun, you needed to like what you saw in the mirror.

As Jane undressed, she couldn't avoid her reflection. She wasn't fat, but had no curves either. Her boobs were still barely there, making a joke of the bra she was forced to wear. Some of the girls in her gym class had to wear underwire bras, their boobs were that big. Their bodies had silhouettes, where their waists dipped in, then flared out to hips. Jane's body was a cylindrical tube. She stuck her tongue out at the miserable girl in the glass.

The first experiment was a lavender print that fell just past her knees. "Yuck." She opened the door and moved into the hall to show her mother.

Bonnie patted her fingers together as if considering it. However, her nose was wrinkled as if there were a foul odor in the room. "Do you like it?" she asked.

Jane shook her head.

Bonnie exhaled in relief. "Thank God. That shade of violet is not the best color on you. You look like a bruise."

The corners of Jane's mouth twitched. Maybe the day wouldn't be a total disaster.

The second dress was no better, navy blue with an eyelet pattern around the arm cuffs and neck. Her mother laughed when she saw it. "Honey, we might consider that if you have to appear in court one day. But not for a wedding. I saw a dress over on another rack that I thought might look pretty on you. I know your taste and mine differ, but will you at least try it on?"

Jane sighed. "Fine. It better not have any flowers on it, though."

She returned to the dressing room and sat, cradling her head in her hands. She would rather be forced to sit through American History for an entire day than do this.

"Where are you?" Bonnie called.

Probably pointless to try and hide. "Over here, second one in."

Her mother draped the dress over the door, and Jane pulled it in. The fabric was pretty, a soft, silky blue the color of the cornflowers in their yard. She felt a mild surprise that she liked it. She slipped it on over her head and looked at her reflection, feeling suddenly shy. The neckline ran straight from shoulder to shoulder. The body was fitted close to the waist, and the skirt flared gently downward. The effect was startling, giving her the illusion of shape where none existed. She felt like Ginger Rogers in those old Fred Astaire movies, with her gowns that moved like water. Jane couldn't help herself – she twirled around on her tiptoes, struck dumb by a rising sense of hope.

Jane stepped out.

"Turn around for me," Bonnie ordered. Jane pirouetted. "Wow." Bonnie slowly walked in a circle around the dress, examining it from every angle. "It's very pretty on you. But don't you think it might be a little old for you?"

"Geez, Mom, you're the one who picked it out. Do you want me to look nice for the wedding or not? I like it." She should've known this would never work. Closing herself back in the cubicle, she tucked herself back into her sweatshirt and jeans.

"Where's the dress?" Bonnie asked when Jane emerged from the booth.

"It's still in the room. Why?"

"Well, you usually need to have the piece of clothing with you in order to buy it."

Jane did a double take. Had her mother actually listened to her opinion? Or had she been willing to let her get the dress from the start?

Bonnie put her arm around Jane's shoulder and squeezed. "Quick, go get it, so we can pay for it and find something to eat. I'm starving."

As they made their way to the store's café, Jane wondered, who was this girl holding a garment bag as if its contents were the most fragile, sacred thing imaginable? Had she loosened some boulder of girl-dom that would accelerate down the mountain of who she had been up to now? It starts out with a dress. Next thing, would she be hogging the bathroom? Painting her fingernails? Passing notes about hunky boys? A worse fate she could not imagine.

She caught Bonnie watching her while pretending to pore over the menu. She had a weird look on her face, sad and happy at the same time. "What is it?" Jane asked.

Bonnie sighed. "All this wedding stuff has me in a nostalgic mood. Did I ever tell you the story of my wedding day?"

It was a rare treat for her mother to reminisce about the past. Jane could only think of a few times where she'd told stories, and those were all from when she or Davey were babies. "No. I think I saw a picture of the reception once, before you put the pictures away. It was outside, wasn't it?"

"Right. But that wasn't the reception. That was the wedding."

This seemed very unlike her parents. "You got married outside?"

"Oh, yeah. Your dad and I were post-hippie-hippies. I always resented that I was too young to really be a part of the sixties. So when the seventies came, I just kept pretending it was the sixties. After Watergate–"

"That was the Nixon thing, right?"

Bonnie nodded. "God. A generation where Watergate is just history. Mind-blowing. Anyway, after Watergate, being a hippie wasn't very in anymore, but I didn't care. And then I met Joe, and it was like finding a second half of yourself that you never knew existed."

Jane's mind was ripping open at this revelation. "Dad was a hippie, too? Eww."

"Oh, you'd have hated us. We'd spend hours playing guitar out on the quad, singing John Denver songs. I'd make bread, and he'd be outside, stripping and refinishing old furniture that he'd sell from the back of his van."

She felt like she was in a *Star Trek* episode where the crew had stumbled into some alternate universe. Mom, playing guitar? Dad, doing something other than tennis or golf, or hitting on women? Would she change so much when she was grown up?

Her amazement must have registered with Bonnie, who chuckled. "Is this too much for you to take in?"

"No. I gotta hear the rest of this." Jane leaned forward. She wanted to find out what had happened to these strangers.

"When Joe asked me to marry him, I knew I didn't want a traditional church wedding. I wanted it outside, where the forest could be our cathedral."

Jane grinned. "You've got to be kidding."

"I know. It sounds totally Greenpeace of me, but it's the truth."

"Wait a minute. Where was Grams? I can't imagine her at an outside hippie wedding. Is that why she's hated Dad all this time?"

Bonnie chuckled. "She was livid. Just one more way for me to disappoint her. Not that she wanted me to have a church wedding – given her atheist leanings, that would have been equally repugnant to her. I think she thought we should have had a quiet justice of the peace ceremony."

There was something her mom wasn't saying. Jane decided to just get it over with. "You were pregnant with me, weren't you?"

Bonnie looked down at the table. Then, as if coming to a decision of some kind, she directly met Jane's gaze. "Three months. I wasn't really showing, but I looked a little chubby around the middle." She took a sip of her iced tea. "I'm sorry about the way you found out. It wasn't supposed to be like that."

Jane took a deep breath. "It wasn't *why* you got married, was it?"

The response tumbled out of Bonnie in a rush. "Oh, honey, no. If anything, finding out I was pregnant with you seemed like a sign that we were meant to go ahead, like we'd been blessed."

Shrugging, Jane said, "Then it's not a big deal." She held onto the glow that had settled inside her. "Anyway, you were talking about Grams… "

"Right. She threatened not to come. Frankly, I would've been okay with that. But she did come. Go figure.

"The day before the wedding, it started to rain. Not just showers here and there, but a steady, non-stop downpour. Now, I may have been an Earthmother, but I had no desire to be sopping wet while I gave my vows. Joe was great, though. Without saying a word to me, he went out and got one of those clear tarps, like you use if you're going camping. He decorated it with white paint, found fringe from a blanket to edge it with, and hung it back between the trees, above our heads, to keep us all dry. In the end, the rain stopped, and the sun came back out in time for the ceremony, but we still kept that tarp up. I had mud spatters up to my knees. That's why in all the pictures you only see us from the waist up."

Jane cocked her head, confused. "Dad never wanted to do anything like arts and crafts with us. When did he change?"

Bonnie smiled. "I don't know. Probably little bits here and there. It was fourteen years ago, after all."

This was so weird. Good, but weird. "It's bizarre hearing you say nice things about him."

"Jane, I don't want you thinking I hate him. I mean, clearly, I think your father is an imbecile. But I also know he loves you and Davey. I should probably cut him some slack. I won't, but I should. But, boy, back in the day, he was something to behold."

She looked off in the distance at a painting over Jane's head. Jane knew she wasn't really looking at it. She was looking at something Jane couldn't see, some time long ago, long out of reach.

-17-
BONNIE

Bonnie sat at her desk at work, sipping her coffee, ignoring the filing, and reminiscing about Joe in his better days. She supposed she'd hit a milestone of sorts: this was the first time in over a year she'd thought of Joe at all without picturing him with that pert little chiropractor. So the accompanying urge to throttle him was gratifyingly absent.

The electronic chirp of the telephone jostled her out of her reverie. Although the caller asked for her by name, Bonnie couldn't identify the voice. "Ms. Stanton, this is Margaret Pulaski from Whispering Woods. I'm afraid I have some bad news. Your mother appears to have had a stroke overnight."

Oh, Jesus. This was it. Bonnie had nightmares about this kind of call, so realistic that she would awake gasping and immediately call the home despite the hour to have them check on Elizabeth. And now this woman was on the phone and Bonnie couldn't seem to catch her breath, much less process the information being given. The woman on the other end appeared not to be bothered by the silence, for she said nothing. After time had dripped off the table like a Dali painting, Bonnie sufficiently gathered herself to ask, "Is she dead?"

"No."

"Well, can you tell me how bad it is?"

Papers rustled. "We only just discovered her, when the shift changed and the day nurse went to check on her. Actually, we need to know what you would like us to do."

Bonnie was confused. Surely they'd already handled whatever needed to be done. She wondered if she'd blanked out on some part of the conversation. "What do you mean?"

"Well, your mother's paperwork is outdated *and* incomplete." The patient, measured tone of the woman's voice was disappearing. "Do you want us to transport her to a hospital where she can be better assessed, or do you want her to remain with us?"

Oh, shit. The *form*. Bonnie hated that piece of paper, and all the power and finality it represented. So she'd bypassed the "Do Not Resuscitate" box, relying on the belief that Elizabeth was just too ornery ever to have her body betray her as completely as a stroke or heart attack. Besides, her mother'd always said things like, "I'll be dead soon and then you'll be able to forget about me good and proper" from the time Bonnie was a teenager. So it felt obvious that she would outlive them all. She realized Ms. Pulaski was still waiting for an answer. "Please, yes, take her to the hospital. She'll go to St. Elizabeth's?"

"That's correct." Now that the bad news was delivered, Ms. Pulaski was beginning to sound impatient, in a polite, no-nonsense way.

"Fine. I'll meet her there."

After hanging up, Bonnie stood, then sat down again. She cast her eyes around the office, unsure of what to do or the order to do it in. Clearly, she'd have to get someone to cover her desk for the day, maybe longer. And Vivian – she'd have to call Vivian. What about Jane and Davey? She decided to wait to tell them until later, when she had some news. She ran her fingers through her hair, tried to isolate what she might be feeling. But she couldn't pinpoint anything – except "rushed." Maybe feeling would come later.

Bonnie picked up the phone. Blessedly, Vivian answered on the third ring: Bonnie had been fearful that she'd be out on a run or at the church.

Vivian made a little choking sound upon hearing the news. "Oh, dear God. How bad is it? Will she survive this?"

Now that her sister was on her way up the worry scale, Bonnie felt herself slide back from her own tumbled emotions for the moment. "I don't know. I'm heading out there right now. Can you meet me there?"

There was silence on the other end, just long enough for her to realize that Vivian was actually considering it. She gripped the phone receiver as if it were a skull she could crush. "Good God, Vivian, that was a rhetorical question. 'No' is not an option right now. Get your ass over to the hospital. I can't do this alone." She hung up before Vivian could come up with one of her excuses.

As Bonnie drove to the hospital, her mind was jumbled. What if Mother died? How would she feel? Relieved, sad, regretful? She could see herself feeling all of these things, even maybe a little satisfied, as inappropriate as that was. Maybe she could design a T-shirt that said "I survived my mother," since it would be true on both the physical and emotional levels. Of course, Mother wasn't dead yet, and it seemed morbid to dwell on the possibility for too long.

Her eyes welled up with tears. No, she needed to keep it together. She needed to be strong. She wasn't sure why she felt this way, but even if it were some coping mechanism, she was going to honor it. She needed to think about something practical, details, like whether Elizabeth would be able to return to Whispering Woods. God, she hoped so. She'd have to check and make sure they would be able to take care of her in a more debilitated condition. The possibility of having to find someplace new for her mother would rank somewhere in Dante's circles of logistical Hell.

And what was this relationship between Vivian and their mother? Bonnie had friends who were estranged from their parents, but they took pains to erase them from their lives: moving across the country, refusing to allow them in their homes, removing any evidence of a shared history. But when Bonnie tried to pin Viv down on why she refused to visit, she'd slip out of the cornering with a born grifter's skill, going on the offensive. "This isn't about me," she would say. "This is about you. Why do you go there every day? Do you think she's ever going to see you and thank you, tell you she loves you? Finally give you some affirmation that somewhere underneath it all, she approves of you and the choices you've made? Because if that's why you're doing it, you're delusional."

Bonnie's thoughts had been churning so violently that she had turned her driving over to auto-pilot, trusting that her reflexes and motor memory could handle the drive to the hospital by rote. But after the second near-miss at a crosswalk, complete with the person attempting to cross the road giving her the finger and yelling, "Stupid bitch!" she attempted to devote her sole attention to getting to the hospital in one piece, and doing no harm to others in the meantime.

When she reached the floor where her mother had been admitted, she stopped, surprised to see Vivian already sitting in the waiting room. She was alternating her gaze between the television set tuned to some talk show and the window, with its view of the construction of a new parking garage. She exhibited the "fight or flight" posture of a trapped animal, perched on the chair's vinyl as though she might spring at any second. Bonnie was struck not only by the fact that Vivian had beaten her to the hospital, but also by how unkempt she appeared. It was the first time she'd seen Vivian since childhood without her trademark red lipstick and artfully-arranged hair. Yet here she was, with dark raccoon mascara smears and lipstick rubbed off. Her hair was newly short, but looked as if she'd been dragging her fingers through it.

Bonnie cleared her throat, and when Vivian looked up, said, "Hey. I'm glad you made it."

Vivian gave a tearful smile. "Yeah, you should be."

She placed her hand on her sister's shoulder, startled at the visible grief on her face. Vivian had never been a huggy person, and Bonnie did not feel bold enough to provide physical comfort more central and encompassing than the hand she offered. "Have you been in to see her yet?"

"I started to, and then I just froze. I couldn't. I couldn't do it alone." She stared at Bonnie as if she wanted to say more, her mouth slightly open, then closed it and shook her head. "Never mind."

Bonnie shrugged, frustrated with trying to figure out her sister. "Well, I'm going in now. Come if you want to."

She paused a moment at the doorway of her mother's room, steeling herself for what she might see. But after mentally girding herself, she was taken aback when the occupant in the bed nearest the door was in fact, not Elizabeth, but apparently, her roommate. The elderly woman's eyes were fixed ceilingward, toward the mounted television. The privacy curtain between the beds was drawn, and all Bonnie could see was the outline of her mother's feet under the blanket.

Before Bonnie and Vivian could cross the room, the curtain was pushed aside and a nurse came bustling out with a hospital chart. She started when she them. "I didn't hear you come in." She moved by the bed to let them pass into Elizabeth's half of the room. "Are you relatives of Mrs. MacKenzie?"

"We're her daughters," Bonnie said. Vivian pulled the visitor's chair into the corner of the room next to the radiator and sat, staring at Elizabeth. Bonnie glanced over, and feeling those rebellious tears rise up, quickly turned back to the nurse. "How is she doing?"

"She's sleeping at the moment, but when she's awake, she's really confused. And she gets agitated easily. She doesn't understand what's happened. I'll page the doctor to come talk with you."

Bonnie thanked her and went to Elizabeth's bedside. Even asleep, one side of her face drooped and pulled downward as if the skin itself were trying to slide off her skull. She had apparently been trying to twist, as evidenced by her hospital gown, which had shimmied off one bony shoulder in a sad satire of high fashion. But the detail that sent a chill up Bonnie's spine was the cloth restraint that bound her mother's left hand to the cold metal bedrail.

Elizabeth opened her eyes. Bonnie wondered if she'd sensed their presence. She looked at Bonnie, but there was no spark of recognition in her eyes. Elizabeth tried to raise herself in the bed. Her left arm strained against the cloth cuff while her right arm lay motionless on the bed, cast under a permanent sleeping spell. Widening her eyes in alarm, she yanked on the restraint again. Having no success, she began hurling herself around the bed, trying to free herself.

Bonnie felt sick with helplessness. She tried to grasp her mother's hand to calm her, but the thrashing did not abate. She looked at Vivian, who looked terrified. "Go get a nurse!" she pleaded. She ran from the room.

By the time Viv returned with the nurse, Elizabeth had collapsed back on the pillow in defeat. The nurse checked to make sure she hadn't pulled her IV out, then readjusted the blanket, patting her on the knee. "You're all right now, Mrs. MacKenzie. Everything's going to be okay." As she left the room, she told Bonnie and Vivian that the doctor would be there in a few minutes.

Bonnie stroked her mother's hand. Elizabeth tried to speak, but all that came out was a garbled mass of consonants. Tears leaked out of her eyes, tracking down her temples to the pillow.

"Hush, now, Mother, you're going to be just fine," Bonnie said, as if trying to calm a wild horse finally penned in a corral. "I'm here now, and look who I brought with me – Vivian."

Vivian cracked her knuckles slowly, one at a time; Bonnie remembered her doing that when they were kids before exams, field hockey games, anything that worried her. "Come over here, Vivian," Bonnie said.

"I don't think I should. What if she gets upset again?"

"I don't think she'll recognize you."

Vivian walked over to the bed. She reached a hand out to touch Elizabeth's shoulder tentatively, as if she were afraid her mother might take a swat at her. When nothing happened, no reaction at all, she exhaled and whispered, "Hi, Mother." Bonnie was moved at the warmth in her voice.

A young man ducked around the curtain into Elizabeth's half of the room. He was wearing a long white lab coat, so Bonnie presumed he must be the doctor, but he looked so young, barely older than Meg. He walked to the other side of the bed, and addressed Elizabeth in the loud, over-articulated voice people use when they think someone is hard of hearing. "Good afternoon, Mrs. MacKenzie. How are you feeling right now?"

Elizabeth writhed and croaked an unintelligible reply.

"These must be your daughters visiting. I see they inherited your looks. May I borrow them for a few minutes? Your nurse will be back in just a minute to check on you."

He turned to Bonnie and Vivian. "I'm Dr. Cavanaugh," he said in a normal tone of voice. He motioned towards the door. "There's a conference room just down the hall. Why don't we go in and talk for a few minutes?" Vivian had set her shoulders in a fashion that suggested she was currently at high simmer, soon to pass into a rolling boil of anger. Sure enough, before they had even taken seats, she lit into the doctor, so angry she could barely articulate the words. "Why do you have my mother tied to the bed like some psychotic? That is absolutely the most inhumane treatment!"

Bonnie winced. While she was glad to see Vivian finally taking an interest in Elizabeth's welfare, that didn't give her the right to alienate her doctors by questioning their decisions. And though Bonnie had been taken aback by the restraint, she was certain that its use had been warranted by her mother in some fashion.

The doctor pulled a chair out for Vivian and stood there calmly until she grabbed the chair away from him and sat, glaring.

"I understand how upsetting this must be for you," he said. "Please know that the Posey was necessary to ensure your mother's safety. Before we got it on her, she'd managed to pull off her monitors and was attempting to climb out of bed – no easy feat for a woman in her condition. She also assaulted the technician who was trying to draw blood for lab work. This is not uncommon for someone who is as disoriented as she is."

"What can you tell us about her condition?" Bonnie asked.

The doctor consulted his notes. "It was a pretty severe stroke, as they go. It inflicted some fairly global damage. You no doubt have noticed the hemiplegia on her right side. It also has affected her language skills, certainly in the expressive arena and possibly in the receptive as well. It's too hard to tell at this point. And it seems to have made her even more disoriented than the Alzheimer's made her prior to the stroke."

"So what happens now?" Vivian asked this question with the same kind of defensive hostility in her voice as if the DAR were getting ready to kick her off its board. "What are you going to do to help her?"

The doctor directed his answer to Bonnie. She knew this would not endear him to her sister. "That's what we need to discuss." He paused. "Which one of you has the medical power of attorney?"

"That's me," Bonnie said. Vivian bit her lip and ducked her head as if embarrassed that it wasn't her.

"Okay. As you know, your mother's Alzheimer's is a terminal condition, something she would eventually die from. But with this stroke, she has lost her ability to swallow and eat. So we've hit a point now where we need to decide what kind of life-saving and life-sustaining measures we will implement for her."

Bonnie nodded.

"If you believe that she would not want any extraordinary measures taken in the event of another stroke or a heart attack, then we should put a Do-Not-Resuscitate order in her chart."

Vivian interrupted. "Isn't that CPR? Her heart's perfectly fine."

The doctor acknowledged her comment with a glance. "As life-saving measures go, yes, we look at keeping the heart and lungs working. That would be cardiopulmonary resuscitation, and artificial respiration, such as intubation. But we also need to consider life-sustaining measures. Here, I'm talking about providing nutrition and hydration through a feeding tube. And that is what is most relevant to your mother right now."

He began to gather the chart and his papers together as if to leave. "What you and your sister need to decide is what your mother would want. We can keep her alive by putting a feeding tube in her stomach. She is not going to understand what it is there for, and probably will have to continue to be restrained to keep from pulling it out." Vivian opened her mouth as if to argue the point, but the doctor held up his hand. "I know you have concerns about the restraint. But it will be a non-negotiable point if the feeding tube is inserted. And that will keep her alive. If you believe she would not want to be kept alive like this, then we will do nothing, release her back to her nursing home, and let nature take its course."

Bonnie squeezed her eyes shut. There was no happy ending here, no way that she was ever going to be able to live with herself.

"You mean she'd starve to death." Vivian sounded as if she was being strangled.

The doctor spoke slowly, as if he were choosing each word with great care. "She would die, yes. But it would not be unpleasant. What we know is that in the final days, when someone is no longer able to eat, they begin to sleep more and the body draws on an endorphin that blunts the nerve endings so that there is little or no discomfort." He rose. "I will leave you to discuss the options. Let the nurse know when you've reached a decision, and she'll page me."

After he'd left, Bonnie laid her head on the table, letting the cool slickness of the laminate act like a soothing balm. She was so tired of being the one every decision fell to, the one everyone turned to. She knew she'd asked for it, accepted the role when it was offered over and over again, that she could have said no. But that knowledge didn't make her any less exhausted; she just wanted to fall under a sleeping spell and let tiny dwarves care for her until this was all over.

Vivian was not about to let that happen. "I can't think in here. It's too white," she complained. "Let's go for a walk and talk this out." She roosted beside Bonnie until, at last, she raised her head wearily and nodded in agreement.

The cafeteria was connected to a labyrinthine set of hallways topped by a glass sunroof. As they wandered through, the light spilling into the expanse lifted Bonnie's spirits, gave her a small – but welcome – sense of optimism. The hall, with its color-coded lines leading to various destinations, resembled an airport runway. She wondered if Vivian had the same thought, for she began accelerating up the hall, pumping her arms briskly. The pace set by Viv's long legs left Bonnie about fifteen feet behind her, struggling to keep up.

Panting, she caught up to her sister. "I thought the purpose of this walk was to talk about our options, not to give you your aerobic activity for the day."

Vivian slowed down without looking at her, although Bonnie still had to power-walk to maintain the pace. "This is how I think best," she said.

"So what do you think we should do?" Bonnie asked.

Vivian stopped cold and faced her. "If she dies now," she said, her voice breaking, "she's going to hell. You know that, right?"

Wow. Bonnie felt like she'd been kidney punched. If this was what Viv was thinking about, no wonder she was so bothered. Still, she didn't want to believe it could be true. "She's an atheist. It's probably a little late for her to convert."

"You don't know what miracles God can perform. That's why we have to keep her alive. If she can recover enough to have even one more lucid moment, she can ask God to enter her life." She spoke with fervor, as if she were already seeing Jesus cradling Elizabeth in his arms.

Bonnie didn't know how to respond to this. They began walking again, this time at a not-quite-so-breakneck speed. When they reached the end of the hallway, they turned, like swimmers doing laps. Bonnie could feel her shirt start to stick to her underarms and pulled at her sleeves. Finally, she said, "I don't know, Viv. That seems awful unlikely to me."

Vivian turned to head to look at Bonnie, never breaking stride. Bonnie wondered how long she could do that without crashing into something. "Do you believe in heaven and hell?"

Bonnie stopped. "I gotta sit." She sank onto one of the benches lining the hall.

Vivian remained standing, towering over her like a vengeful archangel. "Do you?" she repeated.

God, she so did not want to get into a big theological debate with Viv right now. She had never been content to accept Bonnie's more Unitarian way of accepting all beliefs as valid, carping at her about why she was wrong until Bonnie wanted to strangle her with her cross. But this was a question she had to answer. "I honestly don't know," she said. "I tend to look at what Mother is currently going through as a kind of hell. And I would like to think of her being at peace for once after she dies. But heaven and hell in a literal sense? Beats me." She paused, waiting for Vivian to say something.

Vivian knelt at her feet. Her tone, soft and gentle, belied words that burned like acid. "The doctor told us to think of Mother's best interests. It cannot be in her best interest to doom her to hell. So no, I do not think you should sign a DNR order. But you know what? I wash my hands of this. This is on you."

Bonnie opened her mouth. When no words would form, she thought of Elizabeth, trapped in a haze of sounds with no meaning.

Vivian rose. "I'm going to find the chapel and pray." Her voice broke. "Tell Mother I said goodbye."

Bonnie watched her move slowly down the hallway as if in a funeral procession. When Vivian finally disappeared, she raised her head to the harsh glare of the sun beating on the ceiling and lifted a prayer to God for the glass-filtered heat to burn her clean.

~18~
MEG

The sounds of Crowded House were blaring from the stereo, and the juicy aroma of cooking steaks teased the air. Meg dropped her purse on the couch and followed her nose to the balcony, where Brady was turning the meat on a miniature grill. The balcony was smaller than their bathroom, yet he'd managed to cram the grill as well as a deck chair and table onto it. It always made her feel oversized, like Gulliver in the land of Lilliput.

"All I ask is to live each moment, free from the last," Brady sang, loud and off-key.

As Meg pushed open the sliding glass door with its rubbery wheeze, he grinned at her. "Don't call PETA, 'cause we're eating meat tonight!" He put down the tongs and grabbed her around the waist.

She laughed as she leaned down to scratch Barkley's ears, watching Brady. "Lord, who changed your meds?"

Barkley rousted himself from his shady position underneath the lawn chair and stretched in front of her, like a liege bowing before his queen.

Brady turned his attention back to the grill. "Mock me if you want to, but I have had the best day. I feel great!"

She didn't quite trust the extremes of this mood. Might as well throw out the trial balloon. "Have you taken Barkley out yet today, or should I do it now, before dinner?" she asked, knowing the answer damn well.

He didn't rise to the bait. "He's fine for now. Mother let him out earlier." He paused to take a look at the steaks. "Why don't you go uncork some wine for us while I get these off? They're almost done."

Meg backed off the balcony, watching her step.

Pouring two generous glasses of wine – Brady had sprung for the good stuff, she noticed, a fifteen-dollar bottle of merlot – Meg gazed at her fiancé through the glass door, trying to figure out what was giving her a sense of unease. Maybe it was the suddenness of the change. He'd been so mopey over the last week that he'd started to resemble Barkley. If she pointed out some beautiful flowers, he talked about how they'd never survive in the smog. They hadn't spoken any more about moving since the fight, but it was still out there, hovering in the shadows. Meg had stopped trying to pull Brady out of his negativity; nothing ruins a good bad mood like the efforts of some do-gooder. But the pity party was getting old. She had planned to give him one more week before she broached the topic of postponing the wedding.

Brady breezed in with the steaks, depositing them on the dining room table. "Sit, sit. I've taken care of everything." Meg watched with one eyebrow cocked as he took a Styrofoam take-out box from the fridge and scooped salad out into bowls. He brought these and a crusty loaf of bread to the already-set table.

"Nice spread," Meg commented, tearing the heel off the multi-grain loaf. Cocking her head, she searched Brady's face for some kind of sign that might explain this turnaround, but found nothing. She still didn't trust it, though.

"Thanks. Hey, watch me be all sensitive-guy now. So, honey," Brady said in a mock adoring tone, "How was your day?"

Meg smiled. He really was trying. "Actually, kind of weird, thanks for asking. I had to get Carla to cover for me for almost an hour while I tried to talk my mother down from the proverbial ledge." She told him about how Vivian had showed up in the store mid-afternoon, completely unhinged over her grandmother's stroke.

"I mean, Mom was ranting about hell and Jesus, and she was crying so hard she was hiccupping, and I had to get her into the back room so she didn't scare what few customers we had. It was bizarre, especially since Mom seems like she tries to forget Grandmother exists most of the time."

"I still don't get how you've never had any contact with your grandmother. It's not like she lived out-of-state or anything."

Meg shrugged. "I guess it depends on what you grow up with. Mom and Grandmother haven't been on speaking terms for years. Mom always said if I wanted to strike up a relationship with her, I was free to do so as long as she didn't have to be involved."

"So why didn't you? That sounds like something you would do, especially considering how badly you get along with your mother."

"Yeah, but you know how you're allowed to bitch and moan about your relatives, but if anyone else says the same thing, you're all over them with a stick? I came across some letters from Grandmother to my mother from years ago, and they were so nasty. Bitchy and judgmental. Not terribly surprising, I guess. I mean, there has to be a reason she and Mom don't speak. But I can't say they gave me much desire to go get to know her. Somehow, I didn't think she'd end up the cookies-and-apron Granny type."

"Well, I'm sorry to hear about her stroke, anyway. It can't be easy on anyone."

Meg smiled at him and took a sip of wine. She cut into her steak. "So tell me why your day was so good."

"Well, I found out I get my cast off next week, for starters. Then Mother told me that my cousin Chip, my best friend who moved to California, will be coming to the wedding. And I got a call from Daedalus Falls Elementary School asking me in for a second interview. So it's all good."

Meg's knife scraped the plate, the jagged screech sending an electric charge up her spine. She held the steak knife in mid-air. "You've lost me. Why are you talking with other schools?"

"Well, I can't wait very long to find another teaching position. School starts in a month, you know." He said this with a maddeningly patient tone.

"I'm aware of school calendars. What I'm unclear about is why you need to find a job when you already have one."

Brady maneuvered the salad around his plate, avoiding eye contact.

"About that. I never signed the contract. I'm not going back."

Realizing she was still clutching the knife, she laid it down silently on the table. What she needed for this news was a drink. She took a gulp of wine, wishing it were stronger. It tasted rancid in her mouth. "Thanks for telling me."

"I'm telling you now, aren't I?"

"You know what I mean. Why didn't you say anything to me earlier?"

"Because I knew you'd try to talk me out of it, when what I would've needed from you was support."

The air felt sticky and hot around her, toxic as blame. "So you decided it was better to sneak around with this? Great move, hon."

Brady slammed his fork on the plate, rose, and limped into the kitchen, muttering. She knew he hated when she got sarcastic, but fuck it. If he was going to creep around, making secret plans, she was not going to censor herself for his benefit.

She felt like the room was converging in on her. That he would make a decision like that, something that affected their life together, and not even tell her, hurt her as forcefully as if he'd punched her. He could run, or at least limp quickly, from what happened to him this summer, try to erase the memory like so much chalk dust, and Meg might not be happy about it, but she could acknowledge it. But she couldn't accept the deception, the fact that he'd kept news about his life – *their* life – a secret for weeks. She rose and walked into the bedroom, shutting the door behind her and catching the lock. She could hear Brady's muffled curse through the door as she sat down on the bed and cradled her head in her hands.

She heard the lock jiggle as Brady tested it. "What is your problem?" he shouted through the door crack.

She opened the door. "Tell me one thing. Did your mother know about the contract and your applying for the job in the Falls?"

"Of course." His tone made it sound like the question was self-evident. "She helped me line up the interview. It's not that easy finding a position this late in the summer."

"So the only one out of the loop here was me. Gee, way to make a fiancée feel wanted."

He started to speak, but she turned away. She didn't want to hear him anymore; there was no fixing this. She spied a Zimbel's bag shoved under a chair in the corner. Shaking out the contents, Meg began shoving bras, T-shirts, any evidence of her residence into the bag. When the seams threatened to split, she sighed and hoisted the bag onto her shoulder.

Brady blocked the door, still jabbering excuses – he hadn't intentionally not told her about the contract, it was his business anyway, it had nothing to do with their relationship or how he felt about her, they weren't planning on staying in this apartment anyway, and on and on and on.

"Please move." Meg started to duck under his outstretched arms, but he finally shifted, flattening himself against the wall so that she could push past him without knocking against his cast. She continued down the narrow hallway, pausing at the dining nook. Barkley looked up at her from under the table. She shook off the feeling that she saw judgment in his eyes: he was just a Basset, for pity's sake – they always looked judgmental. But she really didn't want the dog to bear any more trauma than he'd already endured.

Brady hopped slowly down the hall. She turned to him. "Are you going to be okay here with Barkley?" she said. "I can take him with me, if you want."

"He's my dog. I'll take care of him."

"Well, then." She shrugged, moving to the door.

"Yeah." Brady turned his back to her and limped slowly down the hallway.

Meg left.

*　*　*

"So why can't you just go drinking like everybody else does when they fight with their boyfriend?" Carla complained as she and Meg sped down the highway towards the stadium.

"Don't want to. Besides, you can drink at the game."

Carla rolled her eyes. "If you can call that piss-water beer."

Meg was silent for a minute as she drove. "Thanks for the bed for tonight."

"T'ain't no big thing." Carla kept her voice light. After a short pause, she added, "So is this it, you think?"

"Dunno. Maybe." Meg maintained her gaze on the road.

"You want to talk about it?"

"Nope."

A few minutes later, they'd gotten tickets and were winding their way to their seats behind right field. They'd arrived late – it was the bottom of the second inning, and trying to balance a bag of peanuts and a beer as she scooted past knees, Meg slopped a little beer on the neck of a man in full Cleveland Indians' get-up. He cursed and turned in his chair to glare at her. She found her chair and folded the seat down with her elbow. She glowered back at him, but Carla apologized.

"You know, a little politeness goes a long way, even with assholes," Carla whispered, settling next to Meg.

"Just let me watch the game."

The Indians had not been having a good season. Even so, the stadium was crowded. An influx of talented new players had given the city hope for climbing out of the cellar. But Meg had been a fan since she was kid, when the Indians had ended every season firmly locked into last place. It had been one of the few things she and her parents did as a family, and she still loved to come to the games, buy a program, and keep her own scorecard.

Carla nudged her when the third inning began. "I'm loving these seats. Look at the ass on that guy."

Meg nodded. A fly ball crested close by, easily catchable. The ass in question, a right fielder named Enrique Vasquez, loped toward it. He moved into high gear only once the ball bounced on the outfield ten feet away from him. "A little hustle!" Meg shouted, her message drowned out in the crowd's general collective groan. He was so infuriating. She had seen him make some truly spectacular plays; but most of the time, Vasquez was just playing to get by, waiting for his next at bat, when he'd drive the crowd into a frenzy with a double or a home run.

Carla was engaged in a contest with the two frat boys sitting next to them, throwing peanuts and catching them in their mouths. Meg was relieved she wasn't bored; she felt grateful that Carla, who tended to call the umpire "the referee" when she talked about sports at all, had agreed even to come to the game. Brady had come to the home-opener with Meg, and while he made an effort to get into the game, he'd spent most of the time searching out coffee and complaining about the cold. God. She should've booted *his* ass right then and there and saved herself a lot of heartache.

The Indians were up now, making decent contact, but driving the ball right into the gloves of their opponents like leather-seeking missiles. A pop fly and double play later, the inning was over.

Vasquez trotted back to right field, tipping the brim of his cap to a group of giggling teen-age girls who had unfurled a banner from the front seats. "Just do your job and catch the damn ball," Meg muttered.

Carla nudged her elbow. "You okay?"

Meg lied, nodding. She was having difficulty keeping the fight at bay.

A few minutes later, with two outs on the board, a single came flying into right field. It looked as if Vasquez could just stand there and catch it, but the ball started to tail off toward the foul line. He could still make the catch if he tried, if he hauled ass toward the corner. The crowd around her stood as one in their seats, screaming encouragement. But Vasquez barely even reached for it, instead waiting for the ball to bounce, and then winging it back toward second base to hold the batter.

Meg was the only one left standing as he threw the ball, tears streaming down her face as she screamed epithets at the right fielder. The ball's bounce on the field had jarred the feeling of betrayal buried deep inside, shaken it loose. Fans in several rows around her turned to stare. Most of their faces scowled in disapproval but some of them, perhaps unnerved by her tears, wore expressions of concern.

Carla stood and took her by the elbow. "Come on, Meg," she said gently. "Let's get out of here."

Meg allowed herself to be led from the section. Carla tried to shield her from the taunts of the spectators. "You've got a beer bong on your head," she told one of them. "Like your opinion matters to me."

Meg swiped her face clean as they exited. "You don't get it," she told Carla. "He really could've made it if he tried. But he didn't try. He didn't try at all."

"I get it, girlfriend." Carla put her arm around Meg's shoulders. "Men suck."

~19~
JANE

Jane trudged up the hill toward Charley's house, trying to let the cloud of music coming from her headphones shroud her from her own thoughts. Her thoughts weren't being very cooperative, though, and kept breaking through Michael Stipes singing about "shiny happy people holding hands." She didn't know of many shiny happy people these days, that was for sure. The whole weekend had been like one of those bad dreams – the ones where there are standardized tests being given, but she arrives late, and when she finally does sit down, all her pencils have broken tips. When she finally gets a chance to look at the test, she doesn't know any of the answers anyway.

Mom had been crazy-wiggy since finding out about Grams. It hadn't started out so badly. Bonnie had been calm at the beginning, and sat Jane and Davey down to explain how Grams had had a stroke. Then she told them what a stroke was, and that this one had been really serious. Davey had snuggled in against their mom and asked if Grams was going to die. He could be so stupid sometimes. Bonnie had dropped her head and shaken it, her hair flopping back and forth like windshield wipers, whispering, "I don't know. I don't know what to do."

It was kind of scary. Jane had never seen her mom this way. Grams was probably going to die. She should be sad, right? She wondered if she was a bad person for feeling nothing. Probably.

All weekend, her mom had stayed really scattered. She would get vegetables out of the fridge and forget she'd done it, and then shout at Jane and Davey to stop moving her stuff, for God's sake. Three cups of coffee, all cold and barely touched, sat in various rooms because Bonnie kept misplacing them. She'd talked to Aunt Viv on the phone two or three times, conversations that involved yelling.

There had been a phone call from Meg as well; she'd apparently had a huge fight with Brady and the wedding was off. "Shit happens," Meg had said, and tried to laugh it off, but Jane wasn't fooled. She felt bad for Meg, but her overriding feeling was relief and hope that she might have more time for her now. Those emotions were iced with a layer of guilt that she could be so selfish. The whole thing made her woozy.

Sunday night, Bonnie finally called the hospital. Jane wasn't supposed to be eavesdropping, but she figured it was her grandmother, too, so she picked up the phone in her mother's room and held her hand over the mouthpiece so she wouldn't hear her breathe.

Bonnie was talking to a man. "I've been thinking about this all weekend, and I just can't make myself be at peace about this."

"I need to be clear on this," he said."You do not want a DNR order at this time?"

She hesitated, then said in a defeated voice, "That's right. I mean, can I change my mind later, or is this cast in stone?"

"You can change your mind at any time. We will insert a nasogastric feeding tube into your mother's nose tonight, and she can be transferred back to the nursing home tomorrow. If you change your mind, you can discuss it with the nursing home, and they will remove the feeding tube."

Jane put her finger on the clear button sticking up from the phone's base so Mom wouldn't hear her hang up. She wasn't really sure what had just happened. It didn't sound like Grams was going to die, though, if she was going back to the nursing home. Jane felt a little bit better for that.

She was happy to be going to Charley's, though: there was no way there could be this much drama at his house.When she arrived, she was surprised to see Pam sitting at the dining table sipping her coffee. Usually, she had her purse ready and was on her way out the door.

Charley was sitting on the floor, making butterflies with his hands. Jane ruffled his hair as she stepped over him. Pam smiled at Jane. "I'm going to be staying home this morning."

"Oh my gosh," Jane said. "I totally forgot about Charley's doctor's appointment. Should I just go home, then?"

Pam smiled. "Actually, if you'll stay, I think I might need you. The car hasn't started in a couple days, so we're going to have to take the bus to the doctor's. I could use an extra set of hands, just in case."

Jane raised her eyebrows. Talk about changing the routine on Charley.

Shrugging her shoulders, Pam scrunched up her face in apology. "It's the best I can do. I made Charley's neurologist appointment two months ago, so canceling is not an option. The office is right on the bypass." Pam inhaled. "Will you help?"

"You betcha." Jane looked over at Charley, and blew some air out of her cheeks. She hoped this was going to be okay. Someone on the bus might jostle him, or God forbid, try to bully him. Pam might know how to shield him from things that freaked him out, but geez, this was a *bus*. Besides, if he went all head-banger on everyone, it was *not* going to be pretty.

As they got him dressed, Charley began to giggle – not a normal giggle, but a high-pitched crazy man giggle. He sensed this was not their normal routine.

Jane tried to show him his bus schedule to calm him down. "Hey, Charley, if your doctor's office is on Route Nineteen, which bus schedule do we need?"

He stopped giggling and gazed at Jane. She wondered if he ever thought that she was stupid for asking him all of these questions. He walked over to his collection of schedules and flipped rapidly through them, then pulled one out and handed it to her.

"Awesome, Chuck! Now, can you find where we catch the bus? It'll be at the corner of Main and Sunset."

He scanned the bus stops and pointed to the right one.

"Two for two," she said. "Now when does the bus get to that stop?"

Charley intoned without pausing, "Nine forty five ten fifteen ten forty five eleven fifteen... "

Jane stopped him before he could go through the rest of the day. "Good job, Charley."

Pam was sitting on the edge of the bed, watching them with a weird expression on her face, kind of proud and sad at the same time. "You really are good with him, Jane. You get the steps that he has to make to go from point A to point B."

Jane was pleased, but also mildly annoyed with the compliment. What did Pam think she did with him all day? She mumbled a thank you, then helped Charley gather up his schedules and put them back.

Charley allowed them to take his hands as they left the house and began walking down the sidewalk. He took each step like he was on a tightrope, placing one foot precisely in front of the other. But he never lost his balance. Jane was hypnotized watching him. She almost tripped a couple times because she wasn't paying attention to the sidewalk.

When they reached the bus stop, Jane scanned the road for any sign of the bus, but it was just the normal traffic interspersed with the occasional neighbor on the sidewalk walking a dog. One of the dogs, a big shaggy mutt, strained at its leash and bounded up to the threesome. Its owner, a round little woman who reminded Jane of a wobbly Weeble, apologized for the dog's behavior, then began to make small talk with Pam. Jane kneeled down to offer her hand to the dog to sniff, then patted the scruff of his neck. The dog licked her forearm and then began to nuzzle Charley, almost knocking him down. Oh, God. He was going to freak, for sure. She placed a restraining hand on the dog's collar, but let go when she saw Charley's face. He was actually smiling, scrunching his hands over and over in the dog's fur.

The round woman grinned. "It looks like Blackie's made a friend." She let them play for another minute, then gathered up her dog and continued on.

"Wasn't that amazing?" Jane said. "Have you ever seen him do that before?"

Pam smiled. "Oh, yeah, Charley's always loved animals."

"But that's huge. You guys should totally get him a dog." Crap. As soon as the words blew out of her mouth she regretted them. Her batting average with making suggestions where Charley was concerned was pretty low.

Pam ran her hand through her hair. "And who'd take care of him, Jane? I can barely take care of Charley." Sure enough, she sounded irritated.

Biting her lip, Jane nodded.

She felt the rumble of the bus coming up through the sidewalk into her toes. It screeched to a halt with a giant wheeze. Charley looked up at the bus as the door folded open. "Mercy buckets," he said.

Pam grasped his elbow firmly. "We'll watch your show when we get home, Charley. Let's get on the bus now."

But he planted his feet on the sidewalk and locked his knees. Jane saw that if they tried to pull him farther forward and lost their grip, he would go flying backward and hit the ground hard. "Pam, he's about to fall."

Releasing her grip on him, Pam said, "That's enough, Charles! Come on!"

The bus driver leaned sideways out of his seat. "Are you folks getting on or not?"

Jerk. Jane yelled up to him, "Can't you see we're trying? Give us half a second, please!" She turned to Charley. "This is the bus we've been waiting for, buddy. We're going to follow the route now." She took his hand and he relaxed.

Pam picked him up and hoisted him onto the bus steps, hugging him with one arm and holding onto the rail with the other. "I have some bus tickets in the front pocket of my purse. Grab them for me, please."

Pam maneuvered Charley into an empty seat with no people around them. Jane eased into the seat behind them, scrutinizing Charley for any warning signs. He seemed okay for the moment. The bus was only about half full. Jane wondered who all these people were, taking the bus mid-morning. Didn't they have jobs? Where were they going? Were they all poor, so that they needed to ride the bus rather than just drive in their cars? If she looked at their faces, she might be able to get clues, but she didn't want to make eye contact with anyone, especially since she felt like they were all already looking at her and Pam and Charley. As the bus began moving, Jane leaned forward, grasping the head of the chair in front of her to keep from losing her balance and lurching out into the aisle.

"How's he doing?" she asked Pam worriedly.

"So far, so good."

Charley had the window seat, but was short enough that his head didn't reach the top. Half-standing to see him, Jane was surprised and relieved to see him handling the ride okay, slouched with his face plastered against the window. She supposed it was probably pretty interesting to him to watch all the images flash by. Was he focusing on any one object, so that all the rest of the images were a blur, or was he comparing the speed of the road to the speed of the buildings? Of course, these were the things that Jane did; maybe he wasn't doing any of that, but was just off in Charley-world.

The bus seemed to stop about every ten feet to let someone off. It was really annoying, because you couldn't ever relax. If Jane had to do this everyday, she'd want to kill someone.

Charley begin to hum. It wasn't any song, but a single tone at a frequency that exactly matched the whir of the air conditioning. This couldn't be good. He was starting to wag his head back and forth. Pam had laid her arm over his in an attempt to keep him still, but the hum was getting louder and louder. The other passengers were starting to look their way again. Jane wished she had a sheet she could hang up to block the gawkers.

Pam whispered, "I think the A.C. is bothering him. He doesn't filter out sounds very well."

Jane thought about that for a second. If she heard every sound that went on in the world, it would royally suck. "Do you think it would help if he listened to some music? I've got my Walkman."

Pam's expression was tense. "It's worth a try," she said. "We still have a few more stops."

Jane let Pam position the Walkman on Charley's head. The tinny sound of the music bled through them. He immediately stilled and stopped humming. Holding his hands over his ears, he squeezed his eyes shut for a moment, then opened and closed them again. When he stopped blinking, he said to no one in particular, "It's orange."

Jane tapped him on the shoulder and plucked one earpiece free. "What's orange, Charley?"

He patted his ears. "It's orange," he repeated. Smiling, he turned back to the window.

"I guess he likes it," Jane said to Pam, who continued to sit as if there were a ticking bomb sitting next to her.

She was surprised to see Pam tug Charley by the arm to stand up when they got to the bus stop near the Stop-n-Shop. All the times Mom had dragged her grocery shopping, she'd never realized there was a medical office building right next door.

After they stepped down off the bus, Pam paused to adjust her skirt. Jane pointed to the store. "Look, Charley. There's the store where they're going to film *Food Frenzy* next week."

When his gaze did not follow the direction she was pointing, she took Charley's arm and pointed it. Now he saw. "Mercy buckets."

Pam laughed. "God help us all."

Charley began to walk slower and slower the closer they got to the doctor's office, until it almost seemed that he should be traveling backwards. While Pam checked in at the office, Jane sat down and picked up one of those stupid celebrity magazines. Was this really what women wanted to look like? She'd bet they weren't even pretty without all that makeup.

When she looked up after a minute, she didn't see Charley, although Pam was still at the front desk. "Charley?"

Pam looked around. "I know where he is." She peered behind the couch. "You okay, sport?" she asked, placing her hand on what Jane assumed was his head.

When she moved away, Jane crept over to the couch. There couldn't be more than a foot of space between the back of the sofa and the wall, and yet somehow, Charley had wedged himself back in there. How could fear literally give a person superhero powers to mold their body into a substance like Silly Putty? It reminded Jane of Boots, a cat they had owned when she was seven who had an uncanny ability of hiding in tight places on days when she was supposed to go to the vet.

When Charley's name was called, even though he resisted going in – tugging away from his mother's reach – once Pam got him inside, that was it. In the waiting room, Jane halfway expected to hear cries from down the hall, or maybe see him streak out in an unguarded moment. But everything stayed calm.

What must it be like, day in and day out, to live with a kid like Charley? It had to be exhausting, but fascinating too. His handicap, if you were allowed to call it that, seemed so unpredictable. He seemed to find threats in the hum of machinery, but would not even register the taunts of a neighborhood bully. It made Jane tired to think of a world so topsy-turvy. She put the headphones of her reclaimed Walkman onto her ears as she waited for Pam and Charley to come out. The song swirled around her brain, cool and light as sherbet. If she closed her eyes, she could see psychadelic-looking whorls. She stopped, amazed.

"It really is orange, isn't it?" she whispered into the listening air.

~ 20 ~
BONNIE

Bonnie barely bothered to pull her hair into a ponytail today; it wasn't worth the effort of putting on makeup just to visit the nursing home. Even if her mother woke, she wasn't going to say anything about her appearance anymore; Elizabeth's most potent weapon had been defused. But at the last minute, Bonnie couldn't go through with it. She slashed on a quick smear of lipstick before getting into the car.

Even in sleep, Elizabeth could not maintain an appearance of calm. Her muscle function had yet to return, so half her mouth was twisted into a permanently pissed-off expression. Her hair tumbled across the pillow, a few renegade strands remaining loyal to her cheek. Her brow furrowed, as if her dreams both puzzled and disappointed her.

Latrice, one of the aides, bustled into the room carrying towels, a sponge, a wash basin, and some soap. Elizabeth stirred and opened her eyes at the sound, and Bonnie lifted herself out of the worn visitor's chair, both to let her mother know she was there and to help Latrice with the load.

Without ceremony, Latrice dumped the paraphernalia at the foot of the bed. "Time for your mama's bath. You can stay or step out, whichever you want."

Every time Bonnie ran into Latrice on one of her shifts, she felt defensive. It wasn't that the aide was ever rude. But she never chatted, or made small talk with her, like the other aides did. She just said what she needed and did it, no response required. This matter-of-factness made it all too easy for Bonnie to project her own insecurities upon her, and think that Latrice must despise her.

"I'll stay," Bonnie said.

Elizabeth gazed at the two of them, eyes twitching from one to the other, resting on neither. A trickle of spit worked its way down from her lip. Bonnie took a tissue and wiped her cheek, crumpling it in her clenched fist. "Actually, I can give her a bath. You don't need to do it."

Latrice raised her eyelids an extra millimeter. "Fine with me. Just mind you don't start feeling sorry for her and untie her from the bed. Those ties are there for a reason."

She wanted to examine Latrice's face, to determine if she was patronizing her, if her expression provided any corroboration of Bonnie's suspicions. But the aide had already moved on. "Yes, ma'am."

Taking the washbasin into the bathroom, she started running the water in the sink, waiting for it to warm up. Bonnie watched the water gather and swirl around the drain, drops spraying randomly. Stuck in the trance of the water's pull, she relaxed, jerking only when a renegade drop scalded her hand. Adjusting the temperature, she filled the basin a third of the way, being careful not to slosh it as she carried it out to Elizabeth's bedside table. The basin felt like it weighed a thousand pounds, as if the earth's gravitational pull had multiplied exponentially just in the space Bonnie occupied.

She was so goddamn tired. She'd lain in her bed for the three nights since Elizabeth's stroke, praying for sleep, tensing every muscle and then relaxing, but still her mind raced. Even when she dozed, she would dream that she was awake and trying to fall asleep; the only giveaway that she was dreaming were odd details like the orangutan grooming himself at the foot of her bed, or vines winding themselves around the bedpost, which had itself transformed into a giant tree trunk.

Wringing out the washcloth, Bonnie began to bathe Elizabeth in long soapy strokes. Her skin looked fragile enough to rip. As she cupped her mother's sunken cheeks with the washcloth, Elizabeth seemed to focus and rasped an elongated "Gark." While the word itself was without meaning, Elizabeth's intonation held no ambiguity: it said, "Get me out of this bed *right now*, you ungrateful bitch!"

Bonnie winced, ducking her head as if to avoid a slap. It had been easier to live with her decision to leave things as they were when her mother had been unaware in her mental fog. Having Elizabeth present, and aware of her loss – if not able to articulate it – left Bonnie weak with guilt. Realizing the cloth was dripping onto the pillow, she turned to the basin, trying to compose her features. She felt like Elizabeth could see her shame hovering in the room like a wraith.

As she wet an arm, then toweled it dry, Bonnie spoke about Jane and Davey, about the weather, about nothing at all, in a soft singsong chant. Elizabeth's eyelids lowered. The muscles in her neck lost their tension, and her body seemed to sink more deeply into the mattress.

Elizabeth's raised arm, leashed to the metal bedrail, called to Bonnie, a tentative student seeking permission to be heard. She looked so vulnerable and peaceful lying there asleep, the restraint ties a harshness that seemed unnecessary. Bonnie untied the knot to massage her mother's forearm. As soon as the bow slipped from the rail, Elizabeth opened her eyes.

She grabbed a handful of her shirt, reaching faster than Bonnie would have thought possible, pulling her close to the bed. She had a surprising amount of strength, given her condition. "Gark," she repeated in an agonized cry, over and over.

"Mother, that is *enough!*" Bonnie dropped the washcloth and stepped backward, but Elizabeth refused to let go. She tried to straighten her fingers with one hand, but was unsuccessful. She ultimately needed both hands to unpeel Elizabeth's cramped fist from her blouse. The act felt violent. How little force it would take to break those fingers. Once free, she lashed her mother's arm back to the bed.

Elizabeth turned her head away and closed her eyes tightly, like a toddler who thinks he's invisible. Bonnie inhaled – and found she couldn't exhale. She gulped more and more air, like a glutton, choking back sobs, even as she realized tears were showering down her cheeks.

She leaned over the bedrail and laid her head next to her mother's; the discomfort of the awkward position seemed fitting, like a penance. "I'm sorry, I'm sorry, I'm sorry," she crooned. Elizabeth made no response. Laying halfway across the bed, the rail jutting into her ribs, Bonnie realized that this was the closest physical contact she'd ever initiated with Elizabeth since she was a child. And while she knew that Elizabeth would have rebuffed any attempts at such contact, the rejected young girl in her still craved a mother's affection. Regretful tears welled up again. Elizabeth lay rigid beside her, but her breaths were even.

Eventually, Bonnie pulled herself upright, rubbing her side. She felt, if not normal, at least functional. There was no way she wanted to finish this sponge bath, but her desire not to have Latrice return and see her in this state was greater. Picking up the washcloth from the floor, she rewet it and set about the task. Taking each body part in isolation, she worked silently, avoiding looking at Elizabeth's face.

When the job was done, she mechanically rinsed out the basin and wrung out the washcloth, hanging it over the lip of the sink to dry. She couldn't bring herself to utter the word "goodbye." Sneaking out of the room, she strode down the hall with her gaze firmly fastened to the linoleum below.

When she reached her car, conspicuous in the almost deserted parking lot, Bonnie melted onto the driver's seat. As she tried to compose herself enough to drive herself home, a memory kept trying to push its way to the surface: Elizabeth running a wet cloth over Bonnie's brow, sitting next to her and placing a stiff arm around her shoulder, with reticent pats presumably intended to be comfort. When on earth would that have been? When had Elizabeth ever, intentionally or unintentionally, acted maternally toward Bonnie?

It came to her with the suddenness of a thunderclap. Bonnie was pregnant, just before the third trimester, and Janey was barely one year of age. Then the bleeding started, so much of it. At the hospital, masked doctors used words like "placenta tear" as they wheeled her into the delivery room. And then she was holding her stillborn son, purple as a sugar beet, motionless and limp.

At some point, a nurse must have taken Janey, for Joe was there, stroking the baby's hand, hiccupping loud sobs. It occurred to Bonnie that she was cradling a baby that was dead, and the thought suddenly seemed obscene. She pushed the baby back to the nurse, folding her arms around herself to keep her heart from spilling out.

In the aftermath, the only person Bonnie wanted was Elizabeth. She sought recrimination, shouting, blame. She needed her mother to pelt her with "You deserved this." But Elizabeth didn't. She arrived at the house; bathed, dressed and fed Jane; stocked the fridge; straightened the house. All without seeking permission or asking for thanks. In any other situation, Bonnie would have bristled at the intrusion, felt an implied judgment of incompetence. Now, she didn't care. After a few days, Elizabeth came into the bedroom once she'd put Jane to bed, and climbed into bed with Bonnie. The incongruous image of Elizabeth, slacks perfectly creased, sitting with her back ramrod-straight next to her, struck her as funny. The laugh came out deformed, a moan.

Elizabeth had patted her shoulder tentatively, like someone touching a feral kitten. "It's a terrible thing to lose a child," she said. At the time, Bonnie had thought that she was referring to Vivian. After Viv had gotten married and had Meg, she began refusing any contact from Elizabeth, who accepted each returned letter with a stony glare.

As Bonnie remembered the incident now, though, she wondered if her mother could have been referring to Pete. Bonnie bowed her head. She felt cheated, somehow. It wasn't fair that the only positive remembrance she had of Elizabeth came on the heels of tragedy. And she felt remorseful as well, that she had failed her mother now when Elizabeth most needed her. She prayed that if there was a God out there, that he or she would help her know what to do and give her the strength to do it.

Starting on the drive home, she stuck in a CD of Karla Bonoff singing "The Water is Wide," and sang along as loud as she could, to drive back the past – and keep herself awake. The air under the forest's canopy was warm and sticky. Though it was still light out – dark wouldn't fall for another hour – the forest road was so heavily wooded that it seemed later than it was.

Rounding a curve, Bonnie caught a flicker of brown in her peripheral vision. Before she could hit the breaks, there was a heavy, dull thump that jolted the car to an immediate stop. The force threw her into the steering column, thwacking her forehead on the steering wheel.

She wasn't sure how much time had passed. It seemed a good idea to remain motionless, whatever had happened. She didn't think she'd lost consciousness, but she was afraid to move, scared to discover if she'd broken any bones.

Bit by bit, she mustered the courage to open her eyes. Check. She felt groggy, like she was trying to swim in a sea of marshmallow fluff. She pushed through the fog enough to wiggle her fingers. Check. Slowly, she pried herself back from the steering wheel. She felt a piercing pain in her chest.

Bonnie breathed shallowly. Knock wood, it was nothing worse than a broken rib. When she raised a hand to brush her hair out of her eyes, it came back bloody.

Headlights bore down behind her like the glowing eyes of a giant demon. A police car pulled over well in front of her. After what seemed like a long time, an officer emerged and ran over to her car.

"I've just radioed for an ambulance," he said.

Bonnie raised her eyes to his. She didn't seem to be able to move normally; everything was in slow motion. She nodded and reached to open the car door, which looked to be relatively intact.

"Ma'am, I don't think you should be moving," the officer said.

He was probably right. But she felt like she couldn't breathe in here, like if she stayed in the car a moment longer, it would fold in on itself around her, trapping her. She'd take her chances.

Bonnie opened the door, silencing the cop with the "Don't start" look she often gave Jane and Davey. She was *fine*. She became momentarily panicked when she was unable to get out of the car – maybe she was paralyzed, after all. But after a moment of fumbling, she realized she was still buckled in. She reached down to unlatch her seat belt and winced from a shooting pain in her ribs.

Once she was out of the car, the ground seemed to sway. The policeman steadied her, kept her from falling. She nodded in thanks as he released her. "Can you help me? I want to see the damage, but I'm a little woozy."

The officer eyed her with a skeptical expression. "That's not such a good idea, miss."

"Oh, please. Just do it."

"Why don't you just have a seat here, get your bearings first?"

"I'm tired of people telling me what to do! Will you help me over there, or should I just do it myself?" Her head hurt when she snapped at him.

Shaking his head, he offered her his arm. Grasping it, Bonnie let him walk her around to the passenger side, crumpled like a wadded piece of tissue. She grimaced at the damage.

A deer lay in the road, its eyes open, staring off into some unknown distance. It breathed erratically, blood pumping out from a jagged gash in its side. Bonnie would've expected a cry or whimper or some distress noise, but there was only silence. She wanted to heal it, comfort it, take back time, hide from its judgment.

The officer touched her shoulder from behind. Bonnie started. "Ma'am, you're going to need to back away now. I have to put him down, and you don't want to watch."

Yes, back away. She felt a wave of gratitude toward him for taking the decision away from her. She backed away as he jogged back to his car and returned with a rifle. She looked fixedly at the trunk of her car until she heard the explosion. Her ears rang.

She looked back at the deer. It was motionless, but its eyes, still open, were fixed on the falling dusk.

~ 21 ~
MEG

The sliding glass doors to the Emergency Room opened with a whoosh of air conditioning. Bonnie sat alone in the lobby, a row of chairs to herself, her arms folded across her chest protectively. She rose upon seeing Meg. "Thanks for coming to get me. I'm glad you were home when I called."

"Hey, I should thank you for letting me camp out on your couch. And don't worry about the kids; Jane agreed to watch Davey as long as she doesn't actually have to talk to him." Bonnie was paler than the hospital walls surrounding them, and she looked as if a gentle breeze could knock her over. "God, are you all right? Do they want to keep you here overnight or anything?"

Bonnie shook her head as Meg led her to where her car was parked. "Honest, I'm okay. I have a couple broken ribs, but that's all. I'm lucky it wasn't any worse."

Meg hovered as Bonnie lowered herself into the passenger seat of her VW Bug. She didn't know how to assist her without causing pain. Bending over at the waist to keep from hitting her head on the car's tiny ceiling, she leaned awkwardly over Bonnie as she tried to help her fasten her seat belt, fumbling with the catch. When she got behind the wheel and started the engine, Bonnie put a hand on the steering column. "Wait a minute."

She turned the key back, hoping she hadn't broken another of Bonnie's ribs getting her into this sardine can. "What's wrong?"

"I don't want to go home yet."

This wasn't the answer she had expected. "No problem. Where do you want to go?"

"To the nursing home. I'll explain on the way."

* * *

Meg drove five miles under the speed limit, being careful to apply the brakes gradually, well before stop signs. The last thing Bonnie needed was whiplash from a too sudden stop.

Bonnie told her about the accident. "I can't stop thinking about that deer. Every time I close my eyes, I see it struggling to die."

Meg nodded, sympathetic but stymied. How she was supposed to be a comfort in a case like this?

Bonnie swiped tears away from her eyes. Her voice quiet, she asked, "Do you believe in signs?"

Maybe the accident had given her a concussion. This didn't sound like her. Meg chose her words carefully. "Like from God?"

"Yeah, or the universe, or something out there."

Meg nodded. "Yeah, I do."

"I feel like the deer was a sign."

She remembered a time a couple years ago, when Jane had dabbled in astrology and tarot, searching for answers in the exotic unknown. Meg had gotten her a book on I Ching, and Bonnie had angrily confronted her afterward. "I don't want Jane second-guessing everything that happens to her, looking for answers from mysticism to guide her in making decisions. That's not the way the world works." So to hear these words from Bonnie's mouth now was a shock.

Meg let the possibility settle between them like a leaf drifting to the ground. "Maybe it was." She smiled grimly. "Too bad God couldn't have sent a less painful sign."

"Yeah." Bonnie fell silent. The road stretched out before them in the night, petering off into nothingness as it ran to the fore of the headlights. After a few minutes, Meg heard a light snore. She peeked over and saw Bonnie's head slumped on her own shoulder, asleep.

Meg was pretty sure she knew where the nursing home was, but she was going to have to wake Bonnie up soon to make sure she took the right turn. Otherwise, God only knew where they'd end up. Winding down the road into the forest valley, she wondered if she'd be able to spot the place where Bonnie had hit the deer. To hit something with such force that you could watch its life fade away – it was hard even to comprehend. Certainly, it wasn't something to get over easily.

Bonnie stirred. As if beckoned by a silent voice, she turned her head and looked outside. "This is where it happened. Right there." She pointed to a spot on the road.

Meg slowed. She would never have noticed it on her own, but now she could see shards of colored headlight glass punctuating the asphalt like bloody exclamation points. She didn't know what to say, so just squeezed Bonnie's hand.

*   *   *

After Bonnie buzzed them into the nursing home and had moved slowly off to the nursing station, wincing with every step, Meg found the room number and silently opened the door. She entered, leaving it open just a crack, so that the hallway light illuminated the room enough to see. Shrouded under a thin blanket, Elizabeth's form in the bed was so slight that she could have been a child. She garbled nonsense syllables in her sleep. Speaking in tongues, Meg thought, smiling at how annoyed such a notion would make her.

She had no real business even being in here. To stay and pretend an emotional bond where none existed felt voyeuristic and hypocritical. She backed out as silently as she had entered. Leaning against the wall, she waited for Bonnie.

She'd closed her eyes. For how long, she wasn't sure, but now, she felt Bonnie touching her shoulder. Her face was troubled. "Didn't you want to go in?"

"I did already."

"Well, I guess we're done, then." Bonnie sounded upset. As she started to move away from the room, her steps were rapid and she held her shoulders as rigidly as a mannequin.

Meg held back a moment to offer up at a silent wish of peaceful passage to her grandmother. But she didn't dally more than a second, concerned about Bonnie. She caught up to her quickly. "What's wrong, Bon? Did they give you a problem inside?"

"No, it's all set. The order is signed. They'll pull the feeding tube tomorrow. After that, it won't be long, maybe a week or so." Her words were clipped, and she clamped her mouth shut once they were out of the locked unit.

Meg didn't know what she was so upset about, but she was worried Bonnie would aggravate her injuries. She pulled the exit door open and allowed Bonnie to walk through first. "So what *is* wrong, then?"

Bonnie sank down onto a bench – presumably the smoking bench for the employees. She winced at the contact."I'm just tired. I'm tired of the silences. I'm tired of not understanding. I don't understand Mother, I don't understand my sister, and I don't understand you."

Meg didn't understand how she got lumped into that group, but she doubted that arguing about it was going to get her anywhere. She sat down beside her. "What do you want to know?"

"What did your grandmother do to you to make you hate her so much?"

"I don't hate her, Bon. I don't feel anything for her. I barely know her. I've seen her maybe all of five times in my whole life." Meg hoped she didn't sound too heartless, but she couldn't lie to Bonnie. Her mother needed the truth tempered, euphemisms uttered, in order to accept unpleasant realities–"I'm only dropping out until I figure out what I want to do with my life;" "I just fell asleep on his couch last night; nothing happened." Bonnie had always been able to listen to the truth, though.

Now, though, she only looked sad. "Why? How can you not have had any relationship with her?"

"I don't know. I mean, there is the religion angle. I think the last time I saw her as a kid, she'd come to dinner, and after grace, she started arguing that God was just a myth, that we were alone in the world. She and Mom got into this huge fight over it. I wasn't there for most of it, because Dad took me on a walk to get away from them. But there's something else between Grandmother and Mom, some weird dynamic I never figured out. *You* were there. Why should *I* know what happened between Mom and Grandmother any better than you?"

Bonnie smiled bitterly. "And yet... did I not mention this was a family of silences?" She stared at the ground for a long time.

Meg swung her legs vigorously under the bench. She felt horrible that she'd let Bonnie down, even though she didn't know how she could have done anything differently. "Are you really upset with me?" she asked finally.

"I just feel so alone. And I'm so tired. I feel like I'm the only one who loves her, although God knows, eighty percent of the time I don't actually *like* her. It's been so hard, and I don't have anyone to share this with."

"But it'll be over with soon." Meg put her arm around Bonnie, notwithstanding her sore ribs.

*   *   *

Carla had called in sick today. Her message had said something about stomach flu, but Meg knew that was code for evil hangover. Cleaning the windows in front of the store, Meg was feeling fairly lethargic herself. She and Bonnie had not gotten back home until after midnight; the kids were asleep, although Jane's reading lamp was still on. Even though Meg was exhausted, she had tossed and turned on the couch, thinking about feeling like a stranger with Elizabeth. Her thoughts tumbled into each other, clumsy drunkards. *Do I bear some responsibility for not having any sort of relationship with*

Grandmother? Could I have tried harder? Did I split from her in the same way I've broken up with boyfriends? By calling Elizabeth a stranger, by leaving Brady during a time when he was so vulnerable, was Meg consigning her future to follow her grandmother's? Would she end up bitter and alone?

The sun rose a degree, peeking above the store rooftops across the street and casting a harsh glare on the newly-cleaned glass. Meg shielded her eyes. She noticed Mona on the sidewalk, heading in her direction. She stifled the urge to duck back into the corner behind the mannequins.

The bell tinkled, the door opened, and in walked Mona. She stood on the welcome mat with an air of expectancy.

Meg didn't know what she was waiting for – she had to have seen her in the window already. She scrambled to her feet. "Mona. Welcome to my humble place of work."

Mona scanned the racks with a dismissive air, as if she were noting every loose thread, every puckered hem on these cast-asides. "You have an eclectic mix."

"I like to think so. Is it to your taste?"

"No, I'm afraid not." The two women maintained neutral gazes. Was Mona trying to assert a power play already? There was no way Meg was going to let her win a staring contest. She hadn't been the champion at Camp Winot for nothi – Meg blinked first. Damn.

"I'm assuming you're not simply here for a new outfit."

Mona nodded. "May we walk a bit?"

Meg eyed her warily. Whatever was on her agenda, Meg didn't see why she needed to be cooperative. She was still ticked off that Mona had helped Brady make his plans and not suggested that he might include his fiancée. "The store's empty, Mona. Why don't we just stay here?"

"I'd rather walk. You don't know whether you might get a customer, and I need to stop by the florist's, anyway." She added, as if she'd just considered it for the first time. "You're by yourself here. Are you allowed to leave?"

Meg bit back at least three sarcastic comments she could make. "If it's only for a few minutes."

The florist's was only a couple storefronts away. Mona requested to see the manager. Although Meg was standing right next to her as the tiny salesgirl stepped away from the counter to go into the back office, Mona said not a word to her. Meg might as well have been her personal assistant or valet. Actually, *they* probably would've warranted more of her attention.

Meg watched the clock on the wall tick away a full two minutes, with no sign of the salesgirl or manager, and still Mona waited at attention without speaking or acknowledging Meg's presence at all. This was absurd. Why was she even here? "I really can't take a lot of time, Mona."

As she said this, the manager finally stepped out to the counter. Mona held up her index finger towards Meg, gesturing her to keep silent. "I need to speak to you about the disturbing trend of the last several weeks. My flower delivery has either been late or the flowers themselves have been subpar to the extent that I couldn't exhibit them in my home. Last week, the blooms were visibly wilted even before I took them out of the box."

Her tone was that of a school vice principal chastising a perpetually tardy student. Meg wondered if her own presence as witness was intentional, a little extra humiliation for the florist. The manager shuffled back into his office to retrieve his receipt book, muttering under his breath, and Mona pivoted to face Meg. "Now. How long are you planning on punishing Brady? The wedding is coming up quickly, you know."

Meg's mouth fell open as she groped for words that wouldn't surface. Punishing Brady? She made it sound so trivial, like Meg was training a dog, for God's sake.

Mona gazed at her with eyebrows raised and an expectant expression.

"Did he ask you to come here? I don't know what Brady has told you, Mona, but I'm finished. This ... " Meg gestured helplessly with her hands, " ... is done."

"I see." Mona's expression did not change one iota. She might as well have just told her the temperature.

The florist came out to the counter. Mona turned her back to Meg to complete her business with him. No "excuse me," no niceties.

Just a turning away as if Meg were nothing. She stifled a growl. But she stayed where she was. They were going to finish this, by God.

A large refund later, Mona was done. When they reached the store, Meg turned to unlock the door. Mona strode several feet past. She turned her head and pulled her sunglasses down, gazing at Meg over the bridge. "Please?"

"Mona, this is a business. I can't just pick up and go whenever I want." The woman's nerve was Olympian.

"I understand. I will buy something from the shop if you wish, or compensate you for your time. But I don't want to be interrupted by customers. Please?"

Meg didn't bother to stifle the groan this time. She re-locked the door. This time of day was always quiet anyway. The pace didn't pick up until lunch. "You have five minutes. No more."

She padded five paces behind Mona like a lap dog. Finding an empty, clean bench overlooking the falls, Mona perched delicately on the end. Meg remained standing, shifting her weight from one foot to the other.

Mona sighed and rose from the bench, as graceful as a dancer. She moved over the fence overlooking the falls. "Incidentally, Brady did not ask me to come. He has no idea I'm here, and would probably be mortified if he knew." She paused. "I know this summer has been hard on you."

Although Mona was looking at the rapids rushing over the rocks, Meg supposed she was talking to her. Meg replied, "It's been hard on everyone."

"Brady misses you. I can tell."

Meg shrugged. She didn't want to hear about Brady, didn't want to consider what he might or might not be going through. She wanted to know what exactly Mona wanted, so that she could refuse her and go back to work.

Mona hesitated, then said brusquely, "Is there anything that would make you reconsider this unfortunate ending?"

"Like what?" Meg's voice rose slightly. She tried to sound less emotional, not wanting this woman to see her so vulnerable. "Why should you even care, Mona? I would think you'd be thrilled not to have this wedding happen."

Mona turned to face her. Her eyes were clear and cold. "Oh, dear. Believe me, Meg, if I hadn't wanted this wedding to take place, or Brady to marry you, it would never have gotten this far."

She drew back, surprised. "But you don't like me."

Mona flipped her hand as if to shoo away such an irrelevancy. "That's neither here nor there. What is more important is that I do not dislike you. And more important still, in my eyes, is that I respect you. You're strong, and you will be good for Brady. "

Meg wanted to cry out in frustration. "But I don't want to be good for him. I'm not applying to be his teacher or therapist. I want to be his wife."

"Ah, good. So there is hope." Mona smiled, with teeth this time.

Meg felt a little uneasy about that. "I need to get back now."

She pushed herself off the fence and began striding, almost jogging, out of the park. Let Mona struggle to keep up in her little Ferragamo pumps. That smile, with its perfectly spaced pearls, signified success. Mona thought she had triumphed over her somehow. But Meg would not let that happen. There was so much she wanted to know – was Brady back at his parents' house now? Had he changed his mind about the job? Was he mad at Meg, or did he regret what he'd done? She dared not ask these questions, though, knowing that certain answers could doom the uncertain future she seemed to once again be contemplating. No. She wouldn't put herself in this position again, would not let herself get hurt by this family.

Meg was gone, and she wasn't looking back.

~ 22 ~
JANE

Jane arrived at Charley's sporting her school backpack over her shoulder. Pam eyed the new addition to her ensemble. "Getting started on your summer reading list?"

She blushed. "I stopped at the library yesterday and picked up some books that I thought Charley and I could read."

"That sounds nice. It's sweet that you're thinking about Charley even when you're not here."

Jane concentrated on picking at the corners on her fingernails. It made her nervous when Pam complimented her, as if there were some hidden "but... " statement coming that would negate the whole item of praise.

Pam started out the door, then stopped. "Remind me when I get home tonight to talk to you about maybe continuing your job through the school year."

Jane nodded thoughtfully, hiding the grin that fought to take over her face.

"It would take some scheduling on everyone's part," Pam continued, "but if you want to, we might be able to work it out." She kissed Charley again, who gazed at her neutrally, and left.

"That'd be so awesome, Chuck, wouldn't it?" Jane helped him up to the table, moved the day's newspaper out of the way, and arranged his breakfast in a way that he'd eat it – orange juice at twelve o'clock, cereal at three, grapes at nine, all lined up in a row.

Man, it would be so cool to keep this job through the school year. That she had a job where she had responsibility, and even made money – well, it might be just enough to help her hit the bottom rung of cool once school started. She wouldn't have to worry anymore about coming up with an excuse for not going out for field hockey or drama: she could simply say, "Oh, I wish I could, but I need to get to my job." That'd show them.

Charley had clearly been done with his breakfast for a few minutes now, since he'd gotten hold of the salt shaker, and was pouring a thin stream of salt into piles all around his cereal bowl. Jane realized that she'd been ignoring him,

"Oh, Charley, no you don't. Give that to me, please!" She reached for the shaker, but he pulled it onto his lap, a tiny frown etched on his face.

"Pretty please?" She looked him right in the eye. Sometimes that worked. No dice.

Jane got down from the table and grabbed one of his cars. "Wanna trade?"

Apparently satisfied that he had a good deal, Charley handed her the salt shaker and snatched his car from her outstretched hand. As she retrieved the hard-shelled toy suitcase containing his other cars, Jane patted herself on the back. See? She knew this kid. How many other people would have known to trade him something rather than try to force the salt shaker out of his hand? This way, there was no tantrum, Charley had a toy, Jane had the salt shaker, and everyone was happy.

While Charley was lining up his cars in the living room, she unzipped her backpack. She hadn't been lying to Pam – she had in fact gotten some books for Charley at the library – but she hadn't been completely truthful, either. She didn't want anyone laughing at her, and until she'd had some practice, it was just going to have to be a secret.

She gazed at the cover of the plastic case. *Italian for Beginners.* Staring up at her was a photograph of this beautiful landscape at sunset, rolling hills and tall, slender trees sloping skyward. The case held six cassettes, and the liner notes promised that by the end of the last tape, you could travel with ease throughout Italy.

The idea had come to Jane only just recently. She had been counting the money she'd earned so far in her room. Normally, she just stuffed the week's fifty dollars into the twirly ballerina jewelry box that she'd had forever and never filled with a single piece of jewelry. But as July rolled to an end, the box started to resist closing from the thickness of the roll. She counted it. She'd made almost four hundred dollars!

She was staggered at the amount. You could do practically anything with that amount of money. She could buy a bike, or in a couple years, if she saved some more money, a car. Actually, now that she thought about it, she wanted to travel, yes, but farther than a bike or car could go. Ever since her mom had told her about almost going to Italy, she had wondered what it would be like to visit there, wander through the cobblestone streets and alleys like you belonged, eating nothing but pizza and gelato.

And maybe, just maybe, if she saved up enough money, she could present the idea to Mom as a family vacation. Mom had been so sad about Grams. It would be nice to give her something to look forward to.

But first, Jane wanted to learn Italian. Her school didn't offer it – Jane was going to be stuck taking Spanish with Señor Schmidt this year – and even if they did, it would take too long to learn much besides the numbers from one to ten. So *Italian for Beginners* it was.

Charley looked like he was nearing the end of his cars routine. Instead of lining them up, he was just sitting there looking at the line, swaying his head as if he were listening to some song in his head. Jane wondered if he remembered the orange REM song.

She pulled him up off the floor with a gentle tug of his hands. Together, they climbed onto the couch, and Jane pulled out the library books. The picture book about the dog didn't do anything for him. He didn't even look at the pictures. She had to put her hand over his to get him to turn the pages. But he really liked the alphabet book that had all the photographs of fire trucks and other vehicles. "A is for ambulance," Jane read. Well, that was a gimme. She wanted to see what they had found for "x."

After lunch, Charley wandered back to his room. Jane carried his plate with the half-eaten sandwich back to the kitchen, wondering what he was doing. He didn't usually play in his room after lunch. When she checked on him, he had pulled out his bus schedules and was combing through them.

"I've got to finish cleaning up the kitchen, Charley. Are you good in here for a few minutes?" Charley didn't answer, but scooted back onto his bed with his leaflets.

On her way back to the kitchen, her backpack, its zipper open, beckoned her to Italy. She hadn't had a chance to listen to any of the tapes yet, and she was dying to learn a phrase, anything, so that she could say with truth that she knew a little Italian.

She looked backward toward Charley's room. Maybe she could listen to the tapes just for five minutes while she finished cleaning up the kitchen. Jane retrieved her Walkman from the backpack, reverently placed Tape One in the player, and fitted the earphones to her head.

Wow. It was so beautiful. Even a comment like "I need help"– "Ho bisogno d'aiuto" – sounded like water drops hitting a fountain pool.

Jane looked down the hall. There was no sign of Charley. It might be nice to sweep and mop Pam's floor for her, and listen to more of the tape at the same time.

The tape spooled to an end, and the Walkman clicked off. She couldn't believe he was still reading those leaflets. She put the mop and broom away and ambled down the hall. "Charley, let's get some exercise, what d'ya say?"

His bedroom was empty. What the heck? Jane peeked in the bathroom, even though the door was open. No Charley.

"Chuck! Come out now!"

The closet. Of course. She should've looked there in the first place. She went back in Charley's bedroom and slid open the closet door. Still nothing.

Jane's neck and cheeks started to burn. He had to be in the house somewhere. God, she couldn't even get him to go for a walk outside. So where the hell was he?

Racing through the house, Jane checked all the closets and behind any piece of furniture large enough to house a small boy, yelling his name with increasing anxiety. If he were hiding, she'd kill him for scaring her like this.

Please, God, let him be hiding.

Pacing to the phone and back – should she call Pam, or should she continue looking for Charley? – Jane noticed the newspaper she'd folded up earlier was on the floor of the living room. Why was he looking at the paper? Kneeling down, she scanned the wrinkled open page, and when she saw the giant ad for the Stop-n-Shop, she knew what he had done as clearly as if he had spoken the words.

"Oh, crap," she moaned.

Jane raced out of the house and down the sidewalk to the bus stop. There was no sign of him anywhere."Double crap!"

She sprinted back to the house. She reached for the phone, then clenched her hand into a fist. She knew she had to call Pam. But to take that step made the situation real. It wasn't just her own screw-up anymore, something she could use as proof of her worthlessness in private: it was Charley's safety now, too. She swiped the wet off her cheek and dialed Pam's number.

She hadn't even gotten beyond the standard office greeting when Jane interrupted her. "I did something really bad, Pam. You have to come home now."

Pam's voice was rushed, worried. "What's wrong, Jane?"

She could barely get the words out. "Charley's gone."

"What do you mean he's gone?"

"I think he's gone to the *Food Frenzy* taping."

"Oh, dear Lord. Wait for me on the sidewalk. I'll be right home."

Time slowed during the minutes it took Pam to arrive. It was worse than waiting for the bell to ring at the end of algebra on test day. A police car raced by the house, lights swirling.

"Oh God," Jane whispered. "Please let him be okay, God. Please." She kept up this incantation until she saw Pam's Chevette screech to a halt in front of her.

Running around to the passenger side, Jane got in the car as fast as she could. As she buckled her seat belt, she was afraid to look at Pam or say anything. But she had to look, at least out of the corner of her eye. It was like picking at a scab; she knew it was going to do her no good, but so be it.

Pam kept her eyes on the road. Her face was hard as granite, and except for a constant chewing of her lips, she made no movement.

Finally she spoke. "You're sure about this?"

"I don't know what else it could be." Jane's voice quavered as she spoke.

"How did he even know about the taping?"

"I don't know. There was an ad in the paper, but I swear I didn't show it to him."

"Right." Pam took a deep breath and started biting her lip again. "I don't understand, even if Charley knew about the taping, how he got out without you noticing."

Jane bit her fingernail. It chipped at the corner and she peeled it off, drawing blood. She sucked on the finger, trying to hide the damage.

"Jane?" Pam sounded more pissed.

In a verbal rush, Jane exploded. "Look, I know I screwed up. I was listening to a tape on my Walkman, and I thought he was okay in his room, he was looking at his bus schedules like he does lots of times, and I swear I thought he was okay. I never, never would've listened to anything if I thought this would've happened -"

"No more."

The shortness of Pam's tone sucked Jane's breath right out of her. It hit her, really, for the first time, that Charley could be seriously damaged by this. And it was her fault. She balled her hands into fists and ground them into the car seat. She would not cry. She would not cry.

Jane could see the grocery store as they reached the intersection to the shopping plaza. A huge banner draped itself across the sliding doors, and an arch of balloons strained skyward. For once, no stray shopping carts loitered in the parking lot.

She felt like her stomach might actually rip, she was so tense. She tried to focus on the store's entrance as they turned into the plaza to see if she could spot Charley anywhere. Then she saw the metro bus, partially obscured by the bank on the corner lot. Pam swerved the car in the direction of the bus.

A crowd of people milled around the bus, all staring toward the windows. Pam threw open the car door as soon as she parked, grabbed her jacket, and sprinted toward the crowd, not even bothering to slam the door shut.

Jane's legs felt like they were made of Jello, and she wished she had something to hold onto. And why had Pam grabbed her jacket? It was August, for Pete's sake. She was surprised Pam's mind wouldn't be totally on Charley at this point.

As she caught up, Pam was wildly gesturing to a very pissed-off looking bus driver. They were standing in front of the bus doors, and he was pointing at the bus and shouting, although Jane was still too far away to hear what he was saying over the buzz of the rubberneckers.

"Were you on the bus?" she asked one of the onlookers, a young woman wearing a blue sundress.

The girl answered without turning her head. "Yeah. That kid is seriously disturbed, man. He scared the shit out of me."

Jane squeezed her eyes shut. If someone talked that way about her, she would want to die. Hearing someone talk that way about Charley was almost as bad. "What happened?"

"I was a couple seats behind him, and didn't notice him right away, so he must've been okay at the beginning of the ride. But then the bus hit a bump, and he started rocking and holding his hands over his ears."

Something worse had to have happened. Rocking might be a little weird, but not enough to stop a bus. "Then what?" she asked hesitantly. She saw Pam climbing onto the bus.

"Someone sat next to him – trying to help, I guess, y'know, trying to pull his hands off his ears so they could talk to him – and he starts yelling and flipping out. Throwing his head against the window, serious shit, you know?"

Jane closed her eyes. She wished she could keep them closed until this whole day disappeared. But when she closed her eyes, she saw him curled up into himself like a fist, trying to bash his brains out. She wished she could undo all the hurt done to Charley.

She approached the bus door as she would a roomful of spiders. Climbing up the first stair, she peered over the bar.

Pam was sitting cross-legged in the cramped aisle. She had Charley on her lap, her legs wrapped around his and her arms holding his arms immobile against his torso. She had thrown the jacket she had grabbed from the car over his head. He was bucking against his mother's restraints, bashing his head backward against her chest. She was going to have a wicked bruise. The oddest thing, though, was that Pam didn't look mad anymore, or even like she felt the beating that Charley was giving her. She looked like the picture of Mary holding the baby Jesus that was on the wall at Aunt Vivian's house. Light and love spilled from her skin as she whispered, "shhh, shhh," over and over and over.

So awed by watching Pam and the way she handled Charley, Jane almost forgot how worried she was. And Pam's magic was working; he was calming, taking longer breaks between fighting her grip. "Can I do anything?" she whispered.

"We're good," Pam's voice was calm, soothing. "Charley, Jane's here. She was worried about you."

Jane tiptoed down the aisle and knelt in front of them. She lifted a corner of the jacket so she could see Charley's face. His eyes were scrunched shut – Jane knew the feeling – but at least there was no blood or broken glass lying around.

"Hey, Charley, I'm so sorry -" Jane tried to say more, but found her voice couldn't say anything else. She lowered the jacket over his face again.

Pam continued holding Charley, his human rocking chair. "Why don't you go out and tell the bus driver we'll be out in a couple minutes?"

Jane nodded manically. Even if she couldn't help Charley, she'd do anything to try to undo the damage to her reputation with Pam. She jumped down the last step onto the curb and ran over to the bus driver.

"Charley's mom says they'll be out in a minute."

The man glared at Jane. His nostrils flared, as big as a hippo's. He spoke."Yeah, well, the ambulance will be here soon, anyway. They can always sedate him if she's wrong and can't get him off the bus."

"She's not wrong! She's his mother."

"Some mother, letting a kid like that go off by himself. She's lucky I didn't call the cops."

Jane opened her mouth to say something in Pam's defense, then shut it again. She didn't want this guy blaming Pam, but she didn't feel like advertising how stupid she'd been, either.

As she tried to figure out what to say, she saw them emerge from the bus, Pam carrying Charley in her arms like he was two. The crowd erupted into applause. Charley buried his head further into Pam's chest. She shook her head angrily at all the people.

They bundled Charley into the car. As Jane climbed into the front seat, she noticed that Pam had lost her loving Mary look.

"Is there anything you left at our house, Jane? Otherwise, I'll take you home now."

Jane had dreaded this moment, when there was nothing left to care of but lay out the penalty for her inattention. "I still need my backpack." She paused. "I guess I'm fired, huh?"

"Yeah."

Jane tried to apologize, but Pam cut her off. "I can't talk to you right now, Jane. I'm so angry that I – I just can't."

They continued the ride in silence. The solidity of the day's consequences hit Jane like a rock. But rather than trying to deflect it, she absorbed the impact, let her body take the hit, welcoming the numbing pain.

As she sat slumped, defeated, it occurred to her that Charley had never even seen the taping he'd gone to so much trouble to get to. He'd never even made it in the door.

-23-
BONNIE

Bonnie had taken a mental health day off from work, and had been hoping that puttering around the house might help her feel like the world was falling back into its orbit. So this white envelope with its return stamp bearing the mark "Public Records" was not what she wanted to see today.

Still, she couldn't bring herself to file the letter away for a better time. The contents of this envelope held at least part of the answer to the question of the mysterious Pete. Maybe it would be enough to loosen Vivian's tongue.

Before she could tear open the flap, though, Jane came racing into the house like a blur, ran into her room and slammed the door. Bonnie couldn't imagine what could've happened at Charley's to upset her to such a degree. She laid down the envelope on the corner of the table and knocked on Jane's door.

"I don't want to talk about it!" Her voice sounded ragged, clogged with tears.

Bonnie opened the door an inch. "I'm coming in anyway. Talk or don't talk, either's okay." Such hysteria was extreme, even for Jane. What more bad news could the week bring?

Jane was folded up on her bed. Her knees were drawn into her chest and she swaddled herself with her arms, head bowed. She looked like one of those mimosa plants Bonnie had seen, whose leaves fold in upon themselves at the slightest touch from an outsider or any other kind of stress. She scooted onto the bed so she was right next to her. "Are you okay?"

Jane's fragile composure collapsed. She leaned into Bonnie and sobbed. Alarmed, she wrapped her arms around her, tried to stabilize her heaving body. Jane never cried like this. For the last several years, the only times she had seen her cry at all were when she was frustrated – with story problems she couldn't solve, with unrepentant pestering from Davey, when she couldn't talk Bonnie into letting Joe move back home. But these weren't frustration tears.

Jane was trying to say something now, but she couldn't get the words out between the sobs.

"Honey, breathe. Don't talk yet, just breathe." Bonnie spooned her daughter to her chest and inhaled deeply, then exhaled with an audible "ssh," as if she could imprint her breaths onto Jane. She was gratified to see her breathing even out, and slow. "Now, what happened?"

"I got fired. I can't ever see Charley again." She began to cry again.

Bonnie stroked her hair. "Tell me what happened."

As Jane told her about the day's events, Bonnie could imagine herself as Pam and Jane, feel the blinding panic both of them must have experienced.

Here on the bed, Jane's lashes shimmered with nascent tears. "Mommy, could you talk to Pam for me?"

Bonnie would've done anything to keep that sense of benevolent omnipotence, the implication that she could make all things okay – she hadn't felt that from Jane in probably six or seven years. But she doubted her abilities in this case. "I could, but what would you want me to say?"

"Tell her I'd never do anything to hurt Charley. See if there's anything I can do to make it up?"

"Oh, honey." Bonnie cradled her. "You can't make it up. I know it was an accident, and I know you're hurting, but –"

"But Charley's hurt worse, and it's my fault. He was getting better, and now he's worse again." Jane hung her head, her face hidden behind a waterfall of hair.

"I don't know that autism works that way, Jane." Bonnie kissed Jane's forehead. "But I'm sorry you're hurting. I wish I could fix this for you, honey."

Jane snuffled and nodded, looking thoroughly miserable.

She climbed off the bed and quietly left Jane to her thoughts. Back in the kitchen, she rubbed her eyes. It was so hard growing up. She pulled out a mixing bowl and automatically gathered sugar, flour, vanilla, eggs and chocolate.

The batter in the oven filled the room with the rich, deep smell of dark chocolate. Bonnie turned her attention back to the envelope. She carefully ripped the envelope at the seam. Inside was a copy of a birth certificate.

Bonnie scrutinized the name for any particle of familiarity: Peter Jonas MacKenzie. Nothing. She had never seen nor heard this name. But here were her parents' names listed. And the birth date: September 16, 1951. He had been born seven years before her, almost to the day. So what had happened to him?

She felt like stuffing the document back in the envelope, pretending she'd never opened it. Now that she knew he actually existed, she was not at all sure she was ready to hear the rest of the story. And yet, a part of her couldn't let it go.

She couldn't believe Vivian had never said anything about a brother. She was only a year older than he. Where was he? Was he dead? Had he been given up for adoption? If so, why? Was something wrong with him? Bonnie was seized with a sudden hope that maybe Pete was out there somewhere. Maybe she could find an adoption registry somewhere, look for her brother, save some part of her family.

Pictures. Maybe a picture of Pete existed someplace. Bonnie remembered old photo albums when she was a kid, with brittle charcoal pages, and photographs of her parents before the war, held in place by confetti-shaped corner tabs. Where had they gone? When they'd moved Elizabeth out of her ancient house and into the nursing home, she didn't recall having seen the albums. Of course, that had not been her focus at the time. Getting Elizabeth settled in her room and calmed enough to unpack, trying to keep her from running down the corridor like a sparrow trapped in a living room – that had been her focus. Anything that hadn't fit in her new "apartment" had gone into storage, packed and moved by a bunch of beefy college boys. She supposed the albums must be in the unit.

She put her head in her hands. How could she have been so stupid? She should've been raiding the storage unit this whole summer, taking pieces in to Elizabeth to provide a connection to home, spark memories.

Maybe she could find the photos today before heading out to the nursing home. Maybe it wasn't too late. In the week and a half since the feeding tube had been removed, Elizabeth had lost interest in nearly everything. Even when she was awake, she looked at Bonnie with indifference. It hurt so much to watch her mother die, a physical ache, like part of Bonnie was dying as well.

She'd thought maybe she could share this with Vivian. When she had called to tell her about the DNR order and her accident, Vivian had not ranted as she'd feared. She'd sounded gentle, and told Bonnie that what had to be done was done, and that she'd keep praying for them. But when Bonnie asked if Vivian would come to the nursing home with her, Vivian said no in a sad, broken voice and then she had hung up.

So Bonnie was in this alone. But maybe, if she was able to show Elizabeth some pictures from her past, it might wake her up a little. Maybe even ease her transition into death.

Jane wandered out of her room, her eyes pink-rimmed and swollen. "Do I smell brownies?" she asked with a tinge of her normal self in her voice.

Bonnie nodded. "I'm about to take them out. After I do, I thought I'd go over to the storage place where we put all your grandmother's things. I'm looking for photo albums. Wanna come?"

Jane hesitated.

"I could really use your help." She hoped Jane would say yes. It might be a way to keep her from obsessing over Charley.

She shrugged. "I guess so."

A few minutes later, as Jane was trying the first warm brownie, the phone rang. Bonnie froze, momentarily afraid to answer it. Like some twisted lottery, any phone call could be the one that would both relieve the waiting and renew her grief.

Davey's sweet voice was on the other end. "Just checking in," he said. "Brian's parents said I can go to the batting cages and spend the night, if it's okay with you."

After talking with Brian's mother and making sure Davey hadn't imposed himself on their household, Bonnie hung up the phone. She turned to Jane. "It's you and me, kid."

Jane didn't look pleased, but neither did she look unhappy about it.

*   *   *

Bonnie unlocked the padlock and began hoisting up the door to the storage unit. The unit was mashed with furniture and cardboard banker's boxes seven feet high. Bonnie groaned. In a less stressful time, she might have found the sheer volume of the chaos inviting, like wandering through an antique store. But now, it just felt overwhelming and disorganized. She'd forgotten how many possessions her mother had been forced to leave behind. She began wedging her way through cramped columns of space. "God, I hope this stuff is labeled," she muttered.

Jane was being no help, standing at the door, staring at the stacks of boxes over her head.

"Honey, we'll be here all day if you don't start looking. Start pawing through boxes. Look for any kind of photo albums or boxes of photos."

Jane heaved a theatrical sign. Shoulders slumped, she moved deeper into the unit.

She began pulling down boxes and rifling through the contents. There were a few books, mostly presidential biographies, and about ten years' worth of old *LIFE* magazines. Another box held a partial set of Correlle dishes and three booklets filled with S&H Green Stamps. Bonnie remembered going to the A&P with her mother the day they redeemed the stamps for the cheap china, and how Elizabeth had dressed as if she were going to a business interview. As if her clothes could disguise the truth of their economic standing.

She didn't have time to get lost in the memories the boxes held. Annoyed at herself, Bonnie knew she could have – should have – come here long ago to sort and inventory Elizabeth's belongings. Maybe if she'd done it earlier, she could have found insights into her mother's brain from the material possessions she'd amassed. Maybe the boxes could have helped her decipher which stories were truth and which were dementia-induced fiction. But it was too late. Now, all Bonnie felt was impatience to find what she had come for and close the door on this place for good.

"Mom, I found something!" Jane's voice was muffled through wood and cardboard. Bonnie wove her way back to the doorway, where Jane sat on her knees, with an open box in front of her.

She wiped a cobweb off her sleeve and knelt to give Jane a hug. "You have a keen eagle eye, my dear." Jane gave her mother a look that clearly said she could save the praise. Bonnie ignored the look, secretly pleased to have Jane reverting back to more normal behavior.

Settling onto the floor beside Jane, with her back cooled by the concrete wall, Bonnie took the photo album out of the box. The cover was warped and faded, cool to the touch.

"I didn't think Grams would be much of a photo junkie," Jane said.

"As far as I know, she wasn't. I can probably count on the fingers of one hand the times I remember a picture being taken. I doubt there's even a camera in these boxes."

Jane peered at the unopened album on Bonnie's lap. "So who's in there?"

Bonnie opened the album to the first page. A sepia-tinted photo of a serious man and woman stared out at them. Clearly a professional portrait, the woman was seated on a wooden chair with a curled back; her hair was carefully coiffed into an upsweep, and a cameo graced her long neck. She had a severe looking expression, and shadows filled the hollows in her cheeks. If she were twenty pounds heavier, with some softness around her sharp edges, she would have been an attractive woman. The man stood behind her, his hand on her shoulder. He wore bifocals, and the pronounced hook to his nose reminded Bonnie of a craggy mountain crest. The two were dressed formally, although the man's collar stays were frayed, and his wife's print dress was faded.

Jane sounded awed. "Geez, was that Grams?"

"No, the picture's too old. I would bet that those are your great-grandparents." Bonnie traced the stern faces lightly, as if trying to massage them into giving her a smile.

"Didn't you ever meet them?" Jane looked at her incredulously.

"No. Your Grams was pretty old when she had me. Her parents had died several years before."

"They look pretty mean. Maybe Grams got it from them."

Bonnie smiled. "Maybe."

They turned the page to a couple more candid photos of the same couple with a young girl. In one, the girl – probably six or seven – was standing next to an automobile. Even at this young age, the girl held herself erect, like a poster child for exemplary posture. Her eyes possessed a depth that made her appear much older. "That's Grams," Bonnie said.

"She looks like me!" Jane said, surprise in her voice.

She examined the photo more closely. "Yeah, you're right. I think it's in the jawline. I don't think I've seen this picture since you were born."

Jane peered at her. "Don't take this the wrong way, Mom, but I'm not sure I want to look like Grams. Looking alike might mean we're alike in other ways, too."

Bonnie sighed. She understood how she felt, but somebody still had to defend Elizabeth. "I don't know, Jane. I think it's okay if you're like Grams in some ways. The way you tell people what's on your mind reminds me of her, and I think that's a good thing. Her good parts are just overshadowed by the other stuff."

Jane squeezed her. "I'm sorry about Grams, Mom."

Bonnie squeezed back. "I'm sorry, too."

She sniffled and flipped over the album page. Here was a shot of Elizabeth standing tall, looking proud in front of an ivy-trellised, Doric-columned structure. She was clutching several books to her chest. Unlike the women in the background of the photo, she was wearing long, wide-legged trousers in the style of Katherine Hepburn. Bonnie couldn't help but inhale – she'd never seen her mother this happy, eyes blazing, lips pursed in a take-no-prisoners smirk. She was stunning.

"Whoa," Jane breathed. "She looks like she could take over the world. Where was this, do you know?"

"I think this might've been where Mother went to college." Bonnie briefly flashed back to the conversation with not-Eleanor and Elizabeth, where she'd talked about her dreams of becoming someone important. She wondered if Elizabeth's friend, Camilla, had been the photographer of this shot.

As Bonnie shifted to accommodate her aching behind, she caught a glimpse of her watch. "Damn. I meant to have us gone by now. I don't want to get to the nursing home too late." She began flipping through the pages more quickly, looking for baby pictures. There was nothing. No Pete. There weren't even any pictures of Vivian, who as first-born, would have been most likely to have been photographed.

Jane gripped Bonnie's forearm. Her eyes were wide with alarm. "You didn't tell me we were going to the nursing home."

"What did you think we were going to do with these pictures?"

"Do I have to see her?" Jane looked close to tears.

Bonnie leaned close to Jane, her voice soft. "I'm sorry, honey. I wasn't thinking. No, you don't have to see her. You can wait in the lobby, or the residents' lounge, or even the car, if you want. It's okay."

Jane nodded, biting her lips as if that could somehow stop tears.

*   *   *

As they reached the nursing home, an ambulance was idling in the circular drive. Bonnie's brain registered that it could be for any one of the residents. But her gut told her something else. "Oh, God," she whispered, unaware that she'd spoken aloud.

"Mom?" Jane's voice, small and afraid, startled her. Bonnie swung the car into a parking space, not caring whether it was centered or whether the car ate up a space and a half. Quickly glancing at Jane, she said, "Stay here. I'll be back as soon as I can." She threw open the car door and sprinted for the entrance.

Rodney stopped her as soon as she set foot in the door.

"Is it my mother?" Bonnie demanded.

"Ms. Stanton, maybe you want to sit down for a second. I'll tell the nurse you're here."

He guided her gently onto an upholstered loveseat, then walked away for a moment and said something in tones too low to hear to the person behind the desk. He came back and sat beside her.

A nurse strode out into the lobby and pulled up a chair next to Bonnie. "I'm so sorry, Ms. Stanton. Your mother passed about twenty minutes ago. We tried to call you but you must have been on your way here already–"

She spoke more sentences, but the buzzing in Bonnie's head drowned out the sound of her voice. She was aware of nodding, of looking like she understood what was being said to her, but the buzzing got louder and louder until she had to wrap her arms around her head.

Bonnie didn't know how long she stayed like that – it could have been minutes, maybe less – but she brought her arms back down to her sides only when Jane's voice penetrated the drone surrounding her head. "Mom? Mom. Mommy. You're scaring me."

She opened her eyes. Jane's face was tear-streaked and pinched with worry. She realized Rodney had his hand on her shoulder.

"Do you feel like a sedative might help? It's mild, but you'd have to call someone for a ride."

She shook her head slowly. She needed to be able to feel, couldn't have it tamped down. Her mother was dead. She was free of her at last. As a child, Elizabeth had criticized her B grades, her lack of any semblance of school spirit, her dowdy braids. As much as she'd been in love with Joe when they married, an equal part of her was passionate with the idea of escaping Elizabeth.

But there was no way, really, to hide. However Elizabeth had raised her, she had a sense of duty, the need to be a good daughter, and that overshadowed the desire to cut out her mother like a tumor. And then the Alzheimer's. Family just shouldn't leave each other. Even if they couldn't stand one another. Even if her mother continued to act as if every ill – from the shabby state of her room to her deteriorating memory – were Bonnie's fault. Maybe Bonnie's commitment was a symptom of her never-ending quest for approval, as Vivian hypothesized, but to her, it still felt like love. How would she explain this to anyone, the contradictions of her feelings, love and resentment and relief and rage all balled up together? How could she begin to contain the gaping loss? She didn't know how to begin.

And yet, here was this child – her child – facing the loss of her grandmother as well as a job that had clearly meant the world to her. If ever there were a time that Jane, who tried so hard to need no one, needed her mother, today was that day. And Bonnie knew she could provide for that need in a way that Elizabeth had never been able to. So she gathered Jane to her, held her head close to her own heart. And uttered a silent prayer of thanks that the suffering was over.

-24-
MEG

Meg needed an escape from her parents now, badly. She realized this was not a helpful response. But she acknowledged it; that ought to be worth something. Bonnie had switched into organized arrangements mode, and seemed to be postponing her grief, or any feeling at all, until after the funeral. Her own mother, on the other hand, had been decimated by the news. Meg's arrival at her parents' house earlier that day had been met by her mother's frequent tears: some silent and graceful, others punctuated with loud, gulping sobs.

Preparing a cup of tea, Meg suppressed an urge to roll her eyes at the theatricality of Vivian's hysteria. For whose benefit was she performing? After all, her mom hadn't had contact with Elizabeth, but for the hospital, in years. She walked into her room, trying to keep perfect posture so as not to spill the Earl Grey. With one look at her mother, who was curled up on her bed, quietly keening, Meg changed her mind, feeling chagrined to have been so cynical five minutes earlier.

Vivian acknowledged her offering of tea with a grateful smile, swiping a tissue over her tear tracks. She seemed embarrassed. "I really did not think this was going to hit me like this."

"Do you want to talk about it?" She hoped her mother would decline the invitation. While she wanted to be there for her, and was willing to listen if she really had to, the enormity of emotion in the room left Meg acutely uncomfortable. The humid air itself seemed to be barely holding in its tears.

Vivian looked up at the ceiling. "I know what you must be thinking," she said softly. "That it's insane for me to be this upset about her." She took a tissue and dabbed her eyes. Meg sat down on the edge of the bed, waiting for her mother to resume.

Vivian shook her head, her eyes welling up. "And I can't really figure it out myself. But the thought that keeps coming into my head is that I haven't really had a mom for more than twenty years. I miss having a mom – and now, it's forever." She quietly sobbed, as Meg held her hand while the tea grew cold. Eventually, her father relieved her of this duty, granting her absolution, and told her to go find something mindless to do for a little while.

* * *

The best place Meg could think of in which to lose herself was the library. She leafed through the New Fiction choices that the librarians had set out, noticing how many titles of the featured books had some mention of death in the them. She wondered if it was always this way, or if she was just being sensitive at the moment. She wasn't going to let herself wallow in guilt for not feeling more grief-stricken for this near-stranger. At the same time, however, she felt cheated and a little pissed, although she was having trouble figuring out the origins of those feelings. She'd been feeling a low-grade achy guilt since Bonnie had blown up with her at the nursing home. Bonnie was right; she should have done more while Elizabeth was alive to initiate some sort of relationship. She should not have been so influenced by her mother's estrangement. But dammit, what the hell kind of grandmother doesn't try to get to know her own grandkid? And if she did try, well, she should have tried harder. Because it was obviously too late to fix anything now.

It was time to distract herself, immerse herself in someone else's woes for a while. She found a few novels that sparked her interest, reading the jacket covers to find stories whose families made her own family's dysfunction seem that much less significant.

From the corner of her eye, Meg spied a man reading, nestled in a shabby upholstered chair in the corner. It was hard to tell from this angle, but he resembled Brady. As she looked more directly, she backed into the stacks with a thud, and he looked up. Meg waved awkwardly.

Brady stood and began ambling over in her direction. Shit. What were her options? His limp was barely noticeable anymore. It would be rude to leave, obviously. She couldn't very well pretend she hadn't seen him. Pity. Her only real choice was to talk to him, exactly what she did not want to do.

"You haven't returned my calls." Brady leaned against the edge of a table, his face quizzical.

Her temper rose. Nice way to start a conversation, putting her on the defensive. "What are you doing here?"

"Same thing you are. Looking at books. You haven't returned my calls." Brady's tone was light, but he wouldn't let her break their gaze.

"I know." Meg shifted from one foot to the other.

"Kind of makes it hard for a guy to apologize."

She clutched her book to her chest and checked her watch. "Fine. Apology accepted. Look, I need to check this out." She turned and took a step to walk away.

Brady grabbed her arm from behind. "Meg, come on. I need to talk to you." His voice was louder and more insistent now. The librarian glanced up at him with a raised eyebrow.

Meg whirled around. "Could you please not broadcast this to the world?"

He grinned. "I'll get louder unless you agree to have coffee with me right now. Go ahead. Call my bluff."

She saw a mischievous spark in his eyes that reminded her of when they had first begun dating, when he was likely to walk up to complete strangers and ask if they wanted to see him kiss the most beautiful girl on the street. It was mortifying but flattering all the same. "Oh, for God's sake. Fine. Let me check out these books and we'll go."

Meg fumbled for her library card. She didn't think seeing him would've affected her this way. She'd been doing pretty well this last week, at least up until the news about Elizabeth. Work was busy, and she'd begun reading a textbook on dress design through history. It took a lot of concentration, but she'd reached a point where she only needed to re-read a passage twice to get its point. This represented progress from a week ago, when she'd reach the end of a chapter and realize she didn't remember a word of it, that her thoughts had been running through how she might've acted differently, whether she and Brady could have worked it out somehow.

* * *

Safely ensconced inside the coffee shop, she sat with her hands wrapped around an oversized coffee mug. Pedestrians outside strode purposefully under their umbrellas; even in the best of weather, this wasn't the kind of neighborhood where you could just stroll and window shop. Brady said nothing, just smiled as he watched her sip her coffee. It was unnerving enough that she broke the silence." So why are you out this way? I thought you'd abandoned Monroe Heights."

"I'm packing up the apartment."

"Right." Meg drew this single syllable out over several seconds to let it contain all the words she wasn't going to say. The apartment that was supposed to have been her home as well, where they were supposed to have inaugurated their married lives. Nice of him to have started packing without her. Although, on second thought, she supposed he might have been calling to tell her that as well as apologize. "When do you want me to come pick up my stuff?"

Brady shrugged. "Up to you. Actually, I'm hoping I can get you to come back."

"Yeah, your mom mentioned that."

He chuckled. "I had nothing to do with that, Meg. Although I think it's kind of sweet of her."

"Sweet. Manipulative. You say 'tomato,'...."

"Why can't she be both?" Brady paused. "Look, Meg, I don't want to spend all our time talking about my mother, especially if this is my only chance with you."

Meg crossed and uncrossed her legs under the table. There was so much she wanted to say to him, nothing nice. That he was a spoiled rich kid who couldn't let go of his mother's purse straps or approval; and a coward as well, for refusing to confront what had happened to him that summer and running away to a homogenized clique of a town. That she hated herself for buying his brand of shampoo and deodorant just to possess the smell of him. That being with him right now made her palms damp with desire.

No. She would be damned before she'd let herself lose control over him again. "Okay. Let's talk about the wedding instead. Why am I still hearing from people who believe they're coming to a wedding in two weeks?"

"Because I want there to be a wedding."

"Yeah. Well, good luck coming up with a bride on such short notice."

Brady ran his hands through his hair, frantic birds trying to find a place to roost. "Look, Meg. I would do virtually anything to make this summer up to you. I really thought if we had a second chance, we could fix things between us–" Meg started to interrupt, but he stopped her. "No. It's my turn now. I haven't even looked for a new place to live, because I didn't want to make a big decision like that without you. See? I get it now. But if you can't forgive me, if you can't let it go, then this is pointless."

He shoved his chair back against the hardwood floor with a loud screech. People in the coffee shop weren't even making an attempt to be subtle. All conversation had halted to let this little drama play itself out.

Was this the place where Meg was supposed to run after him, throw herself in his arms, wait for the applause of the audience, and let the lights fade to black? If he was sincere, then perhaps. She didn't even know if she was the wronged party anymore. But her manipulation radar was tingling; she couldn't help wondering if the scene had been orchestrated for precisely that effect. Look, Brady hadn't even left. He just stood there, glowering.

She raised her eyebrows. "You're blowing the exit, man. Shouldn't a door be slamming right about now?"

Brady sat down again, hunching his jacket around him. "I gave you a ride, remember?"

Meg bit back a smile. It was kind of gallant, really, that even if he was ticked off at her, he didn't want her to get wet. "I can probably walk the few blocks to my car."

"I'll wait. It's still raining, and I don't want to worry about you in this neighborhood. Finish your coffee."

Meg took her time. She wanted to figure out why she wasn't pissed off anymore. If anything, she was trying to stifle a giggle. But what did *that* mean? Was this the big break-up, part two, or did they still have a chance? Did she want them to still have a chance?

As they left the coffee shop, Meg pointedly nodded at all the eavesdroppers. "Thank you. We'll be playing at The Strand until the end of September."

They zigzagged through the raindrops to the car. Meg walked over to the passenger side door. Brady followed her and unlocked her door first. He always had been a gentleman. "Thanks," she acknowledged, ducking in from the rain.

As Brady turned the key in the ignition, there was a grinding noise, then nothing. He tried again, then slumped back in his seat. "Shit, shit, shit. The battery's dead."

"What's your battery doing dead?" If he'd done this on purpose, she'd kill him. The whole "run-out-of-gas" trick was not the way to win her back.

"I must have left the lights on. Stupid shit car."

"Oh." She cleared her throat, trying to disguise the giggle that was threatening to burst from her throat.

"It's not funny!"

"Yeah, it is. Just a little." She pinched her thumb and pointer finger together.

"Fine. What do you propose we do?"

"I can run to my car and come pick you up."

Brady frowned. "That's a half a mile. You'll drown. Let's just wait for the rain to let up, then walk back to the coffee shop and call AAA."

Meg did not cherish the idea of being stuck in a car with him mad at her. "Look. We're in a parking lot. Why don't we just wait for someone to come to their car and ask for a jump?"

"This is not a good neighborhood to do that in, especially this parking lot. A woman got mugged at gunpoint here last week." He pointed to a spot across the lot where a gang of kids huddled under a bus stop's shelter.

Lord, not this again. "What? You think those boys are going to rob us blind?"

Brady tightened his hand around the steering wheel. "Wouldn't surprise me." He tried the engine again, which didn't even sputter.

"Why? Because they're black?"

"No, because they're outside in a downpour in an area with crappy lighting and no security. What else am I supposed to think?"

"That maybe they've got nothing else to do, and nowhere else to go. God. Don't be such a paranoid racist jerk."

"Right. Because I've got no good reason to worry about being mugged." His voice was bitter with the sarcasm.

Meg put her hands to her head; pulling her hair out at the roots would be preferable to this conversation. "Jesus! Yes, Brady, you were mugged. You can play that card for life. It does not mean that every group of kids you see is a gang of thugs." She was so tired of this dispute; it made her want to scream.

A couple of aisles away from them, a figure – she couldn't even tell if it was a man or woman – robed in an oversize Indians-insignia rain poncho, was approaching. Thank God.

"Look, someone's coming out now. I'll go ask him." She made a movement to open the door, but Brady placed a hand on her arm. "Stop," he said. "I'll do it." He closed his eyes for a moment, took a deep breath, and opened his door. Meg watched through the rain-blurred windshield as Brady approached the person and pointed to the car. The figure stopped and stepped a foot back, hands raised, turned his back to Brady and retreated to the safety of his car.

Meg shook her head sadly. "Thanks for nothing," she said to the absent figure. She knew how much it had taken for Brady to take this step. She got out of the car and, not caring about the wet, stood beside Brady, who was standing motionless. He was staring at the boys from the bus stop, currently ambling their way over the tarmac, hands in their sweatshirt pockets.

"Oh, shit," she muttered to herself. It had been much easier to make the argument that these kids were no threat when they were at a distance.

The kids took their time as if the downpour weren't even worth getting worked up about. She quickly glanced at Brady. He had his fists clenched, but he stood firm.

The boys were within a few feet of them. Meg kept focusing on their hands bulged inside their sweatshirts. She felt like she couldn't breathe, terrified that one or both of them might be concealing a gun.

She started to say, "I'll give you my pur–" but the smaller of the boys had started talking at the same time. The rain glistened on his face.

"Hey, mister. You a teacher at the elementary, right?"

Brady blinked as if the boy had just spoken in French. "Yes. How did you–"

"Dude, I knew I recognized you! My brother Davonté was in your class. So you guys got car trouble or you just like getting wet?"

Brady nodded, relaxing just a little. "Car trouble. Battery's dead."

The smaller boy nodded, as if his suspicions had been confirmed. "Wanna jump?"

Meg smiled, feeling light-headed with relief. They were going to be okay. Brady answered, "Yes, but where are you going to get a car?"

The older boy cocked his head and eyed them through heavy lids. "Our uncle works at the body shop 'bout two blocks down. It'll only take a few minutes."

Brady took Meg's hand and squeezed it. As they turned toward their car, the smaller boy yelled, "Hey!" They turned around. "You might wanna lock your doors while you wait." With a face-splitting grin, he said, "This neighborhood goin' to the dogs, you know." He turned back and they loped away in an easy jog.

Meg and Brady got back in the car. Meg wiped the rain from her face, feeling stupidly happy. She leaned over and kissed Brady on the cheek. "You did good," she said. They sat in silence, holding hands, until a truck roared up beside them. The older boy got out and rapped at the window.

"I got your jumpers right here. You wanna pop the hood?"

As the boy began to place the cables on the dead battery, the younger boy walked over to Brady's window.

He rolled it down enough to reach out, hand extended. The boy shook his hand, smiling, then backed off a step. Brady said, "I can't thank you guys enough. Seriously ..." His voice broke a little, and he cleared his throat. "So how is Davonté?"

"Oh, he's cool. He liked your class a lot. Said you were kind of a nerd, but the good kind. He's got Miss Sharpton this year, that skinny-ass witch. No offense, man," he said as Brady raised his eyebrows. Brady started to reply, but the boy looked at his buddy and interrupted. "Okay, you can start it now."

He turned the key, and the engine roared to life. He unrolled his window all the way and leaned out. "Guys, thank you. You have no idea ..."

The boys grinned and waved as they grabbed their cables and climbed back into the truck.

The car idling, Brady leaned back into his seat and exhaled loudly. "Wow. That didn't turn out like I expected at all." He shifted and gazed at her. "So, that little adventure is done. Where to now?"

Meg took his fingers and laced them in her own. "Let's go home."

~ 25 ~
JANE

"Ugh. Why do I have to wear this?" Davey stood at the doorway, tugging at his tie. Jane felt unexpected sympathy for him. He looked miserable. She didn't understand why they were doing a memorial service for Grams with a pastor in the first place, considering that not only was Grams a very loud unbeliever, but she also didn't like anybody. This whole idea would probably have ticked her off but good.

Bonnie tugged Davey's hands away from his neck. "Enough." He held his hands up in surrender as Bonnie tied the tie. "Into the car, both of you." Bonnie's voice was grim. "Let's just get this over with."

Scooting over to make room for Davey in the backseat, Jane hoped no one would care that she was wearing brown cords and a dark blue jersey to the funeral – she didn't own anything dark and funeral-y that wasn't meant for school, and she didn't have any summer dresses other than the one she'd bought for Meg's wedding. Once they were underway, Davey flipped open a notebook and began writing. He showed the page to Jane, its scrawl shaky and looped. "What's up with Mom?" it said.

Jane took the offered notebook and pen and began writing. "Duh. Dead mother, remember?"

The returned notebook came back within a few seconds. "You KNOW what I mean."

Jane did know what he meant. She sighed and wrote one last note to him. "I know. It's not you. Just be cool and let things settle down."

Davey nodded as he read the note. Closing the notebook, he slipped it back into his pocket.

"What're you guys doing with that notebook back there?" Bonnie was eyeing them in the rearview mirror while she waited for the light.

Jane and Davey exchanged glances. "Hangman," said Jane.

*   *   *

Walking into the viewing room at the funeral home, Jane felt Davey thrust his hand into hers. His palm was warm and sweaty, but she squeezed back, threading her fingers into his. This was their first funeral ever. Jane hoped that they weren't going to have to look at Grams' dead body. That would just be too gross. It was hard enough to think about her being dead.

Not because she was so sad. In fact, Jane felt vaguely ashamed, because she'd start off thinking about Grams or death or something deep, and the next thing she knew, she was thinking about movies, or Charley and that whole mess, or school starting. This funeral business was hard. She figured if it was hard for her at fourteen, it had to be really hard for Davey, being only ten.

It was hardest for Mom, that was clear. Seeing her mom collapsed into herself at the nursing home, in some kind of trance, was scary but understandable. But since then, she had become a person who went through the motions – made sure Jane and Davey got fed, bathed, in bed at a decent hour – but spoke so little it was as if she were being charged by the word.

The viewing room was sparse and uncomfortably cold. Jane was glad she was wearing a long-sleeved shirt. At least a couple dozen folding chairs were set up in tidy domino rows. They couldn't possibly expect that many people for this, could they? At the front of the room, a small table stood with the photograph of Grams that she had said made her look like Katherine Hepburn, and a big vase. No coffin, thank God.

Jane pulled her hand from Davey's and tiptoed across the room to her mother, who was speaking with the funeral director. "Where's Grams?" she whispered. She wasn't sure why she was whispering; no else had yet arrived.

"Her ashes are in that urn." Bonnie spoke those words with the same emotion she would have told Jane that the peanut butter was on the top shelf of the pantry.

Jane was saved from having to make any kind of response: Aunt Vivian, Uncle Dave, Meg, and some guy she assumed was Brady. Aunt Vivian looked bad. Normally, she wore a thick layer of makeup at all times; Meg had once told Jane that she wore makeup even when she was the only one home. Today, her face was bare, her cheeks blotchy, her eyes pink-rimmed and wet. She dabbed at herself with a tissue every ten seconds or so. Uncle Dave and Meg wore identical expressions of concern and discomfort.

Meg strode over to Bonnie and gave her a deep hug. "How are you holding up?"

Bonnie extricated herself from the embrace. "As well as can be expected, thank you."

Meg reached out for Brady, circling him around the waist. "I'm sorry this introduction occurs at such a bad time, but Bonnie, this is Brady."

Brady extended his hand and offered his condolences. Bonnie nodded at him, unsmiling. Turning back to Meg, she said, "This was not the time or the place for this. He should not be here."

Jane let out a long, whispered, "Ooh." Mom hadn't even bothered to lower her voice. It was spooky how much she'd *exactly* sounded like Grams at that moment. Meanwhile, Brady smiled politely and moved over to the guestbook, taking extra time to sign his name. Meg said something to Bonnie under her breath, then hugged her again.

She took Brady with her up to the table with Elizabeth's ashes. Seeing Jane, she crooked her finger, calling her over. Jane approached, with Davey tagging along just behind.

At the table, Meg introduced them to Brady and hugged them both at the same time. "You guys okay?"

Jane and Davey nodded in unison.

"Are you making life easy for your mom? She's not her normal mellow self."

Jane shrugged. "I don't know if she's even noticing what we do."

"Well, call me if it gets too bad, or you guys get in a jam. I'll either be at Mom's or Brady's."

Jane sighed. It had been nice having Meg around the house during her break-up. "Does this mean you're really getting married now?"

Meg grinned. "Yup. Back on schedule."

While they were talking, a few more people had entered the room and were chatting quietly. Some of them wore ID badges, as if they were coming from work. They were probably from the nursing home.

The minister entered the room and cleared his throat. "If you all would take your seats, we'll get started."

Jane and Davey sat in the front row with their mother. The chairs were hard, and Jane could feel the chill of metal even through the fabric of her pants.

The man introduced himself as Pastor Luke, the chaplain at the nursing home. He asked to start the service off in prayer. Jane peeped surreptitiously over at Bonnie while she and Davey were supposed to have their heads bowed. She did not look like she was praying. She stared dead ahead at the minister. She didn't even say "Amen" at the end.

"We are here today to celebrate the life of Elizabeth Moore MacKenzie." The pastor coughed. "I confess that, much to my regret, I did not personally know Mrs. MacKenzie."

Geez. What were they even doing here if the guy supposedly running the event knew nothing about Grams? That seemed disrespectful, somehow, as if she were just a generic old dead woman.

The minister continued. "In such circumstances, I feel this service would be more meaningful if, rather than me speaking, those family and friends who wish to would share stories of Elizabeth's life or of their relationship with her."

He gazed out on the gathering with a small smile and palms outstretched, reassuring those shy souls who might want to talk of Elizabeth.

All around Jane, the small audience lifted their chins to better see and support whoever was going to get up to talk. But no one rose. Faces begin to cast their gaze downwards, toward their laps. Chickens, Jane thought. How long would the pastor let it go before he ended the misery of waiting?

The chair next to her squeaked. Bonnie rose and moved to the tiny speaker's podium; her steps were slow and measured, as if she were carrying hot tea that she didn't want to spill. The pastor looked at her with obvious relief and moved aside.

"I know we are all here to honor my mother's memory. I thank you all for being here, especially you all," Bonnie gestured to the small group clustered in the back row of chairs, "who took care of Mother with such kindness and good will."

Her voice was quiet, almost a whisper, and the words came out one by one, the halting voice of a foreigner learning English for the first time."We are supposed to be here to share in our grief. But maybe we shouldn't be grieving." She was speaking with more force now, although her voice shook. "Maybe we should be dancing and singing, sobbing with relief, not with sorrow."

Jane was hypnotized at the spectacle, then suddenly became frightened as she wondered if her mom had really cracked.

Maybe Davey had the same thought. Jane stole a glance at him, but he was slunk down in his chair, refusing to look at anything or anyone. A couple seats down, Vivian's face was bright red, like she was having one of those coughing fits where you try to smother it in your lungs. Meg was sitting on the edge of her seat, fingers folded under the edge. Jane figured she was getting ready to usher Bonnie off the podium if necessary.

"There's a reason no one wants to talk about my mother," Bonnie continued, her knuckles white from gripping the podium. "She was a loveless woman, as incapable of receiving love as she was of giving it. Ask me, ask Vivian, ask any of her grandchildren – none of whom had any real kind of relationship with her. We were orphans long before she died. So why grieve now?"

Her eyes searched the audience, pleading and wide. No one was willing to look at her. Poor Mom. Even after Grams's stroke, when her mom had the awful job of simply waiting for her to die, she'd seemed stressed, but still strong – not broken, like now. But maybe she could help her mom like Pam had helped Charley. Maybe she could show her that kind of saving love. She lifted her face so that her mother could focus just on her. When Bonnie's eyes met hers, her grip on the podium loosened, and her expression shifted from that molten anger to a deep sadness. She let go and stumbled, tripping clumsily to the floor.

In a couple steps, Jane reached her; Meg also shot up from her chair, arriving at the same time. Exchanging a glance of thanks, she and Jane guided Bonnie back to her chair. Then Jane returned to the podium, feeling like she'd aged a hundred years in the last ten minutes. She was glad it was tall enough that no one could see her shaking behind it. "I didn't know my grandmother very well. She wasn't the type of grandma who bakes you cookies or who you send pictures of yourself in a Halloween costume. We tried a couple times, but when we went to her house, we never saw any of the pictures we'd sent."

Scanning the faces, Jane noted that Vivian was nodding and crying. Meg looked like she might cry, but sent her a thumbs-up sign. Her mom was staring blankly at the rug. Davey gripped her hand.

She took a deep breath. "So she wasn't the grandmother you see on television. And I don't think she was very happy. But she was smart, and she said what she thought. And those are good things that I can remember about her."

Blushing down to her toes, Jane lowered her head so her hair covered her face and returned to her chair. Bonnie did not make any movement toward her, but Davey gave her a grin. She heaved a deep sigh. She'd done something she never thought she could do – she'd talked in front of an audience, even if it was a funeral – and lived to tell about it.

The minister stood and asked if anyone else had anything to share. No one responded. Jane counted to thirty, and still – nothing. She didn't mind as much, this time. Grams had been sent off okay. Finally, the pastor asked everyone to join him in the Lord's Prayer.

Our father, who art in heaven,
Hallowed be thy name.

Even though there were not a dozen people in the room, all the voices combined with one another, merged to make one. If Jane closed her eyes, she could imagine this mass of voices transforming into a shimmering amoeba, emitting this prayer in a thousand frequencies, a thousand vibrations. Next to her, Jane felt her mother begin to shake.

Thy kingdom come, thy will be done, on earth as it is in heaven.

Bonnie cried and trembled like she couldn't get warm. Jane nudged Davey, and they both shifted so that they were on either side of her. Wrapping their arms around Bonnie's waist, they held her fast until the prayer was complete.

-26-
BONNIE

As Bonnie slit open the envelope to pull out yet another tranquil sympathy card, a wave of mortification rolled over her for the fifteenth time. How could she have behaved like that at the funeral yesterday? She'd always been nine parts sympathetic, one part judgmental of those mourners who seemed to handle their grief in an undignified manner. Yet her own performance had been not only indecorous, but a couple strata beyond. It was as if a demon had possessed her tongue, shut down her brain and any kind of internal censor. She was deeply ashamed.

There was only one action to take, absent personally contacting every attendee and prostrating herself before each one. She turned on the stove and grabbed some bread, slapping butter on it in heavy impasto layers. As she waited for the grill to darken the bread to the perfect shade of golden brown, she placed the cheddar on top and cracked an egg with one hand onto the grill beside the bread. This was more than just a sandwich. This was what she made – fried egg, cheese and tomato on sourdough – whenever she needed grounding. The melding of the creamy egg yolk with the velvety cheese would hit her tongue and flip an internal reset button, recalibrating her psyche.

She'd made this sandwich when she'd finally kicked Joe out for good, when she was in the depths of her post-partum depression with Jane, and on the day she'd left her mother, screaming obscenities and vowing to kill herself, at Whispering Woods nursing home. She hoped it would work its magic with her again.

She sat at the table and lifted the sandwich to her mouth, then stopped. The screen door scraped the mat as it opened, and for a moment she thought Jane must have finished with her meeting at the school early. The sight of Vivian walking into the kitchen, not Jane, threw her off guard, and she felt herself grow flushed with embarrassment all over again.

"Got your sandwich, I see. Mind if I make one for myself?"

Bonnie examined her turned back for any signs of her mood. Neither sister spoke as Vivian stood at the grill. Bonnie hadn't spoken to anyone in the family yesterday after her mini-breakdown, too horrified to say a word to Viv, or Meg, or the chaplain. She'd escaped as soon as the service was over, Davey and Jane flanking her like miniature Secret Service agents.

When Vivian finally sat down to the table, Bonnie wiped her mouth nervously. "About yesterday–"

Vivian held up a hand. "It's done now." She bit into the sandwich. "This is amazing."

She felt oddly moved at the casual compliment coming from her sister. "I know."

"Seriously. This is the first thing that's tasted good to me in a month."

They finished their sandwiches in silence, chewing in synchrony. Bonnie took her plate over to the sink, waiting for the tension that was hovering in the air to settle.

"Good. I feel better," Vivian said. "We should go, if we want to get back tonight."

Bonnie turned to face her sister, confused. "Go where?"

"Put Mom to rest. Come on." When Bonnie didn't respond, Vivian shook her head in apparent impatience and said, "Her ashes. When you took off yesterday, that squirrely little man gave them to me. I don't want them. Do you?"

She didn't feel ready for this. "No, but–"

"So we need to deliver her ashes so that I can be done with her." Vivian's voice had gotten gravelly. She cleared her throat, looking away for a moment. Her voice gentle, she added, "You need to be done with her too. We need to do this now."

Bonnie slumped at the table. Vivian was probably right. "Where are we taking her?"

"The only place she'd actually want to be."

She felt a flash of annoyance. "Screw the games, Vivian. She wasn't happy with anyone or anything, save for the few times I heard her mentioning Pete – whom you refuse to acknowledge."

Vivian picked up her purse. "That's where we're taking her. To Pete."

Bonnie felt suddenly as alert as if she'd just taken in a bolus of caffeine. "How do you know where he is?"

Vivian ignored her, opening the screen door. "Come on. We'll be gone a while. You should probably leave a note for the kids. We'll be back by tonight."

During the drive, Bonnie asked, "No offense, Viv, but what happened to you overnight? You were a wreck yesterday, and today you're …not."

Vivian shrugged, keeping her eyes on the road. "Maybe your little public tantrum was cathartic in a way. Maybe God's finally answering my prayers. Who knows?" And yet, she gripped the steering wheel, white-knuckled, in the lack of any traffic. Bonnie decided she was exorcising demons of her own, and left her alone.

She watched the signs of the city receding. The landscape galloped before her as they drove. She focused on the barns and trees in the mid-field, allowing the grasses and flowers along the curb to blur like watercolors. She knew that they were heading south, toward their childhood home along the Ohio River.

Bonnie had not seen this stretch of road in five years, since she had brought her mother back to Cleveland. She had gotten a call from one of Elizabeth's neighbors, Mrs. Kennedy, who'd taken it upon herself to inform her that her mother was beginning to act strangely. Bonnie had driven down immediately and been soundly berated by her mother for listening to such a feeble-headed busybody as Virginia Kennedy. "That woman has to invent drama to justify her existence. She's ridiculous, and so are you for even taking the time to listen to her."

The next call she received was from the fire department. Mrs. Kennedy had alerted them when she saw smoke billowing out the door. Apparently, Elizabeth had been cooking dinner and forgotten she'd had anything on the stove. When firemen burst into her house uninvited, she was reading in the living room. She'd never even noticed the smoke blanketing the ceiling.

So Bonnie had traveled to retrieve her mother. She'd lied to her about why she had to take her to the doctor, telling her it was a requisite insurance check-up. When the doctor told her it was Alzheimer's and gave her a list of nursing homes to visit, Elizabeth had protested with enough lucid vigor that Bonnie had begun to doubt the diagnosis.

She glanced at Vivian. Oh, how she'd wanted to hurt her back then. When she'd called to ask her for assistance in watching Elizabeth or inspecting nursing homes, or anything remotely helpful, Vivian had informed her that she was leaving with her church group on a South American mission trip and couldn't cancel.

Elizabeth had spent one excruciatingly long month with Bonnie and the kids. She moved everyone's belongings around based on some unknown logic. She'd hoard food in her bedroom. Yet, she still remembered who they were at this point, so she spent much of her time berating them for kidnapping her from her home, and critiquing the cleanliness of the house: "This place is filthy. When's the last time you vacuumed?" If Davey walked into the living room with a glass of pop, she yelled at him that someone as clumsy as he was would surely spill, and banish him back to the kitchen. Jane grew more and more skittish, checking her every movement as if she were about to be smacked. After about a week, Bonnie gave the kids permission to spend as much time as possible outside, and the children gratefully escaped.

She spent those days on unpaid leave from work, watching Elizabeth while pretending to be involved in paperwork or cleaning. The television remained on during all waking hours, first on morning news, then soap operas, then the afternoon talk shows. Bonnie was never certain how much Elizabeth attended to the television – certainly, she had not condoned TV watching while her children were growing up – but occasionally, she would hear her yell at the guest on Jerry Springer. Yet, even with the television to sedate her, Elizabeth had to be constantly surveilled for the moments when she would hunt through the house for matches to light a fire in the fireplace, or rummage through the drawers for scissors to cut coupons. When she would fall asleep in front of the television, Bonnie wanted to weep with relief.

She checked out the nursing homes on the sly, when she could find someone to watch Elizabeth. She called Whispering Woods the day after her mother walked a full three-quarters of a mile down Main Street in her nightgown, at midnight, before stopping to urinate on someone's lawn. Bonnie wasted no time accepting their offer of a room in their Alzheimer's Unit. She hoped that Elizabeth might welcome the change. So she was unprepared for the vehemence of her reaction to the news.

"I am *not* going to any old folks' home. You can take me to the bus station and I'll take my chances with the winos and drug addicts before I'll go to that home."

"Mother, just look at the room with me. You'll love it. It doesn't look like a home at all. It looks like an apartment complex."

Elizabeth paced the length of the kitchen. "You can put a ribbon on shit and it's still shit, miss."

"Mother!"

"You want to be rid of me. I understand. Just abandon me, like every other person in my life."

"I swear, Mother, it won't be like that. I will visit you every day."

"You won't. You hate me. Everyone hates me." Elizabeth strode into her room and slammed the door. Actually, into Jane's room, which they'd converted into a guest bedroom, much to Jane's disgust. She hated having to share a room with Davey.

Bonnie hoped that Elizabeth might forget about the conversation. But late that night, she was awoken by a crash in the kitchen. When she stumbled in, baseball bat in hand, there was her mother, rubbing her hip. Her suitcase lay behind her. It had fallen open and its contents – her cardigan, the shampoo from the bathroom, a *TV Guide*, and Jane's teddy bear – spilled out onto the floor.

"You don't have to worry about me," she announced, triumphant. "I've called a cab, and I'm going home."

Bonnie noticed the stapler on the kitchen table. "Did you call the cab on that?" she asked, nodding at the stapler.

"Of course I did. They said they'd be here immediately. Very good service, actually."

Bonnie felt like she'd been awake for days. She steered her mother back into her bedroom. "You go lie down until the cab gets here. I'll tell you when they arrive."

After securing Bonnie's promise, Elizabeth acquiesced. "It'll be good to get home," she said quietly.

The next day, Bonnie trundled her into the car. She threw her newly re-packed suitcase in the trunk, and they started down the road. As they drove the final few feet, Elizabeth saw the nursing home sign rapidly approaching. She turned to glare at Bonnie. "You bitch."

Bonnie parked the car with a little more force than necessary. "Mother, we can't do this anymore. *I* can't do this anymore."

"I will not stay here. You wait. I'll kill myself before I spend a night here."

"I'll be sure to tell your nurses that, Mother."

Bonnie found that, to her surprise, the longer and harder her mother ranted against her, the easier it seemed to accept this decision.

Once inside, smiling, enthusiastic personnel surrounded Elizabeth and helped her to her room. She yelled at them the entire length of the hallway. Bonnie exhaled.

That first month at Whispering Woods, Bonnie kept her promise and visited every day, trying to bribe her mother with homemade scones, savory cheddar biscuits, gingerbread. Elizabeth remained angry, refusing to speak with her those first weeks. In fact, the first time she talked to her, a month after she'd moved in, it was to ask who she was. Although she always seemed to remember the food.

* * *

Bonnie dozed off in the passenger seat. When she awoke, she did not recognize the passing landscape. It didn't look like home. They were off the highway now. Farmhouses peeked up behind quilt squares of corn fields.

Vivian pulled off the road and parked on the shoulder, in front of a small cemetery next to a copse of trees. It was isolated, with no church adjacent: just a plot of land maybe fifty feet square, with charcoal grey tombstones jutting up from the earth like so many misaligned teeth.

Bonnie got out of the car and stretched, waiting for Vivian. When she did not emerge, Bonnie wheeled around to see what she was doing. She had her head bowed, practically touching the steering column, and was gripping the cross around her neck. Bonnie turned back around and walked away a few feet, feeling like she had been a Peeping Tom, spying on some intimate act.

She made no comment when Vivian joined her. The two gingerly walked into the cemetery. They were the only ones present – not even squirrels or crows interrupted the ceaseless quiet of the place. Vivian processed up the rows, turning at the third one from the back and gently stepping in three graves' width. Bonnie followed behind, feeling that to speak would break the sacred trance of the place. She gazed at the plot where Vivian had stopped. "I didn't recognize this as the place where Daddy was buried."

Two gravestones rose from the ground, the lettering dark with age and neglect.

"It's grown over a lot since then."

Bonnie rubbed her hands over the smaller grave, swiping off the dirt on her jeans: Peter Jonas MacKenzie, Beloved Son, 1951 - 1955.

Vivian had sunk to the ground in front of Pete's grave. She spoke in a monotone, staring at her lap."It's my fault, you know."

Bonnie knelt beside her sister. Taking her hand, she quietly asked, "What happened?"

"He was four. Super cute and funny, but kind of a brat in the way that four-year-olds are, you know? But he could work Mother like nobody else. She wasn't that much different back then – all business, not many smiles – unless Pete was in the room. She actually let him climb up in her lap, can you believe it? Do you ever remember being allowed in her lap?"

Bonnie didn't answer, not wanting to break the mood. She was trying to envision Elizabeth like this, but it seemed so contrary.

"So one day, Mother was tackling chores. It was a pretty day, and she told me to watch Pete. But he was annoying me. I remember him sneaking up right behind me and then yelling – really loud – right in my ear. I told him if he kept it up, I was going to leave him alone to play. And he started to yell in my face, louder and louder. He was four, you know?" Vivian started to tremble.

"I took off and ran into the woods behind the barn. He came looking for me, but I hid from him. It wasn't that hard to do. And he got bored, and yelled, 'I'm gonna tell Mom you're not watching me,' and went back home. At least, that's what I thought."

Vivian set her jaw. Bonnie couldn't decipher what she was feeling.

"I can't do this." She covered her face with her hands.

Bonnie put her hands on her shoulders. "It's okay, Viv. If you can't, you can't. Don't feel like you have to."

She drew her fingers slowly away from her face. "But I do. Because it explains why Mother was the way she was." Vivian took a deep breath. "She found him in the kitchen. She'd been cleaning windows, so she hadn't seen him when he came in. She'd put out some rat poison, sprinkled it on some bread for the rats." Tears slipped unnoticed down her face. She stroked the carved letters on the gravestone.

A low moan escaped Bonnie's throat. She dug her hands into the grass, clinging to the feel of the blades' soft edges. "Oh, Vivian."

The sisters were quiet for a long time.

Vivian shuddered. "You were born a year after Pete died. Mother was so sure you'd be a boy – I don't know if she thought she could replace Pete's love or not. But when you were born, it was like she washed her hands of us all."

Bonnie felt like she'd known this, deep down, her whole life. "Is that why you and she never spoke all these years?"

Vivian's voice was bitter. "Until the day I left home, there was not a single day that she did not find some way to blame me. No one was ever allowed to talk about Pete, of course, but she'd remind me every day how irresponsibility carried serious consequences.

Daddy was starting to get sicker, so he couldn't help. I finally couldn't take it anymore."

"God, Vivian."

"Yeah."

A breeze rustled through the leaves, hushing the air around them. Vivian seemed to wake up as the wind pushed gently against her. She walked to the car, returning a minute later with the urn and a hand spade. She started stabbing at the soil in front of Pete's grave with the spade. After a minute, Bonnie stopped her. "Let me," she said.

Vivian gave her the scoop, leaning back and wiping beads of sweat from her forehead. "Knock yourself out."

Bonnie carved out a small hole just large enough to fit Elizabeth's urn. She placed the vessel down in the earth, hesitating just a moment before releasing her grasp.

Vivian pushed the soil back in place and patted it, as if she were planting tulip bulbs. "There," she said. "Maybe now I'll be able to forgive you, Mother." She sat motionless for a long moment, staring at the grave. Bonnie picked up the spade again, shifting it from hand to hand, taking comfort in its solidity and heft. She felt like she should say something to her sister, but Viv had suffered for too many years all by herself for Bonnie to have earned the right to console her.

Abruptly, Vivian stood and swept the dirt off her hands. "Are you ready?"

"I need another minute," said Bonnie. "Go ahead and wait in the car. I'll be right there."

Vivian strode to the car without looking back. Bonnie returned her attention to the carved soil in front of her and the marble headstone that bore witness to the love of her mother's life. She couldn't wrap her mind around all the ripples flowing out from the story's origin. By all rights, she should hate her mother, for bringing her into this world only to reject her. But as she patted the earth over the buried urn, rolling grains of dirt around the balls of her fingertips, the only feelings she could identify were a deep wellspring of sadness for Pete and for her mother's loss, for Vivian and the undeserved blame she had shouldered for all these years.

As they drove home, the rural trees blurring into the highway and then the exit sign for Daedalus Falls, Bonnie thought about how motherhood had marked her own life. If anything ever happened to Jane or Davey, she would have to struggle to make it through the days. She would be like Daedalus, reaching land broken-hearted, having witnessed Icarus' fiery plunge into the sea. Or Demeter, with her mournful wrath, denying the world its harvest until Persephone, trapped in the Underworld, was released to her. It's hard to hate someone for not being strong enough to get over her child's death.

"Be at peace, Mother," she whispered.

~27~
MEG

Meg had thought bride's rooms were supposed to be cacophonous, girlish slumber parties where excitement bubbled over like champagne. This was more like sharing a bathroom at the airport - everyone went about their own business with no sense of community. Dresses draped over chairs, hair dryers lay on the floor, and an entire department store's stock of cosmetics was lined up on the vanity. She sat on the padded ottoman in her newly purchased lacy underwear and tried to apply her makeup, but the controlled quiet made it hard to concentrate.

Carla was shaking out her bridesmaid's dress, which had gotten wrinkled in its garment bag. Mona was already dressed, and one of Lydia's minions was pinning her hair into an elegant up-do. Vivian was sharing the vanity with Meg, applying her own makeup; she knew from experience that the painstaking detail her mother lavished on her face could take up to half an hour. Lydia hovered around the room like a hummingbird, clipping stray threads and adjusting seams on anyone whose path she crossed. No one was talking to anybody else, save for a random compliment thrown out every few minutes to Meg. She wished Jane had changed her mind about being a bridesmaid; this group could use a dose of her right now. But they wouldn't be arriving at the church for another hour.

The group dynamic was a troubled one. At the rehearsal dinner the night before, Brady had been telling Vivian about the honeymoon plans during cocktails. "We were able to book tickets for St. Kitts. We've got the honeymoon suite at the Golden Lemon."

Meg joked, trying to lighten the mood. "Yes, I hear they have a bathtub shaped like a champagne glass. You have to climb into it with a ladder."

Vivian grimaced. "That sounds awful!" She narrowed her eyes at Meg. "You're pulling my leg, right?"

"Sorry, Mom. I couldn't resist." She squeezed her mother's shoulders with a grin.

Slipping into the group like an eel, Mona had clasped Brady's arm. "I need you, darling. The photographer wants some family shots."

Meg stiffened beside him. This was the first test of Mona's dominance since she and Brady had reconciled, and she didn't know how he'd react. To her immense relief, Brady asked his mother to wait, and continued to talk to Vivian about their plans. Meg pressed her lips to his palm in thanks. He glanced at her in surprise, then pulled her to him and kissed her hard on the lips.

Mona acted as if the embrace had not taken place. "Oh, dear, you must remember to contact the Cadwells while you're there. I know Candace is in Italy at the moment, but John should be around. He can take you both out on the catamaran. It's a wonderful place to snorkel."

As Mona described their friends' estate, Vivian downed the remainder of her wine spritzer. She broke into the monologue in a rush, as if she might not get a chance to speak otherwise. "Bob and I got to go to the Bahamas once. He got really sick on the conch. Be sure you pack some antacids. And if I were you, I'd pack some plain old American food, like peanut butter, granola bars. You know, just to be on the safe side."

Mona had listened to Vivian with one raised eyebrow during her contribution. She gave a brief nod in her direction, her artificial smile never wavering, then whispered something to Brady. Turning on her heel, she left and rejoined the photographer. Her mother watched

Mona leave, her bright façade momentarily wavering. She reminded Meg of a high school girl who's tried to seat herself at the cheerleaders' table, only to be ignored.

Meg had felt a sharp stab of pity for her mother. "I think your idea is fabulous, Mom. I don't know if we have anything in our pantry right now, though. Grocery shopping hasn't exactly been high on the priority list. Do you have anything we could pack?" Placing her arm around her mother's waist, she walked with her over to her father.

Today, Meg caught Vivian staring at Mona in the mirror with dislike as they primped. The tension vibrating from her mother heightened her anxiety even more than the pre-wedding nerves.

Mona dismissed the stylist and Vivian completed her make-up at about the same time. They joined ranks with Lydia, descending upon Meg to "help," as they put it, in the final touches of her transformation. "You should darken your make-up, dear," Vivian advised as she buttoned up Meg's vertebrae of pearl buttons. "The lights in the church will wash you out."

"And what are you planning to do with your hair, Meg?" Mona asked. "I hired Neil to take care of yours as well. It's a little short to do much, but I'm sure he can do something with it. Don't you think, Lydia?"

"I believe there are some hair extensions in that suitcase, if you'd like. We could give you some more length in the back."

Carla snorted. "Maybe we could braid and coil them like a Swiss maid."

"Sarcasm is not necessary," Lydia huffed.

Meg stood, nearly losing her balance as she stepped on the train. "Look, I appreciate all the help, but I need you to leave now. I just need a little time to myself."

Carla smiled. "That sounds like a great idea, Meg. Ladies, I think I saw the wedding coordinator showing the photographer to the church courtyard for the post-wedding shots."

"Oh, that's all wrong," Mona snapped. "The courtyard has no flowers in bloom right now. There's a lovely fountain with a tiny rose garden surrounding it that will be perfect."

"Honey, are you sure you don't want me to stay?" Vivian asked.

She really didn't want to hurt her mother's feelings, but if she stayed, Meg feared that one of them would say something to ruin their fragile détente. "Honest, Mom, I'm fine. I just want a few minutes to collect myself before heading down."

Mona and Lydia ushered the stylist out, whispering something about an independent streak and not to take it personally. Vivian stopped in the doorway, tears in her eyes. "You look like I've always prayed you would on your wedding day," she said and left.

Carla advanced to Meg. "My turn. I'd give you a squeeze, except I'm afraid I'd break something in this corset."

"I know what you mean. I'm a little afraid to move in this myself." She smoothed down an errant piece of lace on her cuff. "I'll see you downstairs, okay?"

"It's your day, girl. Whatever you want." She blew Meg a kiss. "I'll try to keep the ladies civil."

As solitude settled itself in the room, Meg sank down onto the ottoman, trying to slick down her more wayward spikes. The burgundy ends had not grown out, but she figured the veil would cover them up sufficiently to satisfy the blue-hairs.

The only thing left to do was put her shoes on. She took the creamy satin pumps out of their box, feeling like Cinderella. *But when do I turn into the princess?* In truth, she dreaded donning the heels, as if it were the final step to a transformation that she wasn't sure she wanted. What if it changed her somehow? Maybe Jane had been right, all those months ago. Maybe it had been a mistake to be so laid back about the choice of dress, of shoes. Meg felt like her identity was so swallowed up in the choices Mona had made, that once she put on the shoes, there'd be nothing of her left.

And what about Brady? How could she be really sure of him? Maybe he wanted her to be more like his mother, more like the friends his parents had, his Ivy League ex-girlfriends. Maybe this whole courtship had been his experiment in slumming, the ultimate rebellion against his parents. But once they were married, would he still want her the way he professed to want her now?

The more she sat and stared in the mirror, seeing no one she recognized, the more she felt her heart flutter against her chest like a bird straining to fly against the wind. It would be completely tacky to bolt now, she knew, but still better than realizing afterward what a mistake she had made.

She stood suddenly and began pacing the room, trying to decide whether she were brave enough to abandon the imminent spectacle. As she walked on tiptoes to keep the dress from any stray specks of dust, she noticed a wrapped present perched atop one of the cabinets. The box was on the smallish side, about the size of a lantern. It must be a wedding present that one of the mothers had stashed here and forgotten to move. Over everyone's line of sight, it would be easy to miss.

Meg reached as high as she dared and gave the box a small push, just enough to bring the edge over the molding. She grabbed the end with both hands and pulled it down, hoping it wasn't heavy or breakable.

The tag on the box was addressed to Meg alone. The giver's name was absent.

Intrigued, she pulled at the silky white ribbon and watched the bow diminish and disappear. She pulled the paper away in a single swoop and took the top off the box. Nestled on top of the tissue paper that hid the present was a note in Brady's handwriting. "I know it's more traditional to get you a wedding present like a fancy bracelet or diamond earrings. But when I saw these, they seemed so much like you that I had to get them for you. I hope you like them."

Meg pushed aside the pastel tissue paper and sighed in appreciation. Inside the box were two pristine, white Converse high-top sneakers rimmed with silver sequins and studded with rhinestones. The shoelaces had been embroidered with "The Bride" in silver. They were perfect.

Cradling the shoes in her hands, she turned them around and around, admiring the handiwork and feeling the comforting solidity of the cotton canvas. She noticed the cross by the door, and even though spiritually she was more a questioner than believer, tears filled her eyes, and she offered a silent thanks. Unlacing the shoes, she donned her gift as fast as she could, double-tying the shoelaces for insurance.

Standing up, Meg twirled around, craning her neck to try to view the dress from all angles. Good. The shoes were not visible under the dress at all. They could be their secret, hers and Brady's.

There was a knock at the door. "Hey, Meg, you ready?" Carla called.

Meg took her veil and settled it on her head. She took one last look in the mirror and smiled. "I'm ready."

~ 28 ~
JANE

The United Methodist Church of Daedalus Falls loomed majestically skyward as Jane and her family drove up. A cornerstone of the town square, its deep red brick and slender steeple gave the impression of history, money and tradition. Jane wondered if its churchgoers were as rich as she assumed. As they moved into the sanctuary, she paused, overwhelmed. Sun streamed through stained glass panels, casting the air itself in a golden light. The pews and altars were decorated with ornate carvings of grapevines and wheat. She could see individual chisel marks on the carvings. Intimidated by the wealth of detail, she worried, because this didn't seem at all like Meg.

An usher escorted them to an empty pew on the bride's side, handing each of them a program on heavy cream-colored paper. Jane looked around the sanctuary at the rest of the congregation. Everyone looked old, fifty and up, and there were almost no people seated on Meg's side yet. This bothered her: what if people were looking at it like a popularity contest? It wasn't Meg's fault if they didn't have a lot of family to invite.

Bored of watching strangers in Sunday clothes, Jane let her mind wander. School would be starting next week, and for the first time she could ever remember, she was actually looking forward to it.

When the high school had called and asked her to come in last week, Jane hadn't known what to make of it. She'd wondered if her guidance counselor was identifying the problem kids ahead of time. But she'd shown up as directed, and a gray-haired man with a big walrusy moustache had walked down from his classroom to meet her. He'd introduced himself as Mr. Donnelly.

"Are you my guidance counselor?" she asked, after he'd guided her outside and they'd found a table without bird poop all over it.

"Yuck, no. You couldn't pay me to do that job. I teach in the Multi-handicapped Classroom, down in C Wing."

Oh, God. He was going to lecture her about Charley. News traveled fast in a small town. Warily, she asked, "So why do you want to talk with me?"

"I wanted to talk to you to see if you'd be interested in acting as a student aide for me this year. I know Pam Burke, and she told me what a terrific job you'd done with Charley this summer."

Jane looked away towards the football field. "Did she also tell you she fired me?"

Mr. Donnelly waited until she looked back at him to answer. "We all make mistakes. That's one I doubt you'd ever make again."

She bit her lip. "Did you see Charley? Do you know if he's okay?"

"Pam said he was doing fine. You could always give them a call..."

Jane shook her head. She didn't want to talk about this anymore; she'd obsessed about her failure enough in private. "The student aide job?"

Mr. Donnelly stroked his moustache. "You don't know much about the high school yet. It's kind of a big deal to be asked to be a student peer for our kids. You get out of study halls, lunch, too, if you want, to be in our class, and you actually work with the kids. We only take people by recommendation."

Jane bit her lips, trying to hide the smile that revealed how flattered she was.

"Actually, I don't think we've ever asked a freshman before. There's always a bunch of kids who want to get out of study hall, but they just want a free social hour."

She couldn't believe it. This seemed too good to be true. She was being invited to do something no other freshman would be asked to do. Pam didn't hate her. And she'd get out of study hall and lunch. No more struggling with which outcast table to pick. She said yes without hesitation.

The trumpeting of the organ brought her attention back to the present. The organist, who'd been playing slow, boring classical music so far, announced with loud fanfares the commencement of the wedding. Flourishes – musical loop-de-loops – layered atop one another other like icing swirls on a wedding cake. This wasn't the usual dum-dum-de-dum. It sounded like a queen's entrance. Jane looked in her program and saw that the music was called "Trumpet Voluntary." She loved it. She felt like she had always known this tune but had never heard it.

Davey hopped and squirmed in his seat. "They're starting!" He could be such a girl, sometimes.

The minister, Brady, and several tuxedoed men stepped over to the altar, turning to observe the processional. Even though this was Jane's first wedding, and had nothing to compare this to other than pictures she'd seen in magazines, the whole thing just seemed wrong for Meg. She shouldn't be getting married in a big fancy church. She should be exchanging vows while bungee jumping or up on top of a mountain peak that she had just finished climbing.

Meg's friend Carla slowly swept down the aisle. Jane liked the combination of her dreadlocks with the fancy green silk bridesmaid's dress. That was the way to be yourself.

The music swelled once again. This time everyone stood, and there she was: Meg. Jane barely recognized her. She was pretty sure that her dress was one of the ones she had made a "ychhh" gagging noise over while leafing through that bridal magazine. Meg had removed three of her four pairs of earrings, leaving only a set of pearl studs. Her hair was slicked back under a fluffy veil; you could only see the purple tips if you looked really hard. She looked calm and happy as she glided up the aisle on Uncle Bob's arm.

Jane felt like she'd been kicked in the stomach, sucker-punched by a fist in a long white glove. She watched blankly as Meg and Brady took each other's hands, said the "I do's," and exchanged rings.

The rest of the wedding was swift, but kind of boring, anticlimactic after the grand entrance. When they kissed at the end of the ceremony and the congregation applauded, the couple looked out at their audience with vague surprise, as if noticing for the first time that anyone else was present.

Davey chattered happily in the receiving line. "Brady looked like James Bond. Can I get a tux? It'd be cool to be a super-spy. Can I have some wine at the reception?"

Bonnie ruffled Davey's hair. "Nope. They'll declare me an unfit mother, drag you off to juvie where you'll be sold into white slavery and trained as a certified public accountant. I can't have that on my conscience." She turned to Jane, tiny lines of concern etched around her eyes. "You're awfully quiet. What did you think of the wedding?"

That it was a circus without soul or personality, manufactured for the benefit of Brady's family. "It was okay, I guess. The music was good. Meg had on too much makeup."

When they finally reached the bridal party, Bonnie greeted Brady with a massive hug. Considering the whole funeral incident, Jane expected him to keep himself at arm's length, or make the sign of the cross in front of her like in those monster movies. But he seemed okay with the hug.

"Welcome to the family, Brady, such as it is." Bonnie turned to Meg. "Honey, you look absolutely gorgeous."

Davey pumped Brady's hand fast and furiously. "I like your tux."

Now it was Jane's turn. She looked down at the ground. "Congrats," she muttered. She shook Brady's and Meg's hands – Meg looked so different that she might as well have been a stranger – then turned and hurried out the side door to the steps. She felt awful. Her Meg was gone.

Bonnie appeared beside her, her forehead furrowed. "What's going on? That was pretty rude."

Jane couldn't speak. She shook her head and faced the brick.

Bonnie softened her tone. "Look, honey, I don't know what this is about, but this is Meg's day. This is not about you. Take a minute, and we'll meet you at the car. You can apologize to her at the reception."

She hung her head. To endure an entire reception, watching Meg, who would be taking a path that Jane couldn't follow, seemed cruel.

She cringed when they reached the waterfront ballroom that had been booked for the reception. Okay, the wall of glass overlooking the Cleveland skyline and the Detroit-Superior bridge was fairly cool. But the arch of silver Mylar balloons? The square of hardwood flooring that would serve as a dance floor? What was this – Homecoming? The food had better at least be edible.

Jane accepted a Coke from the bartender and cased the perimeter of the room. Her mom and Davey were laughing like crazy with some friends of Meg's. Jane didn't want to talk to anybody, and wouldn't know what to say even if someone talked to her, so she pretended to be admiring the view. Her dress, which she had felt so right in when she bought it, felt sweaty and limp.

Finally, the lights dimmed, and the meal was served. Salmon. She hated fish. She moved pieces of pink around on her plate. Everyone was either talking to one another or happily tucked into their dinners. Brady's dad – Jane remembered him from the rehearsal dinner – was walking back from the bartender's station at the far side of the room, and tripped over a taped-down speaker cable. Jane bit her lip to keep from smiling as he dipped and righted himself, glancing around to see who had noticed. His eyes met Jane's, and he bowed with an elaborate flourish. Jane clapped, and the two shared a smile.

"What are you clapping at?" Davey asked.

"Nothing." Jane glared at him, and he shrugged and went back to his mashed potatoes.

After dinner, Jane observed the bouquet and garter tosses with dismay. At least her mother knew better than to prod her into trying to catch a leftover bunch of dead flowers. After the cutting of the cake came the dancing. Davey immediately bounced out of his seat and onto the dance floor, flailing around as if enthusiasm would make up for lack of talent. Brady's dad was dancing with his wife, spinning her gracefully around the floor.

Meg walked up to Jane's table. "Hey, guys. Sorry I haven't made it over here before now. You having a good time?"

Bonnie nodded. "This is lovely, Meg."

"Thanks. Mona arranged it all, so I guess I better say I like it. I'd rather have had a giant cookout, myself. What about you, Jane?"

Bonnie hit Jane with one of those "Be nice or die" stares. Jane played with her spoon. "I like the view. And the cake's good."

"Of course. It's the only thing I refused to negotiate on. Chocolate or nothing." Meg sat down in an empty chair. "God Almighty, I'm tired of standing and smiling."

Jane scanned the room. "Where's Brady?"

"Making the rounds, I'm sure. Sucking up to his parents' social circle. I probably should, too. Make nice with the in-laws and all that." She stood, her shoulders sagging. "What I really want to do is tell everyone to go home. I'm tired. Thank God, Brady gave me these today. Heels would've been murder." Meg lifted the skirt of her dress a couple inches, just high enough for Jane to see high-top sneakers. As she dropped her skirt, she winked and raised a finger to her lips. "Don't tell. Mona would have an attack."

Jane walked over to the bar to get another Coke. She felt kind of guilty for thinking Meg had sold out. But she *had* let Mona do all the planning. So hadn't she tried to camouflage who she really was? But then, there were the sneakers. But Brady had given them to her. It was too complicated. She couldn't get her head around all the corners.

As she stood at the window sipping, Brady's dad appeared at her shoulder.

"I've always liked this view," he said.

Jane froze. She always felt so invisible that it startled her when someone talked to her.

"We met at the rehearsal." He extended his hand. "I'm Arthur, Brady's dad, but help me remember your name? I know you're one of Meg's family."

"I'm Jane. Meg's my cousin."

"She'll be a welcome addition to our family, I assure you."

Jane didn't know how to respond to that, so said nothing.

Arthur watched the dancers for a moment. "Is that your brother out there on the dance floor?"

The gyrating spaz? She sighed. "Yes."

"It must be hard, being the only young people here. Although your brother looks like he's having fun. Why aren't you dancing?"

Jane snorted. "I don't know how."

"Well, that can be fixed. Would you do me the honor of dancing with me?"

Jane started, spilling a little bit of Coke onto her hand. She set the glass on the table, wiping her wet hand on the back of her skirt. "I-I don't know," she stammered. "It looks hard."

"It's not. The music will show you the dance it wants. And I can help."

Jane tentatively took the arm Arthur offered her and let him lead her to the dance floor. A fast song had just begun, but the floor had attracted few couples. Davey noticed her and waved. She waved back, making a face at him.

"Now, this is a good song for a two-step," Arthur said. "You move your feet just like this – right-left-right. Now, left-right-left. We're just going to repeat that over and over, and let the music tell us if it wants us to spin or twirl."

He slipped his arm around Jane's waist. She didn't have much of a choice: she placed her arm around him as lightly as she could, trying to strike a compromise between not touching him and not falling, and they began to circle in time to the music. He smelled nice, like a dad, a faint woodsy aroma wafting close to her. Right-left-right, then left-right-left. Arthur moved with grace and ease. Slowly, she felt herself relax into the rhythm, letting her body dip a little into each step.

"Jane, you're a born dancer."

The praise made her blush and stiffen, but she loosened up as soon as she shut out everything but the music. Without warning, Arthur twirled her around, briefly letting go of her arm and then catching it again.

Her skirt flared out around her. She gasped. "Oh, my goodness!"

Arthur chuckled. "Fun, isn't it?"

He twirled her again, but this time Jane was prepared and stepped into it, completing the turn with a small bobbed curtsy. She felt the music bubble up inside her, like a fizzy soda, and suddenly felt content, almost happy. The music continued to press up inside her, making her lighter and lighter, until she couldn't hold it back any longer. She laughed.

THE END

MORE GREAT READS FROM BOOKTROPE

One Week **by Nikki Van De Car** (Coming-of-age novel) Celebutant Bee wants nothing to do with fame, so she takes off from LA to find her own identity. Little does she know that one week can change everything.

Grace Unexpected **by Gale Martin** (Contemporary Romance) When her longtime boyfriend dumps her instead of proposing, Grace avows the sexless Shaker ways. She appears to be on the fast track to a marriage proposal… until secrets revealed deliver a death rattle to the Shaker Plan.

Spots Blind **by Linda Lavid** (Fiction - Short Stories) Stories about being blindsided -- sometimes by family, friends, and lovers; sometimes by our own refusal to see the truth.

Lark Eden **by Natalie Symons** (General Fiction) A play chronicling the friendship of three Southern women over seventy-five years. At once a deeply moving and darkly comic look at the fingerprints that we unknowingly leave on the hearts of those we love.

Thank You For Flying Air Zoe **by Erik Atwell** (Contemporary Women's Fiction) Realizing she needs to awaken her life's tired refrains, Zoe vows to recapture the one chapter of her life that truly mattered -- her days as drummer for an all-girl garage band. Will Zoe bring the band back together and give The Flip-Flops a second chance at stardom?

… and many more!

Sample our books at:
www.booktrope.com

Learn more about our new approach to publishing at:
www.booktropepublishing.com

CPSIA information can be obtained at www.ICGtesting.com
Printed in the USA
LVOW08s1706030714

392893LV00002B/398/P